LOYALTY

AVI

LOY

ALTY

CLARION BOOKS

An Imprint of HarperCollins*Publishers*

Boston   New York

Clarion Books is an imprint of HarperCollins Publishers.

Loyalty

Copyright © 2022 by Avi Wortis Inc.

clarionbooks.com

Library of Congress Cataloging-in-Publication Data has been applied for.
ISBN: 978-0-358-24807-1

The text was set in Fournier MT Std.
Map illustration by Tristan Elwell
Cover and interior design by Celeste Knudsen

Manufactured in the United States of America
1 2022
4500843602

First Edition

For Bruce Coville

CONTENTS

PART 1   1

PART 2   49

PART 3   105

PART 4   171

PART 5   205

PART 6   275

PART 7   315

AUTHOR'S NOTE   337

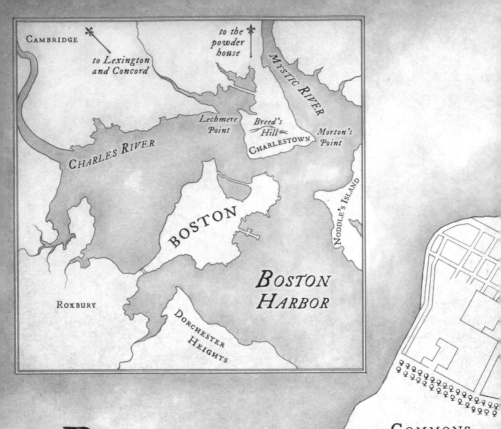

CAMBRIDGE

to Lexington
and Concord

to the
powder
house

MYSTIC RIVER

Lechmere
Point

Breed's
Hill

CHARLESTOWN

Morton's
Point

CHARLES RIVER

BOSTON

NODDLE'S ISLAND

ROXBURY

DORCHESTER
HEIGHTS

BOSTON
HARBOR

COMMONS

Frog Ln.

Hog Alley

Newbury

Hollis St.

White
Horse
Tavern

Beach St.

Liberty
Tree

Essex

Orange St.

Walner's
Wharf

Byle's Wharf

Neck

BOSTON
and
SURROUNDINGS
1775

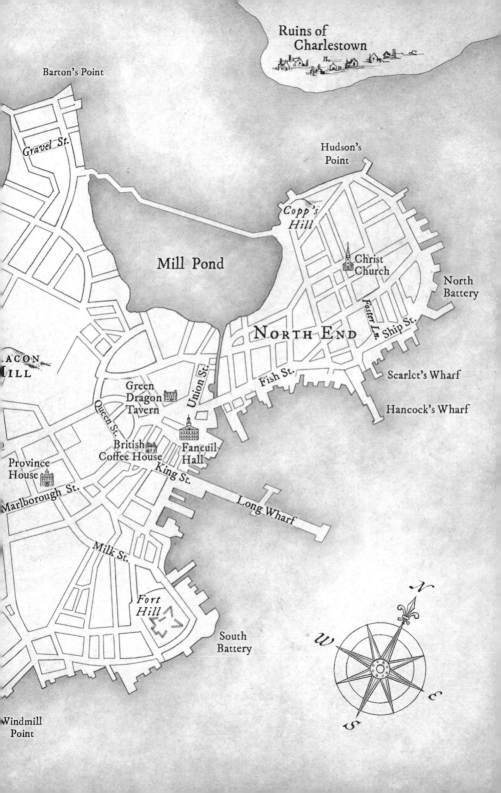

PART 1

1774

Friday, April 1, 1774

On this day, my father was murdered because he said a prayer.

It happened in our town of Tullbury, a few miles west of Concord in the Province of Massachusetts Bay, the British colony in North America. A crowd of some fifteen angry men had gathered outside our door. "Death to tyrants!" they were chanting. "Keep our freedom! Down with King George!"

Not only did I smell wood burning, but smoke was drifting into our house. I didn't know the reason for the fire but feared the worst, since I knew that houses were being burned and looted by such mobs. Father had told me that.

Despite the uproar outside, my father, Solomon Cope, the parish minister of Tullbury's Grace Church, had gathered our family — my mother (Clemency Cope), my two sisters (Mercy and Faith), and me, Noah Paul — about the table for our regular pre-dinner prayer. We struggled to keep our attention on Father because, since it was spring weather, our two front windows had their shutters open and some of those outside men were leaning in to listen to what Father was reciting: a prayer from a book called *Morning and Evening Prayers for Families, Wives, Children and Servants.*

For as long as my memory reached over my thirteen years of life, Father had read that prayer to us each day. It was, he believed, his duty to do so. Being the absolute head of our family, even as he was the head of his church, he was a strict father, an ever-correcting teacher, sure of himself and unemotional in his ways. But at that moment, I was witnessing his fright, something I had never seen before. Let it be said: a frightened parent is — for a child — a terrible thing to behold.

In a shaky voice, he read: "'Help me daily to increase in the knowledge and love of thee, my God, and of my savior, Jesus Christ. Show me the way in which I should walk while I am young and grant that I may never depart from it. Bless whatever good instructions have been given me, that I may be ever-growing in knowledge, in wisdom, and in goodness.'"

Knowing what words came next, I nervously flipped the hair out of my face and tried to keep my eyes on Father, even as I stole glances at the men at the windows.

As if seeking strength, Father took a deep breath, gripped the book tightly in his small hands, and completed the prayer: "'Bless, and defend, and save the king and all the royal family.'"

No sooner did the men leaning in hear Father utter those words than the door burst open — we never had a lock — and some of the mob rushed into our front room. Two held muskets.

With a hand clamped over his mouth to prevent him from speaking, Father was dragged from the house.

Were these assailants strangers from another country or province? No. Every man was from our town of some fifty families. I knew them all. A few were parishioners in my father's church. One of them, I was shocked to see, was Mr. Downs, father of my friend Micah, who often visited my home. "Sons of Liberty," these men styled themselves, insisting that they — and they alone — were preserving our freedoms from the tyranny of England. A large portion — though not all — of the town supported them.

As Father was hauled outside, my sisters burst into cries of dread along with torrents of tears. My mother, a small woman with gray hair, shrieked, jumped up, and tried to hold Father back but was flung aside. I, too, used all my strength to keep Father in the house. But two large men — William Harwood and Ezekiel Trak — grabbed hold of my arms and marched me outdoors even as they kept me from Father.

"Come see how we deal with Loyalists, boy," Mr. Harwood hissed into my ear.

You may be sure I fought to free myself, but against such large-made men, it was useless.

Was an entire troop required to subdue Father? Was he such a person of strength? Nothing like. Rather, he was a tall, skinny man of modest power with a smooth-shaven face that projected, beyond all else, self-confidence. The strongest thing about Father, his voice, expressed deep conviction. His sermons were always forceful while pleasing to the ear. Although the word was no longer fashionable, he liked to refer to himself as a "Puritan."

And now, having spoken his beliefs, he was pulled from his home.

Once Father was outside, he was encircled by the crowd. "Curse the king!" they demanded. "Renounce England!" "Defend our sacred freedoms!"

All the while, Father was being pushed and shoved so that he bounced from one man to another like a shuttlecock in a game. It was appalling to observe.

To these demands and battering, Father, though he gasped for breath, stayed mute. He was trying — I knew him well enough — to maintain his self-respect as well as his religious oaths.

In contrast, the faces of the men who had seized him were flushed with anger and elation, each man encouraging others to greater brutality. Then, to my further horror, some of the men, Proctor Davenport, Thomas Radcliff, and George Gardner, began to strip Father of his clothing.

Father was dressed in his usual black clerical garb: coat, waistcoat, britches, stockings, and shoes. No wig. Not one bit of neck lace or fancy upon him, not so much as an iron buckle on his shoes.

Within moments, all his clothing — including shoes and linen — was taken from him and flung upon the ground. Father, milk pale, stood naked as Adam, shivering from fright and chill without so much as a fig leaf to cover his privates while he tried to hide his shame. But he was not standing in the Garden of Eden facing his Creator; rather, he stood in his own front yard before uncompromising rebels. And let it be noted that I was being held in such a fashion that I was forced to witness Father's humiliation. Indeed, I was sure his dishonor was mine, too.

"Tar him!" shouted Ananias Neale, our local blacksmith.

The crowd parted, and Ebenezer Goodman and Samuel Skelton, both brawny men, came forward. They were holding the handles of a blackened iron pot from which I saw shimmering heat rise, which told me why they had made a fire. The next moment, Richard Poor and Ezekiel Trak stepped up with large horsehair brushes in their hands.

Father made desperate efforts to free himself. Once again, I tried to help. Neither he nor I was successful.

"Denounce the king!" someone shouted. "Tell us who else in town supports him!" called another.

At last, Father spoke. In a gasping voice clogged with sobs, he cried out, "God save our king!"

That further infuriated the crowd. Two of the men clutched Father's arms and held them out as Mr. Goodman and Mr. Skelton set the iron pot down near him. Those with brushes dipped them into the boiling tar and began to splash and paint Father's body, bringing forth ghastly cries of pain. It took but seconds for him to be covered in scalding pitch from his balding head to his small, narrow feet, some of it dripping down over his face like black tears.

Oh, you who read my words: may you never witness the torture of your father. I don't pretend I suffered anything like his agony, but at that moment I felt like my soul was being ripped from my body.

Then George Deaver raised a plump bag and tumbled out a cloud of chicken feathers. These feathers were scooped up instantly and daubed on Father so that he looked like a grotesque bird of giant size.

Released, Father fell to the ground, writhing in agony.

Someone shouted, "So be it to all enemies of our sacred liberties!"

With more cries, such as "Down with King George—God save Massachusetts!" the crowd dispersed, laughing and shouting insults. Our nearest neighbors—who must have observed what happened—had remained in their homes throughout the clash.

I flung myself down by Father, who was moaning and writhing, but there was nothing I could do. My mother and sisters rushed out with a blanket and wrapped it around him. Then the four of us carried his convulsing body inside.

Once within the house, Mother tried to remove the still-warm pitch from his skin. The process was not just agonizing but failed. In three days, my father, never free of mortification or suffering, died.

I tell you truly, "God save England" were his last words on earth.

Monday, April 4, 1774

We laid Father's body out in the front room. During the two days that his remains rested there, we stayed by his side. Not one person from our town came to pay respects or offer so much as a sip of sympathy. Tullbury, the town in which I had spent all my life, my home, treated us as outcasts.

Numb from the dreadfulness of it all, I didn't know what would happen. Full of confusion and despair, I was unable to see how my family could exist without Father, for he had guided us in every way every day. The intense shock of the sudden loss brought on a kind of blindness: I could see only the past, not a future.

I must admit I felt one splinter of doubt: Why did my father have to be so unlike the other men in town, and preach against the things they believed? But no sooner did I have such a thought than I was ashamed and dared not give it voice. Indeed, I rebuked myself for failing Father in his hour of martyrdom.

The people I most wanted to see, wishing reassuring acceptance, were my best friends, Micah Downs and Nathaniel Farrington. That

Micah's father had been part of that assaulting mob made the attack even worse. To be sure, I had known Mr. Downs was a radical. It had mattered little to me before. Now it mattered greatly.

I trusted none of our neighbors and feared leaving our house lest I, too, be assaulted as another Loyalist. With Father's tar and feathering, I hated the town of Tullbury and all the people who lived there. Moreover, I feared them.

Wednesday, April 6, 1774

When two days passed, our church sexton, eighty-year-old, white-haired Mr. Bellwright, brought a pinewood coffin that he had fashioned with his knobby hands. Continually bobbing bows and whispering words of woe, he bore Father away on a screaky cart.

Mother, my sisters, and I followed, walking upon the town's one road until we reached the cemetery next to Father's Grace Church. No one was on the street but us, though you may be sure I knew all who resided in the houses we passed. In a few homes were particular friends. That day, doors were shut, windows covered. But as we went along, an occasional curtain twitched, which told me we were being watched.

There was another church down the road, the Congregational one, where most of the community worshiped. But Grace Church was where my grandfather, Pastor Obadiah Cope, lay. My great-grandfather, Jeremiah Cope, a pastor too, was also buried there. That was where we took Father.

In the churchyard, Mr. Bellwright had dug a deep and narrow grave surrounded by multiple slate stones that bore images of death's-heads with wings, weeping willow trees, and anguished angels. Using ropes, Mr. Bellwright and I lowered the coffin that held Father into the grave.

Since there was no minister—indeed, no one but us—Mother asked me to read the service. Pushing my hair back, I did so. Finding it hard to say the words, I haltingly read the funeral text over my murdered father. Then we covered him with earth. I can assure you that dirt falling upon a coffin lid is the deadest sound on earth.

My sisters held hands and cried. Mother wept. So did I. But by the end of the day, I was bereft of tears, a deep well gone dry.

Throughout, I kept thinking, *Where are my friends?*

Then into my head crept a further thought: *How did the mob know my father always read aloud that prayer with those words about our king?*

Someone had betrayed us.

I needed to know who.

The burial over, we four walked back home. Mother insisted I lead the way. Then came Mother. Finally, my sisters together. Eyes set straight ahead, we went in affrighted silence, walking slowly despite fears we might be attacked. Though I was sure we were being watched, no one came out to us, not even our neighbors. It was a great relief when we arrived home unharmed.

Our modest wooden house—on a stone foundation—had been built by my great-grandfather when he first came to Tullbury. That tells you how old it was, and how long the Copes had lived there. Indeed, my father grew up in our house.

Beyond the front door, there was a room to the right where we ate meals. In one corner stood a cupboard where the old family Bible always lay open. My great-great-grandfather, Jacob Cope, brought that Bible with him when he came from England in 1652. On the inside of the cover was a lengthy list (in many hands) of family names with dates of births, marriages, and deaths, our family history. Not a profound memoir, but a chronology of our lives. The earliest date was 1623, in England.

Our cupboard held some pewter dishes, cups, and candlesticks, everything old. Newness was not our nature. (My sister Mercy once complained to Father about that, only to be chided for her vanity.)

Also in that room was a table upon which Father wrote his sermons with his small hands, slender quills, and never-changing convictions.

Against the east wall was the hearth in which my mother cooked. Blackened pots hung from chimney hooks. From ceiling beams dangled herbs whose leaves were as dry as old butterfly wings.

To the left was the parlor, with its own hearth. Also, a spinning wheel, which my mother used. The room having straight chairs and a settle, my family gathered there most evenings. Many a night my sisters worked their samplers by candlelight. Mother guided them. All the while Father read aloud to us from some worthy book (such as Bunyan's *Pilgrim's Progress* or Edwards's *Freedom of Will*). I was expected to answer questions Father put to me about the text, and since he was my teacher, he corrected me when I was wrong, which, by his lights, was most of the time.

We learned reading and writing at the town's little grammar school. Father gave memory training by having me repeat Bible verses. His expectation was that when I turned fifteen, I would study at Harvard College and continue the Cope line of ministers. My sisters would marry pastors.

(I admit, sometimes I fancied I might go to sea before I became a minister. I imagined running away from my family to distant islands with friends and having adventures. You may be sure this was something I never shared with my father.)

At the rear of the house was a smaller room. My sisters and I were born there, Mother's mother serving as midwife. There was also a pantry. Out back was a vegetable garden. And the privy.

Between the two front rooms were narrow steps that led up to the second floor. Under a low, slanting roof there were two modest spaces. One was where my parents slept. In the other, my sisters and I reposed. It was hot in the summer but made comfortable in cold winter by the brass bedwarmer, which another grandmother had brought across the sea from England years ago.

My father insisted we live a self-effacing, simple, and solemn life, saying we must set an example of humbleness. Displays of affection were frowned upon. Smiles rare. Sorrow silent. Laughter nonexistent. If my parents disagreed, I never knew it. Father's most oft-repeated maxim was a quote from an ancient church divine who said, "It was pride that turned angels into devils and humility that made men angels."

Once when Father said that, my sister Mercy replied, "Then I am glad I'm not a man." That brought a sharp rebuke.

From then on, whenever Father quoted the remark — it was his favorite — my sister looked at me and shared a secret eye-smirk. I had to look away, fearful of Father's disapproval.

In short, Father was forever telling me what was right and what was wrong. Now the one who had always instructed me on what to do was gone. I had been thrown into an unknown wilderness, and I was left to find my way.

I hardly knew how to take one step.

After the funeral, the family gathered around our table. Mother, pale and faint in voice, began with a recital of the same prayer Father had been reading when he was attacked. You may be sure this time the window shutters were closed.

Her voice unsteady, she read, "'Help me daily to increase in the knowledge and love of thee, my God . . .'" She went on to read the whole prayer, but as she approached the end, she hesitated, afraid or unwilling to say those fateful words. After some moments of what seemed a struggle, she read the last sentence: "'Bless, and defend, and save the king and all the royal family.'"

How curious that those words, which I had heard so often for so many years with very little thought, were now fraught with frightful hazard. It was a lesson: what we never notice can become all we see.

I understood Mother to mean that we must go on being loyal to the same faith and convictions that Father practiced, that *nothing* in our lives should change. "My advice to you all is," Mother said, her eyes on me, "be true to yourself."

The only way I could understand her was that being "true" meant being like Father.

And yet—and yet—so much had already changed. I knew it more when my mother set out the family Bible as well as quill pen and ink and told me to write down the date of Father's death next to his birth and marriage days: his entire life in stark numbers. When I finished writing them, I was sure I was meant to start a new chapter, but as far as I was concerned, our story was done. The end.

But Mother said, "Your father left a will."

"What's a will?" Faith, my younger sister, asked.

Being eight years of age—five years younger than me—Faith was the family baby and looked it. Though I was young at the time, I well remembered that when Faith was born, Mother had almost died, as many women did during childbirth. Those had been fearful days in our family, with great tension, dread, and constant prayers. Father named the baby Faith because he was sure it was our deep faith that saved mother and child. Those nerve-racking days were seared upon my heart.

Round-faced, somewhat small and delicate, Faith had dimpled hands, pink cheeks, and a way of blurting things out, asking questions Mercy—my elder sister—and I wanted to put forward but didn't, in fear we would reveal, despite being older, our ignorance.

Mother replied, "A will is a legal document that determines where Father's property should go when he dies . . . which has happened."

"Isn't the property yours?" was Faith's next question. That was what I assumed.

"When a husband dies," said Mother, "the family property goes to his wife. For the moment, everything rests in my hands. But when Noah turns eighteen, Father's will states it all goes to him."

Her words astonished me.

Mercy was equally surprised. "All?" she cried out.

Being three years older than me, Mercy thought herself a young woman and tried to act as such. Looking much like Mother, but already taller, she had dark eyes, a somewhat stub nose, a pouty mouth, and a sharp tongue. Though she and I were fond, Father, who insisted on restraint in all things, always cautioned us about expressions of affection within the family. Instead, Mercy and I were forever bickering, jockeying for authority, with her trying to tell me what I should do. Since Father was constantly preaching, Mother always deferential, and Faith so childish, Mercy, despite her sharpness, was the one with whom I felt closest. Only with me did she share her many complaints about Father's firm rules, objections I listened to with guilty (if silent) agreement. Though I never *said* I sided with her, she must have sensed I did so secretly, because she took pleasure in telling me such things.

"And," continued Mother, "there is something else."

"What?" I asked.

"As the eldest male, Noah, you are now the head of the family."

"Me?" I yelped. Being but thirteen, I considered myself far too young to take Father's place.

"I don't expect you to make judgments at this time," Mother continued. "But from now on, I'll consult you on all matters of importance. So, strive to have wise thoughts and be brave. And both of you"—she looked at my sisters—"must acknowledge your brother with new respect."

Faith gazed at me with alarm or disbelief, perhaps both.

As for Mercy, the firm set of her mouth and the slight narrowing of her eyes suggested hurt resentment at my new position. There was a tiny upward tilt of her sharp chin that showed (I thought) rejection of my elevated status. I was sure she was telling me: "I dare you to try to be superior to me."

Let it be clear: she said nothing, but I fear that I (from habit, not malice) may have answered her reaction with smuggery. Moreover, as I pushed the hair out of my face, I was unable to keep from sitting a little taller while Mercy and Faith considered me with their different gazes.

At the end of the day, I was left with sad thoughts. I noted how empty our home felt. And what folly it was to think I was head of the family. How I wished nothing had changed. Moreover, I was unable to free myself from the fear that we would be attacked. Since I was now the only male in the family, I was fearful that the Sons of Liberty might think I knew what they had asked Father about: who the town's other Loyalists were.

Before I proceed with my narration, you must know some things to better understand all that happened.

To begin: Father—as I have related—traced his ancestry back to England, to the Dorset town of Weymouth. His forefathers immigrated to Massachusetts in the year 1652, so the Copes had lived there for 122 years. However, although my father lived his entire life in New England and had never visited old England, three thousand miles away, he, as did most Massachusetts inhabitants, considered himself a citizen of what he called "our mother country." England, Great Britain, was for him "home."

When Father was ordained—at Harvard College in Cambridge—he swore upon the Bible to uphold the Church of England. He held no promise more sacred than to defend that church and its leader, King George III, the anointed monarch of Great Britain's American colonies. Father used to say, "The church is England, and England is the church. Inseparable."

As pastor of his church, he was strict but willing to listen to any man who came to him for comfort or dispute. But always, always, he clung to his fundamental beliefs—the principles of the Church of England—sure that his life on this earth and in the hereafter depended on it.

You may be sure he taught his children to hold to this faith. It never occurred to me to question him or his beliefs. His word was our law. Our way of being. It pleased me when people said I was made in his image.

His views were further shaped by recent history.

Following a successful seven-year war against the French, which ended in 1763, the English empire, bigger but poorer, used new taxes to raise revenue. The English government's reasonable—Father's word—message to her American colonies was "We defended you. You must help pay for that defense."

But many in America objected, insisting they had a right to be included in that decision but had been left out.

As I would learn later, the king and his Parliament believed that the colonies' hostility to England's new taxes came primarily from our province, Massachusetts, with Boston being the center of what they soon called a mutiny. It was true: many an angry meeting to oppose England's authority was held in Massachusetts. More than a few citizens were ready to take up arms.

For radicals—called Whigs—the villain was Great Britain's Parliament, three thousand miles across the sea. The nearby enemy was the English army. But increasingly, I had heard words objecting to our king.

My friends and I heard constant whispers about radicals marching and mustering in our community and nearby towns. There were rumors of musket collections and hidden gunpowder. The secrecy about all this excited us. We bantered about such talk—echoing our parents' views—and sometimes argued, but it was a concern for adults, not us.

When Father attended town meetings (he allowed me to come, not my sisters), he was not shy about speaking in public about politics. His views were not appreciated. All the same, he instructed me about the issues that so provoked people and caused such anger.

Those who defended King George III and his government were called Tories. For them, Parliament was showing firm resolve in the face of mob anarchy, and they believed that the British army provided protection against the rebellion. They also proclaimed their devotion to King George. Tories were also called Loyalists. Father asserted he was one of them.

"And Noah, note that these rebels and their leaders are double-dealers. They talk about liberty all the time, but some of the rebels—these Sons of Liberty—who protest that England is trying to enslave them, who cry 'Down with slavery,' are themselves enslavers of Black people. They are hypocrites. Slavery is absolutely wrong. A Christian outrage."

Father not only supported efforts to abolish slavery in Massachusetts; he preached a few sermons against it, which added to his unpopularity and also, so it was said, angered the town's richest man and sole lawyer, Mr. Hosmer.

I also knew Father's thoughts regarding what had happened the previous December when, in defiance against the tax on tea, about a hundred Boston Sons of Liberty flung chests of tea into Massachusetts Bay. The water, people said, stayed brown for days and the fish never slept.

"It is wicked to destroy property," Father lectured me. "And I'm sure London will insist that Boston pay for that tea. But it's not right that others suffer for what a few fools did. Times are hard enough. Punishing Boston will make things worse. The truth is, Noah, despite the government's tea tax, the cost of tea was made *lower* than it was before. Only smugglers suffered."

I listened mutely.

He went on to say there were hints of more laws coming, what the rebels were already calling "the Coercive Acts." One such law would be that any royal official accused of a crime would be brought to trial in England, not Massachusetts.

"To be sure," Father told me, "they will get a fairer trial in

England than here, where there is prejudice against the Crown government."

He also told me about reports that Parliament was making a law that all Massachusetts official positions—judges, magistrates, sheriffs, and the like—would be filled with people chosen by England, not Massachusetts citizens. In other words, no more elections.

"That may be necessary," Father instructed me. "If people choose the wrong kinds of leaders, they deserve to lose the right to elect them.

"My worry," he went on, "is that London, having left us alone to manage ourselves for so long, must now impose order. It's like a parent trying to control a long-neglected and disobedient son. It will take considerable firmness to set things right. But it must be done. Proverbs thirteen, twenty-four: 'He that spares his rod hates his son, but he that loves him chastises him from time to time.'

"Noah, most important," Father said, "if you ever feel our government is wrong, *any* violent response is sinful. As a father must rule his family with firmness, the king must rule his subjects.

"Put your full trust in the British constitution. Consider: Boston has some sixteen thousand people. London alone, five hundred thousand."

I was unable to imagine such an enormous number.

"And Noah, remember this," he concluded. "The Church of England and the empire are one, with the empire being greatest in the world. Never forget, you are an Englishman. Being invincible, England will protect us. Our church, country, and family deserve your total loyalty."

You may be sure I did not argue with Father. As a dutiful son, I accepted as truth everything he said. Even as Great Britain would triumph over all, it would guard us from harm.

Saturday, April 9, 1774

Though I had been told I must take Father's place, the authority that had been dropped upon my shoulders was a great and unexpected weight. I knew all too well that I was only a boy. Moreover, for my age, I was small and skinny, with more sharp edges (knees and elbows) to my body than a flight of steps. Clumsy, with big ears and forever floppy, longish hair, I thought most people believed I was wisdomless and treated me as such. Even Mercy mocked me by saying my face bore a constantly timid look. "Don't bother so much about what Father says," she once chided. "Make your own decisions." The truth is I didn't want to.

A few days after I had been proclaimed the head of the family, I made myself go outside. Once there, I tried to repair the two wooden steps that led to our door, which were loose. They had been so for a long time, since Father was never one to make quick repairs. He had loftier thoughts. With uncomfortable notions that I must demonstrate my ability to do such tasks, I decided to fix those steps.

As I bent over my inept work, I became aware that two men had come up behind me. I looked around. Ezekiel Trak and Richard Poor had drawn close. The two had been among those who tarred and feathered Father. In other words, I considered them murderers.

The moment I saw them, I was sure I was about to be killed.

"Noah Cope," came Mr. Poor's booming voice. "Come along with us. You are under arrest."

"What . . . what do you mean?" I stammered. "Who's arresting me?"

"I am," said Mr. Poor, who offered no authority other than his height and strength.

"I need to tell my mother—"

"She doesn't have to know."

With that, I was yanked to my feet and had no choice but to be marched down the road, each man holding me tightly by an arm.

"Where are we going?" I asked, my heart beating like a military drum.

"You will see."

"What are you intending to do?"

"We only wish to talk."

I did not believe them.

We passed a few townspeople. Though they stopped and stared, no one intervened. I wanted to call out but was intimidated.

I was led to the town's sole tavern, the Old Oak. The main room, the drinking room, which reeked of rum, was dim and deserted.

My captors pushed me into a small back room, where there were a few barrels, nothing more. A solitary window provided some little light.

Mr. Trak shut the door and stood before it to assert that there was no exit. Then Mr. Poor shoved me hard against the rough back wall. I was finding it difficult to breathe.

"Now," began Mr. Poor, his hot, red face only inches from mine, his drink-sodden breath all but suffocating me, "you must have heard your father speak of the town's Tories. The secret ones who support the king the way he did. We need to know: Who are they? Who has hidden guns and gunpowder?" His yellowing teeth, his bleary eyes, and the sneer of his lips made me think he was the Devil himself.

I had no knowledge of such men or of guns and powder. Let it be repeated: I did *not* have the information they desired. But despite my terror in being held by the men who had murdered my father, I wanted to cling to my father's principle of remaining mute. "I . . . I won't talk to you," I said.

"Lift your hands and put your face against the wall!" Mr. Poor shouted.

"Why?"

"Do as you're told." Not waiting on my compliance, he swung me about and shoved me into the position he wanted.

I stood there, petrified, convinced I was about to be killed. Desperately, I tried to remember one of Father's prayers, but I was too frightened.

The next moment there was a sharp, searing stroke upon my back. Mr. Poor must have brought a rod down upon me. The pain made me gasp. My legs buckled. My eyes welled with tears. Nevertheless, Mr. Poor continued to strike me ten more times. Trying not to collapse, I clutched the splintery wooden wall.

"Who are the town's secret Tories?" came the demand anew.

Wanting more than anything to act the way Father had, I somehow found the strength to say, "I . . . won't talk to you."

For my loyalty, I received five more blows before I crumpled to the floor. I must have lost consciousness. When I opened my eyes, all I saw were my tormentors' boots, and I felt intense pain across my back.

I lay there, too scared to do anything.

"Let him stay awhile," I heard one of them say. "We'll come back later. Maybe he'll have remembered."

I heard footsteps, the sound of a door shutting, a latch clacking, the snap of a lock. As soon as I knew they were gone, I broke into breath-gulping sobs.

I didn't move. I was unable to. The slightest motion caused agony. My thirst was great, too. As for thoughts, I was sure I was dying and only hoped my mother and sisters would know what had become of me and that I had remained loyal to Father's ways.

I don't know how long I stayed on the floor, feeling the pain. But after what felt like much time had passed, and I was still there, I began to ask myself if I should tell the men the truth, that I knew nothing about secret Tories, nothing about hidden guns or powder. Perhaps if I did, they would free me. Then, feeling shame for my weakness, I reminded myself afresh how my father had acted, that more than anything I must do as he did, that is, not give in to their demands. Was I not now head of my family, taking his place? Did I not have a duty to follow my father's beliefs, his ways?

In short, I resolved not to give these Sons of Liberty the satisfaction of telling them I had no information. Let them think what they wished. I would be steadfast to Father — and England — and keep my mouth closed.

It may well have been hours that I remained in that room. At some point, I think I slept. When I woke it was to the sound of the door opening, and a voice saying, "Let's try him again."

Ezekiel Trak and Richard Poor had returned.

The two men repeated what they had done before: forced me to stand up, set me against the wall, and beat me while calling for the names of the town's secret Loyalists, the ones who had gunpowder.

Each blow seemed to pierce deeper until, at last, the pain became too intense to bear. My will gave way. "I don't know anything!" I cried out. "Please stop. I don't know what you're asking for. I can't tell you anything."

I began to weep uncontrollably, as much from agony as because I knew I had failed to act like Father.

After five more strokes of the rod, I felt blood seeping down my back. I was barely able to stand. "I beg you, stop. If I knew anything about guns or Tories, I'd tell you."

"And the king?" demanded Mr. Poor. "Will you denounce him?"

"I hate the king," I cried, sobbing.

It was Mr. Trak who said, "Enough. We don't want to kill another one. He's not worth it."

They grabbed me by my arms and dragged me through the front room of the tavern, where some local men had gathered. These people — I knew them all — must have understood what had happened. I saw them looking up, faces full of alarm and fright. No one said or did anything.

I was thrust out the door and onto the dirt road. "Go home" was shouted into my ears, delivered with a hard push.

With stone-heavy feet, I staggered home, my lungs gulping air, my back a coat of pain, and my face dripping with streaming tears. But more than pain — which was intense enough — I felt a profound shame that I had given way. I had failed Father. I had said what I did not believe: "I hate the king."

My prayer was that Father — who was surely looking down upon me from heaven — would forgive me.

I was certain he wouldn't.

"I love the king," I whispered.

I reached home. My frantic family — who had not known where I was — welcomed me, eased off my blood-soaked shirt, and spread some salve my mother had made upon my torn back. I told Mother about the beating but said nothing as to how I'd given way. I was too humiliated to admit it.

"I am proud of you," Mother said. "You upheld your father." Her words made me feel worse. Believing myself a failure, a coward, I nevertheless fell into exhausted sleep.

I never told my family all of what had happened. I was too ashamed of myself. But somehow, even as I lay upon my bed, tracing the events that had led to this moment, my mind went back to that question: Who had told the Sons of Liberty about my father's prayer? I had to know.

Monday, April 11, 1774

It took two days before I was able to stand on my own. The scars remained. I have them yet, a memory etched upon my back.

During the time of my recovery, my mother and sisters attended me with much tenderness. Let it also be noted that friend of mine, Micah Downs, whose father had been part of the tar and feathering, came to our door. Mother said he asked if I would live. When she told him I would, he stammered that he was pleased to hear it before darting away. Mother said he seemed fearful of being observed.

As I lay abed, still hurting, I kept thinking how I had failed my father. How I had been disloyal. It made me hate those rebels almost as much as I hated myself for what they had forced me to do.

More than anything, I wanted to leave Tullbury. Forever. Simultaneously I told myself that I must be loyal to England and King George, no matter what pain it brought me. Firm loyalty was, I thought, the only way I'd be able to redeem myself.

Once again, Mother gathered us around the table. In a voice so small and halting, I thought she might dissolve into tears at any moment, she said, "My children, we must leave Tullbury. We . . . we cannot live among those who . . . murdered your father. And beat Noah. In truth, I fear for our safety. There has been so much violence of late. I don't think this community will support us in any way. I also have very little money to sustain us."

"Will we be allowed to leave?" I asked, trying to keep my desire to do exactly that out of my voice. I didn't want anyone to know how frightened I was.

"Let us pray so. As you know . . . I was raised in Boston. Boston was where your father and I met when he was a student at Harvard. I still have family there. My uncle William Winsop. Though it's been years since I've seen him, we'll go to him."

"Is he nice?" asked Faith in a shaky voice.

"Is he loyal?" was my question.

"I don't have answers," said Mother. "Let's hope it won't matter, and he'll help as family should. Most important, I have heard that the British army is in full control in Boston, so if we can get there, we'll be protected. Many who remain loyal to the king have already gone there for safety. Your father was determined to stay, but I think we must go." She turned to me. "Do you approve?"

"Yes," I said. Knowing we were running away, I was glad it was Mother's decision, not mine.

"How far off is Boston?" asked Faith.

"About twenty miles," I told her.

"Do we have to walk?" she asked, alarmed.

Mother said, "I shall hire a horse and cart."

Faith puckered her lips in wonder. Father had always said such equipage was frippery.

"But what about our house?" asked Mercy.

"I must sell it," said Mother. "As soon as I can learn how."

The notion that we must leave our house came down upon us like a sudden hammer. The question of where and how we would live filled the air. For some moments, no one spoke.

Mother went on. "Once in Boston, I shall endeavor to make our lives as comfortable as possible. It won't be the same. It will be hard. I may have to seek employment."

"What kind?" asked a shaken Faith.

"I can spin. Sew. Clean."

"I can work too," my older sister added.

"That may be necessary," Mother agreed.

I said, "I'll find a way to earn money."

"You may have to."

"I don't know how to do anything," said Faith in a small voice.

"When shall we leave?" I asked.

"As soon as I can make arrangements," returned Mother. "But we'd best hurry. There have been plunderings and burnings of homes of those who don't agree with the rebels. Look what they have done to us. They may well ask me—as others have been asked—to sign a loyalty oath to their cause before they let me go. I will not do it."

"Mama," said Faith, her voice fraught with fright, "Madam Elger was made to walk through town without . . . without . . . any clothes. They said it was because she wouldn't sign."

"I am aware of that," said my mother, even as her face turned red. "But I can't put my name to such a sinful thing."

"I shall protect us," I said, feeling I was expected to say that.

"What you will do," said Mother, "is keep out of danger."

By way of instruction, she, as Father had so often done, cited the Bible: "Matthew five, thirty-nine: 'Turn the other cheek.'"

"Are we turning?" asked Faith.

"It amounts to the same thing," insisted Mother.

Mercy shook her head. "We're running away," she said.

Though I said nothing, my head was full of thoughts about wanting to avenge my private disgrace. Still, beyond all else, what I most wanted was to get far away from Tullbury.

But before we left, I wanted to know who had betrayed us.

I kept puzzling over the matter. Gradually I began to have a notion.

That night, when we three children went to sleep in our room —Mercy and Faith in the same bed, I in my own—Faith said, "Noah, when you inherit Father's property, will you allow us to live in our house?"

"Goose," said Mercy, "the house will be gone. Mother must sell it. We shall be in Boston." Mercy, as she often did, sounded peeved.

After a moment of quiet, Faith said, "How big is Boston?"

"Very big," I answered. "And crowded. When Father took me there last summer, he said sixteen thousand people lived there. It's like a swarm of bees. Noisy, too."

"How many people live in Tullbury?" was Faith's next question.

"Something like three hundred," I said. "But Concord has more than a thousand."

"Oh."

There was silence until Faith said, "Noah, will you take care of us?"

"Of course," I said, knowing it was the right answer.

"You won't have to take care of me," Mercy announced.

"Why is that?"

"I shall be married."

"Married?" cried Faith. "To whom?"

I was also taken by surprise.

"It doesn't matter," said Mercy. "Somebody."

"Who would have you?" I sneered. "You won't even have a dowry. Or have you a stupid rich man in mind?"

"I shall find someone."

"I'll miss you," said Faith, suppressing another bout of weeping. After a moment she added, "I'll never marry. Noah, will you marry?"

"I'll work. And be loyal to England."

"What shall I do?" she asked.

"You can stop asking foolish questions," snapped Mercy.

There was quiet for a while, and then I said, "They might not let us leave."

"Who?" asked Faith.

"Those Sons of Liberty."

"Why?"

"They might wish to torment us more."

"Noah, do you want to leave?" Faith asked.

"Mother said we must," I said, thinking I would appear weak if I admitted I, too, wished to go.

I heard Mother pacing below. And crying. Until Father's death, I had never known her to weep.

"Mother is so sad," Faith said.

"We all are," I said.

"I don't intend to cry anymore," announced Mercy. "Feelings are a hindrance."

"Will you hold my hand as I pray?" Faith asked Mercy. She began: "Our Father . . ."

After I said my own silent prayers, I lay back and thought about what I might do in Boston—if we got there.

My loathing and fear were all about the rebels, but I had to believe, as Father had said, that British justice and power must prevail. Had not Father said Great Britain was the most powerful kingdom in the entire world? A vast empire, it would avenge his death and protect our family. Thinking all that gave me a momentous new idea. If we were able to reach Boston, I would join the British army. That way I could prove my loyalty and help justice triumph.

What would it be like to be a soldier? I wondered. Was I capable of shooting someone? Killing? Among my friends, we had talked about how British troops were taught to use their bayonets. Would I be able to stab someone?

The thought made me shudder.

As I lay there, I told myself I must be stronger and tried to consider ways to push myself in that direction.

When I was sure my sisters were asleep and my mother had retired to her room, I crept down to the first floor to where our Bible lay open. I placed my hand on the book. "I vow loyalty to Father," I whispered, "to his church, to England, and to our king, His Majesty George the Third. I'll never falter in my beliefs or faith. I will hate the rebels. In the name of Jesus Christ, amen."

It was a long time before I slept. When I did, I had nightmares, seeing my father writhe in pain upon the ground. Sometimes it was me I saw.

In the middle of the night, I woke feeling frightened. For a long while, I stared at the ceiling. I had the sensation that it was falling on me, making the sound of the dirt dropping on Father's coffin, this time burying me.

Tuesday, April 12, 1774

Though we wanted to leave Tullbury as soon as possible, it proved perplexing as to how to sell the house, much less what price should be asked. We never had many dealings in a business way, and the few we had experienced had been undertaken by Father.

Nevertheless, Mother consulted me. "Do you think I should speak to Mr. Hosmer?"

Mr. Hosmer was the only lawyer and the richest man in our town. He was known to support the rebels, and though he wasn't one of those at the tar and feathering, I considered him among our enemies. "I heard him give a speech denouncing Parliament," I informed Mother.

"When was that?"

"The last town meeting Father took me to. And Mr. Hosmer's eldest, Abner, marches with the Concord militia."

Mother grimaced. "Noah, Mr. Hosmer drew up your father's will. I don't know another person to ask. I have to speak to him, but you must come with me."

"When?"

"Before long, we will be out of food, and I don't wish to go to market."

She, too, I realized, feared our fellow townspeople.

"So, I must see Mr. Hosmer soon."

I dreaded that moment. Save for visiting the privy, we had stayed inside our house since my beating. Going to Lawyer Hosmer meant we would have to walk through town again.

We spoke of it no more that night. Instead, to pass the time,

Mother set me to reading some of Father's religious books to my sisters.

Father had died, but his ways lived on.

Friday, April 15, 1774

A few days later — I think it took that long for Mother to gather up her courage, or perhaps our pantry was empty — she and I walked down the road to Mr. Hosmer's home, which stood adjacent to our town's meetinghouse. Being fearful of neighbors, I struggled to hide my fright when we passed some people. Of course, we knew one another, but they wouldn't look at us. We had become unwanted outsiders. Worse: enemies. My chief thought was *I must get away*. We even went by that best friend of mine, Micah. Soon as he saw me, he shifted about. We might as well have been strangers. I worked to keep my hurt within, along with my shame. How many people, I worried, knew what had happened at my beating and that I had given way? Fearful of another assault, I kept walking and said nothing,

Mr. Hosmer's house — the finest in Tullbury — was a two-story stone building of deep gray, with a gabled roof, windows with fine shutters, and stout chimneys at both ends of the roof. Overall, it was neat and plain but showed wealth.

"Are you ready?" Mother asked me when we came up to the door.

I nodded.

She knocked. I saw a curtain flutter, which told me someone was peeking out.

I said, "What if Mr. Hosmer refuses to speak to us?"

Mother made no response but stood straight, her hands clasped.

We waited. It took some time before the door was opened by a woman whom I knew was enslaved by Mr. Hosmer. I didn't know her name. But no doubt she had asked the question "Should I let Madam Cope in?"

"Mr. Hosmer, please," said Mother.

"Who shall I say is calling?" asked the mobcapped, aproned woman, although I was sure she already knew.

"Madam Cope. And Master Noah Cope."

"Yes, madam. Please come in."

We were led into a room. There was a desk in the center and a row of law volumes on a shelf. Seated behind the desk was Mr. Daniel Hosmer.

He was a large, puff-gut man, with a bagwig, a florid, jowly face — complete with bushy eyebrows and wet, red lips — a wide neck, and hands like flabby bear claws. His constant frown suggested a man who was always about to object, even as his deep-set eyes showed shrewdness.

When we came in, he stood, grunting from the effort, and made as much of a bow as his belly allowed. Hearing his heavy breathing, I thought him tense. He must have known about my father's death and my thrashing. I knew I feared him. I also hated him, but which came first it was hard to say.

"Madam, I am sorry for your misfortune," he muttered without grace, and gestured to an empty chair that had been placed before his desk. He didn't bother to look at me.

Mother, fingers interlocked, sat. I stood behind her. We all waited until Mother said, "Mr. Hosmer, sir, I need to sell my house."

"Ah. You are leaving Tullbury?"

"I am."

"For good?"

"Yes, sir."

"Hmm. Well, well." The man seemed relieved. Perhaps he had thought we were going to lay charges. "I think that's for the best," he said. "These times . . . Where will you be going?"

"Boston."

"Ah, yes, of course," said the lawyer as his eyebrows went up. His unspoken words, "That's where Tories go," hung in the air.

"Have you a buyer?" he inquired.

"No."

"Then, madam, how am I to assist you?"

"I have little ready cash, Mr. Hosmer. By selling the house, I can — among other things — purchase a horse and cart to get my family to Boston with such possessions as we have and survive a little longer with what remains. I'm requesting your help, sir."

Mr. Hosmer pressed his big hands together, no doubt trying to squeeze out some sympathy. "Well, well. Hmm. I fear, madam, that no one in town will buy your house. I have to say your late husband was not . . . appreciated. People would not wish to be . . . hmm . . . associated."

"He was murdered," I blurted out.

"Well, they say . . . indeed," said the lawyer without looking at me. "Anyway, he died. These times . . . are difficult. Tempers are taut. Anger great. Our lives are endangered."

"Not by my husband."

"Hmm . . . well . . . the English army . . ."

"Mr. Hosmer, I have come to you for help, not a speech."

"Well, yes, I appreciate that . . . Perhaps . . . perhaps I can provide some."

"How, sir?"

"If, madam, you would be willing . . . please . . . be under no pressure . . . to sign over your house to me . . . well . . . I might be able to secure you a wagon and horse."

My pale mother turned paler still and was silent for a moment. "Do I understand you, sir? Are you saying that you'll exchange my entire house . . . for a wagon and horse?"

"The *loan* of a wagon, madam. Purely a loan." He breathed deeply. "Madam," he said into the silence, "I am trying to help you."

That was when I said, "Such a trade is not equal, sir."

He turned to me. "Boy," he said, "I'll have no comments from a coward."

He might as well have struck me across my face. My shame surged. My cheeks grew hot. Tears welled in my eyes. To have my disgrace at giving way during my beating proclaimed aloud cut deep. But I had no choice other than to stand there.

"You might think it unequal, madam," Mr. Hosmer said to my mother, "but . . . after all . . . hmm . . ." He opened his big hands wide, as though to prove they were empty. "These times . . . I assure you, I will have trouble disposing of the house. A Tory house is, well . . . tainted. My offer is best. May I add, it would be advisable that you leave . . . soon."

To my ears, that sounded like a threat.

Mother remained silent. At last, she said, "Very well. We shall do so. When can you bring the horse and wagon?"

"Ah . . . give me a few days. You may expect my son to take you. His name is Abner. A most responsible boy. People hereabouts think well of him. Recently voted a captain by the Concord town militia. He shall bring the necessary papers for you to sign."

Mother, shaken, her face pinched with discomfort, stood up, hands on the chair back to steady herself. "Thank you, sir, for your help. Come, Noah. We must go."

As she turned to leave, Mr. Hosmer lurched to his feet and mumbled, "Madam, let me assure you . . . it's for the best that . . ." His voice faded off into hollow silence.

We left.

As Mother and I walked back along the road, I was full of mortification at Mr. Hosmer's rebuke, to the degree that I was trembling. But I'm sure Mother did not realize what I was feeling. I certainly was not going to tell her. From what Mr. Hosmer had said, I was convinced the whole town knew what had happened to me. I also knew that our leaving would be equally known by everyone. My desire to leave grew even greater.

Echoing my thoughts, Mother said, "Noah, I'm afraid we can do no better. I worry for our safety. We need to leave before more terrible things happen."

I said, "Mr. Hosmer's son, that Abner—you heard what his father said. He's part of the rebel militia over in Concord."

Mother said nothing but took my arm.

We continued without speaking until Mother said—letting her thought become audible—"Yes, better for us to be in Boston. We shall be protected."

"The army," I said, as strongly as I could.

"I trust so."

"Mother," I said, "if we reach Boston, I . . . I intend to join it."

"Join what?"

"The army."

She halted and gave my arm a firm squeeze. The expression on her face was sad. "Noah, your father would not have allowed that. He wanted you to become, God willing, a minister. Like him."

Wishing to avoid an argument, the best I was able to reply was "I . . . will try."

We continued walking.

After a while, Mother said, "I will send a letter to my Uncle William—in Boston—and tell him what has happened. That we are coming."

"Will he have us?"

"We shall all pray tonight."

The letter was written but never sent. The post rider refused to carry a Loyalist letter. Said it might contain secrets.

Knowing nothing about this Uncle William, and unable to contact him, we could only hope he'd welcome us to Boston.

Saturday, April 16, 1774
Since we lived frugally, it was no great matter to gather clothing, shoes, hats, boots, and blankets. Of course, the family Bible. Father's

books, his pocket watch (his one vanity). Dishes. A pair of old candlesticks, which were wedding presents given to my parents long ago.

These things were placed in an ancient wooden sea chest that had come from England decades past. Still, it was a matter of waiting two days for the wagon to arrive. Let it be understood, we weren't sure it would.

The hours passed with painful slowness. Mother, dressed in black, sat in a corner, hands clasped, constantly wiping away tears, looking like death's shadow. Faith whimpered and fidgeted. Mercy continued her aloof sulking and refused to look at me. I kept to myself, nursing my anger at everything. Time passed like a long winter.

Sunday, April 17, 1774

The night before we were meant to leave, after Mother and my sisters went to bed, I lay awake. When I was sure everyone was asleep, I crept outside. The almost-half-moon afforded enough light, and I had no trouble walking along the town's deserted dirt road to the meetinghouse.

At the back wall of the house was an open shed in which wood for winter heat was stored. My friends and I had stacked the wood so that there was a hollowed-out section. We used more logs to mostly block off the entryway and create a small closet-like space that shielded us from view, so it was a secret spot for our private talk.

Certain that my friends would have learned that I was leaving the next day, I was hoping that they would show up at our usual meeting place. As I approached, I observed a small flutter of light. Someone was there.

"Who is it?" I called in a whisper.

"Nathaniel."

I was relieved. Nathaniel Farrington was one of my best friends. Though he was taller than me, we were about the same age. Over the years we had done many things together — visited each other's houses (his father made barrels), walked through the woods, fished, hunted squirrels, and battled each other with spinning tops — things I mostly kept from Father. When I was with Nathaniel and my other friends, we prattled, talking about anything. Of course, we also talked about the troubled times, what was happening. Sometimes (echoing our fathers) we disagreed, but it hadn't seemed to matter.

I went around the barrier. Nathaniel was sitting cross-legged on the ground, into which a small burning candle had been stuck.

He looked up at me. "Heard you're leaving tomorrow," he said. "Hoped you'd come." Though the light was dim, I saw he kept glancing at me, only to shift his eyes away. "Micah said he'd try. Don't know why he hasn't come."

"It's all right," I said, sitting down.

"Sorry about . . . what happened," Nathaniel muttered. "I mean. . . your father. I heard my father say they didn't intend to kill him."

"They did, though. And lashed my back."

"Everyone knows. Does it hurt bad?"

"Not really," I lied.

"That Richard Poor is a mean one."

"He is."

We sat for a while, not talking, both of us gazing upon the small candle flame.

He said, "I heard you are going to Boston."

I nodded.

"I don't blame you."

I said, "I'm a Loyalist. I intend to defend the king."

"How?"

"I'm going to join the British army."

"Not the navy?" Nathaniel and I had spent whole afternoons concocting plans to run off and sign on to ships.

I shook my head.

"Maybe you'll come back with the army."

"I'll try not to shoot you."

He said, "Remember that time at Botter's Creek when we floated that log and you fell in and I pulled you out?"

I nodded.

"Saved your life. So, you owe me one." He forced a laugh before lapsing into quiet. Then he said, "Did Micah . . . did Micah have a meal with you and your family?"

"About a week before the tarring. Why?"

"Did your father read a prayer that said, 'Bless, and save, and defend the king'?"

"He always did."

Nathaniel hesitated, then he said, "Micah told his father."

If hearts were able to shed tears, at that moment mine did so. Micah's father was part of the Sons of Liberty and the tar and feathering. In other words, one of my best friends told a rebel what my father had read. That was why my father was killed. Why I was beaten.

Nathaniel looked up at me. In the small light of the candle, I saw tears glisten on his cheeks. He said, "He feels really bad about it." *It* being my father's murder.

Though incensed, I chose not to speak.

We continued to sit in silence. Then Nathaniel said, "Got something here." From behind his back, he fetched out a ball of string. "For you," he said, holding it out.

I knew his string ball well. We all did. It had taken Nathaniel years to collect. It consisted of bits and pieces of twine, mostly short, found here and there, tied together, and then wrapped into the ball. Among us boys, it was kind of a joke. Its sole purpose was itself, but it was his most treasured belonging.

"Sorry you're going," he said, dumping his string ball at my feet. "Keep it."

With that, he jumped up and left, leaving me alone with his gift.

I blew out the candle and sat for a while in the dark. Then I took up the ball, only to put it back down. I wanted nothing from Tullbury, not even string.

I walked back home along the empty road. Once in bed, I lay wondering if I ever would come back. If I did, and I was a soldier, would I have to shoot Nathaniel? The idea of it made me queasy. *Leave . . .* was the thought that filled my head. I would be safe in Boston.

That night I had more bad dreams.

Not long after dawn, Lawyer Hosmer's wagon came. As promised, his son Abner was at the reins. Twenty years old, he was big and lumbering, round-faced like his father. But unlike his father, his large, brown, cow-like eyes suggested simplicity. Since he was older than me, I didn't know him, save that I now considered him one of my enemies. I loathed that it was he who would take us away. For all of that, he was civil and helped me load our chest into the wagon. A pile of Father's religious books was heaped in a corner of the wagon. While we did the work, we didn't say one word to each other.

Abner offered some papers to my mother. "My father says you must sign these. I have pen and ink."

Without reading the conveyance, Mother wrote her name where Abner pointed with his stubby finger. Once she was done, our house was gone. There was nothing to do but leave.

I looked about. Some of our women neighbors had come out of their homes and stood by their doors to watch our going. They surely knew what was happening, but they kept a silent distance, though they had been our neighbors for years.

Our family, the four of us, stood together in front of the closed door of our — no longer our — house. Mother, her face forlorn, her long, narrow hands clasped, spoke a short prayer, looking upward. No doubt she was addressing Father directly in her small, shaky voice. I was sure the moment was agonizing for her, but there were no more tears, only the deepest sorrow in her eyes.

Faith, sniveling, clung to Mother's apron.

Mercy remained silent. She and I stood together but spoke nothing, keeping our eyes on Mother.

Young Hosmer had the decency to wait. I think he even looked away.

Mother made a movement to get into the wagon. I helped her up. She sat next to Abner on the driver's seat. Mercy, Faith, and I sat within the wagon bed.

Abner gathered the reins and glanced around at Mother, waiting for her permission. No one spoke. Our silence was the silence of the grave.

I was thinking: *Move. Get to Boston. Leave. Never come back.* To hide my feelings—I felt like crying—I let my hair fall over my face.

Though Mother was staring straight ahead, she must have noticed Abner's look, because she pushed a strand of gray hair under her bonnet and gave a tiny nod. Abner clucked to the horse—an old, swaybacked, piebald nag—and shook the reins. Never mind my sense of urgency and fear, we set off at a plodding pace, passing our mute, staring neighbors. I hated them. I hated everything. Most of all, I hated myself.

As soon as we started to move, a teary-eyed Faith scrambled to the rear of the wagon. On her knees, holding to the board, she stared behind us, unwilling to relinquish the past. Mercy, the opposite, looked ahead, her body rigid, her face blank, so I could not tell her thoughts. As for me, I refused to look anywhere but at my own feet. Boston would, I prayed, provide safety. If we got there.

I had a sudden thought: *Who will tend Father's grave?*

Hot with anger, I hawked up spit into my mouth and spat onto the road, hoping I was observed. Mercy, noticing, made a fist and struck me on my leg as a reprimand. I ignored her.

I had another thought: After we'd buried Father, Mother had told me that I had inherited all his property. Now, I realized, I had no property. None.

We rolled on. The old road was full of pits that jolted us. No one spoke. Faith whimpered. Mother kept sighing. Mercy remained stonefaced. I shut my eyes and struggled to show — as Father had taught — no emotions. The truth is I was full of grief. I knew very well we were homeless, exiles in our own land.

PART 2

1774

Monday, April 18, 1774, continued

It is oft suggested that on unhappy days—and it was surely a wretched one for me—the weather joins the temper of the moment with gray and gloomy skies. The weather that day, however, was nothing of the kind. The air was bonny mild, the sky a robin's-egg blue. Trees were abloom with new green leaves, while birds savored the slide of sweet air on slender wings. All the beauty of a New England spring was offered. It made me angry.

Why, Lord, I demanded in my head, *are we being treated so harshly?* But, in truth, I did not blame God. Since it was the Sons of Liberty who had murdered Father, it was an easy stride for me to blame all those who were in rebellion. Hardly a surprise, then, that I set my loathing on the radicals while constructing fanciful plots of retaliation. Once again, I promised myself that I would join the king's army.

During the previous summer, I had gone to Boston with Father when he attended church business. "With you destined for the ministry," he had told me, "it's never too soon to make connections and let them know you are my son."

As I had not been so far from home before, that trip had been memorable. Having walked the road then, I somewhat knew the way we were now taking. That meant my alarm increased because it was common knowledge that the Sons of Liberty were active in such places as Concord, Lexington, and Lincoln, towns through which we must pass. I knew no one in the towns, nor did I want to. But

I worried that information had been laid against my father, against my family. Me. It was well known that the radicals were in constant communication. I feared that we would be stopped, questioned, or worse. I prayed I would have the courage to protect my family.

As if to mock my desire to move fast, we continued unhurriedly along the bumpy dirt road, plodding past houses, farm fields, stone walls, and stands of trees. We entered Concord by its North Bridge and went through the town slowly, which increased my anxiety. We passed the mill, the town meetinghouse, a tavern, the pond, a church, and then continued on the Boston Road. No one paid us any heed. All was calm, except me.

Having passed Concord unmolested, I felt my tension ease.

At some point, Mother asked for a pause. She left her seat and came into the wagon bed to comfort Faith, who refused to be consoled. Though Mother said nothing, I sensed that she, too, feared being attacked. By comforting Faith, she took her mind off her own fears.

Mercy sat next to Abner.

Preferring to remain aloof, I stayed where I was, doing nothing but watching the world we passed, alert for trouble, hoping it would not come.

We continued along the six miles to Lexington, a town with some 750 people (Father had told me that), more than twice the size of Tullbury. We passed the village school, the common, the church, a tavern. I was hoping Mother would not halt for food, because Lexington was another town known for its rebels. That we pressed on toward Boston gave me further relief.

Faith, exhausted by her emotions, slept, her head in Mother's lap. Mercy talked to Abner. To my annoyance, it sounded like cheerful chatter, almost flirting.

Sullen, I kept to myself.

Rather than entering Cambridge on the way to Boston, we skirted it by taking what Abner called the Watertown Road. I was disappointed not to see the Harvard buildings where my father had studied.

By that time, I had replaced Mercy sitting next to Abner. The first thing he did was mutter, "Sorry about your father."

I gave (I confess) only a rude nod to acknowledge I heard him but offered no further response. Even so, Abner tried to engage me in talk, prattling about how, on his twentieth birthday, he had been elected a captain in the Concord militia. I suspected the rank was achieved only because his father was rich. I held my anger, saying nothing, and kept my eyes fixed on the road.

Trying to suggest how knowledgeable he was of military matters, Abner chattered about gunpowder, how it was made of saltpeter, charcoal, and sulfur. "Hard to get or make," he told me. "Most of it comes from Europe."

I refused to be like Mercy and blather, so continued my silence. As far as I was concerned, Abner was no friend. Quite the contrary. Still, his talk made me think about how he was part of the rebels' militia, while I hoped to be part of the British army. Might we, I mused, meet on a field of battle? Who would win? *The British, of course*, I told myself with satisfaction.

We moved through Brookline and, after passing through the small town of Roxbury, approached Boston by midafternoon. The strong, salty smell of the sea — so different from inland forest scents — filled the air. Gulls wheeled overhead to welcome us, though there was nothing polite in their screeching, the sound of which put me in mind of the Tullbury town meetings I had attended. With growing eagerness, I told myself I was glad we had left Tullbury and tried to imagine what our lives would be like in Boston. Though in fact I had no idea, there was still an upstirring of my mood.

Drawing ever closer to the town, Abner told me that we would be crossing "the Neck," the thin isthmus that connected Boston (at the south) to the mainland (Roxbury). If the bay water proved to be at high tide, he warned, the Neck would be submerged. If so, he said, we'd have to wait for the tide to turn, or take the ferry from Charlestown to the north side of Boston, some six hundred yards across the Charles River. By then it would be night.

The Neck, Abner further informed me, was half a mile long but no more than 120 feet wide. "Nothing but mudflats on either side. Hope the tide is low. Can get squashy."

Though he was, I knew, trying to be friendly, I gave back no more than a grunt. I found his chatty manner irritating but consoled myself with the thought that I'd never have to see him again.

As it happened, the bay tide was for the most part low, so we were able to proceed via the Neck. As we rolled forward, the road smoother, I took note of a windmill and the town gallows. I welcomed the gallows as a sign of law and order and hoped the town hanged murderers. I also observed — Father had previously pointed them out to me — the graves of sinful suicides, buried outside the town limits. That my return to Boston included sights of death fit my mood of vengeance.

It wasn't long before we came to crude fortifications — what Abner called breastworks: dirt piled up a few feet high for defense — the gates of which marked the first entryway to Boston. Reaching it, we were required to halt.

Impeding our way were a few British soldiers, upon whom I looked with admiration. They wore bright red jackets, blue cuffs, white trousers, and, across their chests, white sashes that held ammunition pouches with polished royal badges. In the soldiers' hands were long muskets with glistening bayonets, visibly sharp. To me, the men appeared strong, fierce, and invincible. The notion that I might soon be dressed like that, be like that, filled me with zeal. Having reached these soldiers, I felt my family had attained protection. The fear that we would be attacked dwindled.

An officer approached our wagon. He started to speak to Abner, but Abner deferred to my mother. "Madam," the officer said, "what brings you here?"

"The rebels tarred and feathered my husband, sir," she informed him. "He died. Afterward, they beat my boy."

"Why?"

"My husband and son defended our king."

"Where was this?"

"Tullbury, sir. West of Concord."

The officer touched his brow in a salute. "I'm sorry for your troubles, madam. You may be sure we'll protect you." As he spoke, he gave me a salute as well, inspiring my gratitude and pride.

The officer turned toward the soldiers standing by the gate and waved his hand. The lift-rail went up. Once we went by, it came down again, keeping out our enemies. A surge of relief passed through me. *We are truly safe*, I told myself. I had no doubt the might of the British Empire would, as Father had said, protect us. Our loyalty rewarded by safety and calm.

Even as I had such thoughts, I heard Abner murmur, "Can't wait to shoot a redcoat."

Under my breath, I muttered, "And I to be one of them."

If he heard me, he said nothing.

We continued along the narrow causeway, passing through the true entry to Boston by way of its south side, even as we observed the multiple church spires that marked the North End, the crowded part. Abner, who must have noticed I was looking about, said, "It's two miles from the Neck to the North End. Hudson's Point. That's the wealthy section. The town is one and a quarter miles wide. This section here is Portuguese. Over there, by Fort Hill, that's the Black section. They say there are some eight, nine hundred Black people here." He made another nod: "Lot of chandlers near this spot."

I continued my silence, only then realizing I had no idea where Uncle William's home might be.

Boston houses were crowded together. Buildings were, for the most part, wood, and I could see that a few old ones had survived multiple fires. There were a fair number of brick structures, while a few were stone. They were one, two, or three stories high, many with shops on lower levels.

The streets were narrow and appeared to have been laid out by blind and wiggly worms. The perambulating crowds made it easy to believe that the town had a population of sixteen thousand. My ears filled with constant babble, some in languages strange to me. The realization that we would be living in this disorderly, congested place tipped me back into discomfort. Even I, who had seen Boston before, found it chaotic. Without Father at my side, the town seemed more complicated and overwhelming than I recalled.

The air smelled of bay waters, rum, and tobacco mixed with the stench of the horse and cow dung that lay everywhere. Pigs and honking geese roamed free.

Large numbers of people were going about their business midst horses, wagons, wheelbarrows, sedan chairs, and even a few coaches. Though I was sure I observed more people than when I'd first been to Boston, I tried to act as though all was ordinary.

Laborers—called mechanics—were the majority on the streets. They wore broad-brimmed hats, linen shirts, leather aprons or smocks. They walked with a kind of swagger and were loud when they talked.

The wealthier men I saw—in Tullbury we boys called them "goldfinches"—were topped with bagwigs, though most men had natural hair tied in pigtails and wore tricorn hats, cutaway coats, and tight-fitting breeches. Jackboots or low shoes. Some had canes.

Here and there I saw Black people. Father had told me there were a fair number of free Blacks in town, though most were enslaved. I found it impossible to guess their position by looking.

Women wore long, wide skirts, with tight-waisted bodices and elbow-length sleeves. On their heads, caps or bonnets. They appeared to move about as freely as any man.

As we proceeded down what I would come to know as Orange Street (named for William of Orange—England's former king), I gazed upon the constricted streets and mazy alleys while catching glimpses of multiple wharves sticking out into the bay like so many roads to distant worlds. I remembered Father telling me that each year a thousand ships, laden with cargo, left Boston. It was hard for me to comprehend numbers so large, but the ships, tied up to the wharves, sprouted a forest of masts and spars.

Seeing the vessels, for a fleeting moment I recalled my dream of going to sea. I had the passing notion that it might be best to leave Boston and go to London. In haste, I dismissed such thoughts. Instead, I reminded myself that though I had been to Boston but once, and then only briefly, Massachusetts was my home, where my family had lived for more than a hundred years. This was where we belonged, where I must demonstrate—and prove—my loyalty.

Faith's eyes, seeing all this for the first time, were big as she tried to take in the disorder of the large town. "So many people," I heard her whisper to herself, she who knew only little Tullbury. That Tullbury was insignificant must have been startling for her to realize.

Mercy was stonefaced.

For my part, I worried that when people considered me, I'd be judged as an awkward country lad. I was pleased, then, to see any number of boys dressed like I was, in my trousers, low shoes, and cutaway brown linen jacket (that Mother had made), with its pewter buttons. When I saw other boys, I felt the desire to have new friends. Then I remembered what Micah had done and told myself I needed to be exceedingly careful whom I trusted.

To my relief, no one paid us any mind, and we received looks of neither like nor dislike. Instead, there was utter indifference toward us. That no one knew us gave me, after Tullbury, where I knew everybody, the freeing sensation that I had turned invisible. That said, I also felt alone, all too aware that in crowded Boston I knew no one.

I looked to Mother, who had once lived here. Her face was full of tension, which, I belatedly realized, was likely because she didn't know how we would be received. New thoughts jolted me: *What if Uncle William turns us away into the night? Will he be Whig or Tory? What kind of world is it when you don't know if family are enemies?*

"Is Uncle William married?" Faith asked abruptly. "Does he have children?"

No one answered. No one knew. Not even Mother.

"Where to?" Abner asked my mother.

"Hog Alley," she replied. That being the first time I heard the name, I imagined the worst.

"I think I know it," said Abner.

———

We went farther along Orange Street.

To the left, Frog Lane headed west. To the right, Essex Street went east. We passed something I had seen the previous summer—the Liberty Tree, so celebrated by the rebels, and where they often met. To my disgust, I saw crude paper figures of miniature, red-coated soldiers hanging from the tree by their necks.

How violent the rebels were.

Orange Street now became Newbury Street, paved with pebbles that made our wagon bobble and jerk. Other streets either were surfaced in the same fashion or were dirt. Narrow walkways were separated from the street by wooden posts.

We made a sharp left turn, at which point Abner announced, "Hog Alley."

A quick glance assured me that Hog Alley had no swine. It was simply a dirt street no more than eleven feet wide, enough to allow Abner's wagon to pass. Nor was it long. The western end was open. A few wooden houses stood on both sides of the street. A couple of these had two stories. The others had but one.

"There," Mother called out, pointing. "Uncle William's house. I remember it." She indicated a shab-rag one-story wooden house, set upon an old stone foundation.

Compared with our Tullbury home, the house seemed mean and small. Covered with clapped boards, perhaps white at construction, it had dulled to gull gray. At its center was a single broad chimney, set against an angled roof covered with wood shingles, some curled with age. Two windows (with old, thick glass) fronted the street.

One shutter was askew. A wide front door was approached by a single stone step, which was crooked. Though I had not known what to expect, I felt disappointment.

Abner brought the wagon to a stop.

"Does Uncle William like children?" whispered Faith, her voice full of disquiet.

"I'm sure he does," said Mother. But she was squeezing her hands so tightly they had turned white.

"Beggars can't be choosers," said Mercy in her caustic voice.

"Are we beggars?" asked Faith.

Mercy and I exchanged looks that said, "Yes."

I asked, "What does Uncle William do?"

"It doesn't matter," said Mother, who, I only then realized, had no idea. "Noah, knock upon the door. Say what I told you. We need to know if he'll have us."

We need to know if he'll have us. A simple statement, but the hinge upon which our lives now swung.

Apprehensive, I climbed out of the wagon, went to the door, pushed the hair out of my face, took a deep breath, then knocked three times, pausing between the raps, making each one louder than before.

I waited.

When no one answered, I turned around, thinking, *We have no home,* even as my look asked Mother if I should knock again.

She gave a tense, curt nod, telling me I must try once more. But before I could do so, the door opened.

In front of me stood a short and stout old man. He was wearing a stained green coat and an unclean wig in lopsided fashion (it must have been hastily clapped on), which gave him an almost comical appearance. His small, wrinkled face bore the ill-shaved stubble of gray whiskers, while his eyes were rimmed with red. His cravat was untied. Buttons were missing from his coat. His right-hand fingers were smeared with black. Overall, he appeared old and careless, with little resemblance to Mother.

"Yes, boy? Is there something I can do for you?" said the man in a croaky voice.

I bowed. "Sir, do I have the honor of addressing Mr. William Winsop?"

"Aye, that's me."

"Sir, my name is Master Noah Paul Cope, son of Madam Clemency Cope, your niece, who is the widow of the late Pastor Solomon Cope." Those were the words my mother had bid me say. Once I spoke, I moved aside and gestured to her. Uneasy, she had remained sitting in the wagon.

Mr. Winsop took a limping step out his door, leaned forward, and peered at Mother in short-eyed fashion. She returned a weak, pathetic smile while lifting fingers in a timid greeting. Mercy and Faith, on their knees in the wagon, gawked at the man. Faith, I was sure, was about to cry. Mercy glowered. What I felt was acute embarrassment.

Mr. Winsop turned to me. "And what is it you wish, boy?"

Before I answered, my mother called out, "Uncle, I cry mercy. My husband was murdered by rebels."

Responding to the term "Uncle," the old man leaned forward a second time and squinted. "Clem? Is that you?" He used the shortened form of my mother's name, something I seldom heard. I was now sure he was Uncle William. Was I relieved? I was mostly disheartened that he was such an old man.

"Yes, Uncle," she answered. "It's me."

"Your husband, Parson Cope, was *murdered?*" His mouth had dropped open, even as he used his dirty fingers to cover it. "How in the good Lord's name . . . when . . . ?"

That was when I blurted out, "Tarred and feathered for refusing to denounce our king, sir."

"How . . . frightful." That Uncle William seemed appalled eased my worry. I was, moreover, glad Abner heard him speak so.

"Dear uncle," Mother said, "my children and I have no home. Would you offer us some Christian charity by way of shelter?"

The man, taken aback by such an unexpected appeal, rolled his small hands one over the other. "My dear niece . . . I am but a bleached bachelor, a simple scrivener with modest means, and . . ."

He faltered and rubbed his nose as if that would bring clear thought. It left a black smudge. "How many," he asked, "are you?"

"Just me and my three children, sir," returned Mother. "I'll keep house for you, Uncle. Sew your buttons. Provide order. We will stay out of your way."

Uncle William rubbed his forehead—he seemed to have a whole alphabet of anxious gestures—which caused his wig to dip. In haste, he pushed it back.

"I own," he said, "I'm not fond of those radicals Mr. Adams or

Mr. Hancock and their ruffians. They have brought misery to this once-happy town. Times, I fear, are perilous."

Though the names he mentioned were nothing to me, I was much relieved by Uncle William's words. He appeared not to be a Whig. Not a rebel.

"I don't know those men," returned my mother. "But we, sir, are in misery too."

"My house is small," said Uncle William. "As am I. Have you much by the way of possessions?"

"A sea chest, sir. Books. Nothing more." Mother held out her hands, a doleful gesture that showed utter emptiness. I felt shame: Mother was begging.

Uncle William's mouth screwed up with what appeared to be difficult considerations. He rubbed his nose again. "My few rooms are not large, Clem. Nor well ordered. I confess I'm neither tidy nor much used to company. And I have a case of gout. Rather . . . painful."

I was sure he was making excuses.

"No matter, Uncle," said Mother. "I assure you. I shall do the cooking. Take care of your house. Ease your age."

The man seemed bewildered. "So sudden," he said. "But if . . . if . . . for a brief while. Your late mother, Clem — my sister — and I were fond. I can recall your marriage day. Your wedding breakfast was a cheerful celebration. As for Mr. Cope, if somewhat dour, he was a gentleman. Murdered? How dreadful. But you are kin . . . and times . . . are perilous," he repeated while rubbing an ear.

We waited in suspense.

"Do tell," he said. "How are you regarding the . . . the . . . shall I say, public disputes?"

"I'm a Loyalist, sir," I exclaimed.

Uncle William looked at me with evident approval. "Ah, well said, young man, well said. Well said. Then we shall be under no obligation to quarrel." Even so, he remained standing on his threshold, once again folding his hands one over the other, molding a decision.

"Now, Clem," he said at last, "best come along. Families have obligations. We must see what we can do. Times are perilous," he repeated with, I think, a sigh of resignation.

With that, he retreated into his house, leaving the door open, which we took as an invitation to follow.

Our relief was great.

Mother and the girls climbed out of the wagon. Abner and I unloaded our sea chest and set it in Uncle William's vestibule. As for Father's religious books, they were stacked in a corner. (I don't believe they were touched by anyone again.) Then Abner went off, but not before Mercy was far too effusive (I thought) in her thanks.

It was thus that we moved into Uncle William's Boston house, which, though a major event, took only moments.

For my part, I felt that, having taken something like a dangerous sea voyage, we had reached safe harbor. But then, as the door shut behind us, I realized I had no idea as to what came next.

———

Great-Uncle William's house had four rooms, two front, two back, all in utter disarray. There was also, as I would learn, a low, dirt basement. The rooms, then, needed much cleaning before decent order was achieved. In other words, Uncle's appearance, not the trimmest, was replicated within his house. All the same, we were glad to be there.

In one of the front rooms was a standing desk, along with multiple candle stubs and a stack of foolscap paper and parchment, because my uncle, as he had said, was a scrivener. That is, he copied letters and documents (correspondence, bills, and invoices) in a neat hand. Spoiled letters were crumpled up and cast off, so the floor had the look of a wilted flower garden. His occupation also explained the large bottle of iron gall ink, a sand bowl, the jar of quills — looking like a turkey's tail — a quill-paring knife, and his ink-stained hands. His wig, like a blob of dirty snow, hung upon a peg. As we were soon to observe, his pencraft was the sole well-ordered thing about him.

Eager to prove our value, Mother, my sisters, and I, despite the hour, set about cleaning his house. We found an old straw broom (unused) and worked it. Some useful rags, the same. I came upon a leather fire bucket, walked out to the main street, found a pump well, and brought water back, then used it to scrub floors. There was the question of food, so Mercy and Faith were sent forth and with some of our scant money somehow purchased cabbage and chips of salted cod.

While all this was happening, Uncle William stood before his desk and lit candles — no doubt wishing to demonstrate his trade—and made fair copies of some letters. "Merchant affairs" was his brief and solemn explanation.

Dinner—Mother prepared a fish-and-cabbage soup—was had around a little table, served with our family's pewter cups and spoons. I took comfort that the room was lit by our candlesticks.

During our meal, Uncle William professed his house had never been so clean. "Perhaps," he said with a shy smile, "we can make a success of this. I rather like it. And you, sir," he added, turning to me, "would you be willing to deliver my work from time to time?"

"Yes, sir."

"Excellent. As you may have observed, my walking suffers. Your assistance would provide a bit of welcome ease."

At one point, Mother asked her uncle, "And what of your brother in Worcester? My Uncle John?"

"A radical Whig," said Uncle William with a frown. "We no longer communicate."

That, too, pleased me.

Even as he spoke, there was the sound of a booming cannon, which made us start.

"Pay no heed," said Uncle William. "It's the army's evening gun. The Commons is close. Upon lowering their flag each sunset, they fire the cannon."

We nodded.

In a back room, we found a rope bed, the ropes slack across the frame. That night, Mother slept on it, while my sisters and I slept upon the floor, huddled together. In time, we purchased another bed. We were also able to string a blanket wall-to-wall to make two smaller rooms: one part for Mother and my sisters, the other for me. It meant I had to forgo my regular evening tattle-talks with Mercy and Faith.

Uncle William had his own room.

The privy was out back.

It had been a long, draining day. For me, having seen my family to the safety of Boston, I felt I'd fulfilled my obligations. What now loomed before me was my plan to join the army. As I lay there, trying to sleep, I thought about that evening gun and allowed myself to acknowledge some anxiety about military life. Then I recalled my oath and told myself it was an obligation and must be done. Thankfully, multiple church bells rang through the night hours and served to soothe me, so at last, I slept.

For the first time in many a day, I had no troubled dreams.

Tuesday, April 19, 1774

The following morning, we breakfasted on stale bread and the bitter, gritty drink called coffee, tea being unavailable. As a response to the tea tax Parliament had levied, people were shunned or attacked by the rebels if they refused to boycott tea. In fact, Uncle William warned us that even *attempting* to buy tea marked you as a friend of Parliament, undesirable among many in Boston. People who went against the boycott, he said, had their names posted in the town's radical newspaper to shame them.

"But don't think all of Boston is radical," he told us. "Far from it. Most, I believe, only wish to be let alone. Happily, there is much support for the Crown government."

I was pleased to hear so.

As Mother commenced a deeper round of cleaning, she sent Faith and Mercy about town to fetch more provisions. For my part, I told myself I must search out a recruiting sergeant, thinking that would be the best way to enlist. I tried to think of a good excuse to leave the house but was fearful of telling my mother of my intentions, worried she would stop me.

By good fortune, Uncle William approached me and said, "Young man, would you oblige me to speak in private? Might we step outside?"

Glad for the excuse and having neither objections nor knowledge of what he desired to say, I consented.

Once outside, Uncle William rubbed an eye, pulled an ear, and said, "Let's walk." So we did, he hobbling from his gout.

We reached the end of Hog Alley and came upon a large, open area of undulating grass bordered by trees. Still silent, we passed through the trees and stepped upon a field and paused. With an all-encompassing wave of his hand, Uncle William announced, "The Commons.

"The army encampment," continued my uncle, pointing to tents. "The Twenty-Ninth Regiment, the King's Own Fifth, the Thirty-Eighth, and the Forty-Third. That's Copp's Hill, with one of Boston's old cemeteries. You can see Charlestown from there."

What I observed was exciting to see. To the north side of this large space were two brass cannons on their carriages. Nearby was a flagpole from which hung Great Britain's flag, called the Union Jack ("jack" meaning flag) insofar as it celebrated the union of England and Scotland.

Beyond the cannons were multiple rows of canvas tents. Among them were soldiers in scarlet jackets. In other words, I had been taken where I most wanted to go: to the British army. But I confess, the sensation I now experienced was akin to having been led to the edge of a steep cliff that I had promised to leap off. That is, I felt misgivings.

Uncle William turned and directed my attention southward. "A new cemetery." Then he pointed across the way. "A fort in which the Royal Fusiliers are stationed."

"What's a fusilier?"

"A soldier who carries a light gun. And that rise is Beacon Hill."

"Whose house is that?" I said, observing a great mansion.

"Mr. Hancock's. No wealthier man in town. Or in Massachusetts. Perhaps in the colonies. A trader, to be sure. And yet one of the chief leaders of the rebels."

"A radical?"

"And a well-known smuggler. Some say he's a rebel merely to free his smuggling from government interference."

"What's that water beyond?"

"The Charles River. Then Cambridge."

There were some cows grazing on the Commons. I watched them until, growing impatient, I said, "Sir, you wished to speak to me."

"Ah, yes." Uncle William rolled his hands in thought, looked away (appearing embarrassed), and said, "Last night your mother informed me of your financial situation, that by your late father's will it's you who have inherited his entire estate."

"It's true, sir. When I turn eighteen."

"May I congratulate you on your good fortune. And . . . and how old are you now?"

"Thirteen."

He looked at me with obvious disappointment, saying, "I hoped you would be older." Then he gazed off into the distance. "Would it be offensive for me to ask how . . . how large is your estate?"

"It is nothing, sir."

He swung about. *"Nothing?"* he cried, the one word conveying disbelief and dismay.

"We had to exchange our house, sir," I explained, "along with almost all that was in it so we might escape. All we own is in your home."

"That . . . sea chest?" he asked with more dismay. "Those books?"

"I fear our fortune is my misfortune," I said. "But, sir, I'm about to join the army."

"Join the army? As a common soldier? Good heavens. Why?"

"I must show my loyalty to England. To support our king."

"Whose idea is this?"

"It's what I think my father believed in."

"No great expectations are to be had by becoming a common soldier," said Uncle William in such an offhand way I wasn't sure whether he was approving, disapproving, or even listening. "But," he said, swerving abruptly to another subject, "just how much ready money does your mother have?"

"I've no idea, sir."

He frowned.

"I think, sir," I said, coming to his aid, "since you've taken us in and you are a close relation, you might ask her."

"Indeed, I believe I must," he said. Then he uttered his favorite phrase, "Times are perilous." With that he turned his back on me and, limping, headed in the direction of his house, leaving me alone. Perhaps it was his trade, but as I had already learned, money was always in his speculations.

"Please, sir," I called after him, "don't tell my mother what I'm about to do." He waved a hand to suggest he had heard me. But I had to wonder if, when he received an answer to his question about money from Mother, my family would still be allowed to stay in his house.

With that troubling thought, I turned my steps toward the army encampment. Did I really wish to join? *Yes,* I told myself. Besides, with my need to earn money, my intent to enlist — to show my loyalty — had become not only necessary but urgent.

As I approached the rows of gray triangular tents, their support lines pegged into the ground, I observed no great sense of military discipline. Any number of soldiers seemed to be wandering about or sitting on the ground, talking or playing cards. Most of these men were in their red jackets, but many did not have them on and were at their ease in linen shirts. A few were washing from water buckets. Some were shaving. One of the men, back toward me, had no shirt on, and I saw multiple red welts on his back, the evidence of a brutal flogging. Reminded of my own beating, I shivered.

I saw a few women, but whether wives of the soldiers or servants, I didn't know, though it was clear they were on familiar terms with the men.

There was also a gathering of young Black men. Their uniforms informed me they were soldiers, though their jackets were not red but yellow. Nor did they have guns, but rather marching drums. When I approached one of them and asked who they were, he said they were regimental drummers.

"Where are you from?"

"Barbados," he said.

"Where's that?"

"West Indies."

I moved on, impressed that the army had men from its far-flung empire; that they were Black, and surely volunteers, suggested liberality on the part of the army and the loyalty of so many.

Here and there, little fires burned, some with pots suspended over them. I also saw many stacked muskets of the flintlock "Brown Bess" kind, which was what British soldiers were issued. About five feet long, they were leaning against one another in a triangular fashion, their bayonets coming to a sharp point. I wondered what it would be like to carry one.

I observed no officers.

I finally came upon a solitary soldier, a white man, sitting on the ground next to a modest fire. His being alone emboldened me, so I went up to him and stood there. His gun lay nearby on the earth. He had a small pot on the flames and was stirring its contents with a spoon. He looked up. "What can I do for you, boy?"

"I want . . . I want to join the army."

He studied me in blank silence, though I thought I detected a slight smile. "Why?" he said.

"I'm loyal to King George."

"Not a rebel, then?"

"No, sir. Not at all."

"Good lad. I'm glad to see you so. As for joining the army, do you know the pay?"

"No, sir."

"Eight pence a day. And there are deductions. Food. Fixing your shoes. Some for the regimental surgeon. You'll not get rich."

I said, "It's not for that."

"You might get killed. Or maimed."

"I know."

"Do you?"

"I think so."

He made a mocking sound. "We have a saying: 'Cross my heart and hope to die.' Do you know its meaning?"

I shook my head.

"That if I'm shot, I'm hoping I get hit on my crossed chest straps so I might die at once and not linger in pain and misery." He nodded to his musket. "Pick it up," he said.

I did, taken aback by how heavy it was and that it was almost as long as I was tall.

"Eleven pounds," said the soldier, who must have read my face. "Ready to carry another fifty more pounds of equipment?"

Though unnerved by the notion, I replied, "I'm sure I can," but I was glad to lay the heavy gun back down.

"The people hereabouts," the soldier continued, "a lot of 'em anyway, they don't like us."

"I do, sir."

"Much thanks for that," he said, and studied me. "How old are you?"

"Fifteen," I lied.

"How tall?"

"About five feet."

"Sorry, lad. Regulations are strict. You must be at least seventeen in age. No shorter than five foot six and a half. And mind, if you disobey rules, the officers lay on lashes. That would break your young body."

That the rebels and the army both resorted to flogging gave me pause.

"Any idea of how many desertions there are?"

I shook my head.

"A lot. Get caught, and the army will flog or hang you. Not your choice."

"I would never desert," I said, continuing to stand there to prove my determination.

The soldier stirred his pot, dismissing me. "Best come back when you gain some height. But too bad, because within six months we'll have drubbed these deluded rebels and have gone back home."

Frustrated, I was not prepared to take one man's opinion. I continued about the camp and announced my intentions to any number of soldiers. In every case, I was given the same answer I had already received: I was too short. Too young.

I left the Commons with something like embarrassment. I had wanted to join the army, but after what I had learned—such things as low pay, the weight of equipment, floggings—I admitted to myself that I felt some relief that I had been prevented from doing so. But quickly, I turned my mind to a vital question: If I could not join the army, how was I to earn a wage? My family situation demanded I find something. Soon.

I returned to Uncle William's house. Since he was alone, and I in need of advice, I told him what had happened.

"That's most unfortunate," he replied, which I took to be mostly an allusion to my lack of money.

"Please, sir," I said, "I must find work to support my family."

He said, "That speaks well of you, but with considerable unemployment in town, paying jobs will be hard to find. Still, you have my word, I'll put my mind to helping you."

With nothing else to hold me, I worked with my family to do more cleaning. Mother liked to quote the adage "Cleanliness is next to godliness," so there was much to achieve. The house being small, however, we soon met her standards.

"Do you like it here?" I asked my sisters when we were done.

"It's not as nice as home," said Faith. "And Uncle William is messy," she added in a whisper.

Mercy said, "I don't intend to stay long."

"Where will you go?" I asked.

"That is my business," she snapped, turning away from me. It was clear that she had not yet forgiven me for inheriting the Tullbury house, even though I no longer owned it. I found her attitude exasperating. It was not I who had written Father's will, but he. It would have been better if he hadn't done so, not least of all because it had caused Mercy and me to be at a distance, and she was the only family member with whom I felt free. I was also aware she would have made a better head of our family than me. Better than Mother. But that, I told myself, was something never to be. Father, though gone, had made sure of it.

"Noah, what are you going to do?" asked Faith.

"Uncle William will find me a situation," I said, hoping it was true.

At a later point, Mother took me aside and said Uncle William had inquired about her funds. When she informed him, he, in turn, told her that if she stayed, she would need to bring some income in good time.

"What will we do?" I asked.

"I don't know," she said, her face filled with apprehension.

Though I didn't mention the army, I was even more anxious to find employment. More than ever, I missed my father: he always told me what to do.

Who was to guide me without him? Mother's rules were almost always about the small things we did. I needed more. I found it troubling that I was at such a loss, unnerved that things had changed so. *I don't like change,* I found myself thinking.

As I sat there, I wondered what my Tullbury friends were doing. Did they miss me? I knew I missed them. Did they even care that I had gone? Did Micah regret what he had done?

When we had come to Boston, I thought we had arrived at a safe harbor. Being in the army would have meant I had orders to follow. Now I felt I had been pushed back into mid-sea, becalmed, drifting I knew not where, no hand on any rudder and no shore in sight. What I wanted, more than anything, was a direction, something for which to aim.

I was all too aware I needed someone to tell me what to do.

Saturday, April 30, 1774

It was helpful that from time to time Uncle William called upon me to deliver his copy work to various places about town: taverns, warehouses, or private homes, wherever business was conducted. It gave me something to do, earned the odd penny — with its image of King George II — and allowed me to gain a better sense of Boston.

You may be sure I worked hard to be fast and reliable and was particular about any monies sent to my uncle. I even gave him the tips I received. He, in turn, more than once, told me how pleased he was by my industry and honesty. "The evidence of your hard work is admirable," he said. "It will help me help you."

As I went about such tasks around town, I often found myself lost and confused, the streets as twisted as a sailor's knot. It didn't help that the town was crowded with a variety of people in look and dress that often proved puzzling, in that I was unable to read their stations or professions. In Tullbury, I knew what everyone was and did. In Boston, I knew no one and nothing of their business.

In my solitary meanderings, I often came upon odd, narrow, corkscrew streets with names like Turn Again Alley, Marginal Road, Sliding Alley, and Crooked Lane. The names were like fingerposts for my new life.

I also wandered out along King Street onto what was called Long Wharf, which was indeed long, sticking out (I was informed) one-third of a mile into the bay. It was the principal wharf among some fifty town docks. Many a ship loaded and unloaded there. It was also a merchant center, crowded with shops and countinghouses, along with dwellings where people lived.

While I took note of the tepid commerce, I heard, or was told, repeatedly (in agreement with Uncle William) that times were unprofitable, that Boston business was dwindling because of the disputes with the Crown.

Also, there being so many taverns — I had been informed that Boston had one tavern for every two hundred or so inhabitants — it meant liquor was on the streets, with many a loutish sot. Multiple shouting matches, sometimes scuffles, ensued, politics being the reason for most. Whigs in opposition to Tories. Tories in opposition to Whigs. Arguments about how to deal with the English government were constant. Talk of liberty and freedom filled the air like confetti. As I could observe for myself, Boston was full of different points of view, at odds, one against another. And though it may seem a contradiction, I found it familiar and bewildering at the same time.

I was also struck by the high number of British troops on the streets. Ordinary soldiers and officers, too. These soldiers rarely walked alone but went about in bands for protection. Let it be said, I observed many an offense against them, Bostonians jeering at or mocking them with harsh taunts: "Lobster coats." Or "Go home, foreigners." "Pigs." I was offended.

For their part, the soldiers were quick to rebuke people, and pushed their way through gatherings of mechanics when the laborers would not give way. The cheapness of rum meant that on more than one occasion, I saw drunk soldiers, which led to further altercations.

The Boston air everyone had to breathe was full of competing politics. I had the sense that the town was ready to descend into a great brawl. I made sure to walk along the margins of the streets, where it seemed safest.

Sunday, May 1, 1774

On Sundays we attended Christ Church—we were told it had Boston's tallest steeple—in the north part of town. It was a great comfort to be there as a family, midst so many who joined the familiar Church of England service. It gave me further pride that several British officers were in attendance. There were also men and women of wealth, of fashionable society. I was pleased to see some younger people as well. But noticing the general wealth, and being dressed so shabbily myself, I was left in no doubt as to how poor we were. Feeling much the outcast, I spoke to no one.

Faith sat with Uncle William. She seemed to be warming to him, and for his part, he clearly found her constant questions amusing, answering them with indulgent patience.

Friday, May 6, 1774

I did not tell Mother that I had been unable to join the British army, nor did I share this information with my sisters. Surely not long-tongued Faith. As for Mercy, she remained distant and hostile, which continued to pain me.

I begged Uncle William's assistance once again.

He was sympathetic to my need for employment, purpose, and funds. Better yet, he offered to seek help beyond the delivery of his work.

He asked me about my reading and writing. I assured him I was capable. "Excellent," he proclaimed. "And your reliable effort in delivering my work and collecting fees makes it easy for me to recommend you."

As it happened, two days later he requested that I bring some letters he had copied to a Mr. Congreve, a molasses merchant who lived on Queen Street.

"One letter," Uncle William said when he gave me his portfolio, "is about you, requesting assistance. Mr. Congreve is an important Tory and is cozy with the British army staff. Be respectful: he's in a position to help you."

I made my delivery of Uncle's work to the north end of town, to a fine brick mansion that suggested wealth and power. When I told the Black servant that it was Mr. Winsop who had sent me, I was taken right to Mr. Congreve and left alone with the man.

Mr. Congreve was dressed in a blue silk coat with a high, wide collar and fine white lace. He wore a stylish powdered wig, as befit a wealthy gentleman. Elderly, his face seemed skeletal, cheeks sunken and scarred with pockmarks. His smile showed few teeth. During my interview, he took snuff, sneezing into a lace handkerchief at his cuff.

I bowed, pushed back my hair, and gave him the copied letters, which he shuffled through. Then he paused. "Ah, this is about you." He read it as I remained standing before him.

I think Mr. Congreve scanned Uncle William's letter twice, lifting his eyes above the paper, comparing me with what was written. At last, he said, "Your name is Noah Cope."

"Yes, sir."

"Lost your father of late."

"I fear so, sir."

"A loyal pastor in the English Church."

"Yes, sir."

"My profound sympathy. I regret these ignorant traitors. They must be put down, and I assure you they will be. Indeed, I hope they all hang. I guarantee they do not represent the true sentiments of British America. What is Mr. Winsop to you?"

"My great-uncle, sir."

"He speaks well of you." He held up my uncle's letter as evidence.

"I hope to deserve it, sir."

"He says you are an ardent defender of our beloved monarch and that you remain loyal to your father's principles."

"Both true, sir."

"Altogether offensive, what these radicals say about our esteemed king. But your uncle tells me you desire to do your part to support England."

"Very much, sir."

"Age?"

"Thirteen."

"You read and write."

"I do, sir."

"The other day some British officers dined here. I may have something I can suggest. But I must ask: Are you willing to undergo some danger?"

"I am, sir," I said without much thought.

"Well, then I promise I shall pass on your name in hopes we shall find a way to put you to beneficial use."

I expressed my gratitude and bowed my leave.

Once home, I asked my uncle, "Can Mr. Congreve truly find me a position?"

"If anyone can, he will" was his reply. "He mingles with the best."

I had to be content with that. But what echoed most in my thoughts were Mr. Congreve's words: "Are you willing to undergo some danger?"

I admit, while I knew the army held hazard, I had not considered my safety in any other situation. In my keenness to obtain employment, I had blurted out that I would not flinch. Now that I had time to reflect, that "some danger" worried me somewhat, but I told myself I must hold fast to my duty.

Tuesday, May 10, 1774

A ship from London brought news to the town of what was called Parliament's Boston Port Act. Word of it flew about the streets like a nor'easter.

Because of the destruction of the tea the previous December, the English government decreed that until Boston paid for that loss, the entire port would be shut down. The fine levied was thirteen thousand pounds, which was immense. If not paid, June 1 would be the last date any vessel would be free to enter Boston. On June 15, ships would not be allowed to leave.

In sum, the Boston seagoing merchant trade — almost the whole economy — would cease to be.

The ship that brought this news was named the *Harmony,* but the intelligence brought anything *but* harmony. Indeed, I witnessed churning anger on the streets, along with the constant, if varied, refrain of "Boston is ruined." I noticed that Tories were equally vocal that all businesses would suffer. But whereas the Tories appeared to be willing to do anything to placate the British government, the Whigs were vehemently opposed to anything that might appease Parliament.

As for the British troops, they alone seemed to enjoy the news and taunted Boston citizens with the intelligence. Several times, I saw fistfights break out. Once, I saw a sword drawn, but the soldier was held back by a comrade.

My father had said such a severe government action would not be right. It was easy to agree with him. I was glad no one asked me to defend the act. England had offended almost everyone. I worried about what would happen next — and how it might affect me.

Friday, May 13, 1774

General Thomas Gage sailed into Boston from England aboard the sloop of war *Lively*, which had twenty cannons. He came to serve as captain general and governor of Massachusetts Bay. This is to say King George gave Gage complete command of the colony, making him virtually king of Massachusetts. He could do what he desired and pay no heed to elected officials. Since, as I understood things, so many of the actions taken by these judges, magistrates, and sheriffs were being thwarted by radicals anyway, that made sense to me.

Gage disembarked at Castle William out in the bay, safe from any turmoil in the town. There, so it was said, he conferred with the departing governor, Mr. Hutchinson, who was planning to leave for London.

Boston's streets throbbed with talk as to what Gage might do. Everywhere I went, both Tories and Whigs claimed the general as their friend. It appeared Gage had served in America against the French during the Seven Years' War. He also had a wealthy American wife (from the colony of New Jersey). Those facts were considered much in his favor. People said he understood America. There was excitement in the town, a sense that something good was about to happen. I was happy to feel that my side was gaining strength.

That said, General Gage arrived on Friday the thirteenth, which I thought ill-omened.

Saturday, May 14, 1774

The Hog Alley house being so small, my mother and sisters easily kept it clean — far more than Uncle William ever did. It meant that other than delivering Uncle's copy work, I spent my time wandering alone about Boston. So it was that I saw the King's Own Regiment disembark on Long Wharf, followed by the Fifteenth and Forty-Third Regiments. They marched through town, music playing, colors flying, bayonets gleaming, with every soldier looking proud, strong, and disciplined. They camped on the Commons. It gave me pleasure to see them.

I tried to count how many were in a regiment. I calculated some four hundred or so, plus officers. I learned that each regiment was divided into ten companies. I also noticed the variations in their uniforms and tried to keep them in my head. I liked knowing these things.

Over the weeks to come, more and more troops arrived. They came from New York City, Quebec, and Halifax, the last two the recently conquered territories of Canada. Boston became crowded with redcoats. While the sheer numbers made me feel well protected, many of the soldiers' voices had thick Irish or Scots accents, which I didn't always understand. It sounded like a foreign army had invaded.

Monday, May 16, 1774

When delivering Uncle William's letters to a merchant at the British Coffee House on King Street — a Tory place frequented by British officers — I stayed awhile to listen to the gossip. That was how I learned that Black Bostonians petitioned the new governor to free them from slavery. I gathered they had done so before to numerous provincial governments. The authorities, Whig or Tory, had ignored such requests. At the tavern, I heard people say it was all the rebel talk of liberty, of Great Britain trying to enslave the colonists, that had encouraged Black people to petition for their freedom yet again.

I had given little thought to slavery other than recalling Father saying it was "absolutely wrong." But I, for one, doubted that any Black person needed to be encouraged to seek their freedom. As it happened, General Gage — from his island headquarters — declined to accept the appeal.

Then I heard rumors that England might offer freedom to enslaved Black men if they ran away from their masters and supported King George.

I did not think about it much beyond the notion that anything that helped England would be good.

Tuesday, May 17, 1774

General Gage came into Boston by way of a ceremonial barge, rowed by Royal Navy sailors. Midst cheering crowds and an ear-thundering cannonade from the royal ships in the bay, I watched his grand arrival on Long Wharf eagerly.

In a fine red uniform with multiple medals gleaming, Gage, a tall, aristocratic-looking man with a high forehead and a long nose, stepped upon the wharf and was met by all kinds of officials — military and government men, both Tory and Whig.

I ran along as his fine coach — which he must have brought from England — proceeded down King Street to the Town House, where he was proclaimed governor of the Province of Massachusetts Bay. To celebrate his arrival, a troop of one hundred mounted soldiers was in attendance along with a company of grenadiers (the army's tallest regulars), as well as Boston militia.

To my surprise, among those who were there to greet him was the Splendid Independent Company of Cadets, which was led by none other than Mr. John Hancock, one of the chief rebel leaders. I took his being there as a sign that he acknowledged the rightful power of England.

With loud and universal hurrahs, Gage was greeted by musket volleys and still another cannonade. A banquet was held in his honor at one of the town's principal buildings, Faneuil Hall. It was a rare moment when Whigs and Tories joined.

Then the new governor took up his residence and headquarters at what was called Province House, situated at Marlborough and Milk Streets.

At home, I regaled my family, including Uncle William, with a description of General Gage's fine arrival. "All kinds of people were there, even radicals. It was a grand display of who was in charge."

It turned out that Uncle William, much neater and cleaner, buttons fixed, wig powdered—all thanks to Mother—had attended the Faneuil Hall banquet. "General Gage," he told us, "gave a speech in which he promised he would uphold all liberties and freedom for British Americans. His remarks were greeted by loud cheers.

"And here's more good news," said Uncle William. "A large body of Boston men—one hundred and thirty wealthy merchants, far more than that so-called tea party, told Gage that they were willing to pay the fine for the tea."

I said, "That would be excellent."

"Indeed," said Uncle William, "if the merchants pay the fine, all will be well. The port will stay open. Our peril will be averted. But we shall have to see. The Sons of Liberty have vowed to oppose the action and threaten all who offer to pay."

"What kinds of threats?" I asked.

"Public shame. Boycotts. Physical violence. You saw that in your former home. The Sons of Liberty oppose so-called tyranny with a tyranny all their own."

I understood and agreed.

Then Uncle William took me aside. "You requested a way of being helpful to the Loyalist cause. At the dinner, Mr. Congreve informed me that he may have secured employment for you. Once General Gage has settled in, you must go to Province House, which is to become the army headquarters."

I asked, "Is it paying work, sir?"

Uncle William put a cautionary finger to his nose. "I smell money.

Mr. Congreve sent me a letter that you are to take to Province House in a week or so. Noah, this suggests real promise."

I could hardly wait to go.

Wednesday, May 25, 1774

A Royal Navy convoy sailed into Boston Harbor ready to enforce the Port Act. First to arrive was Admiral Graves's flagship, *Captain*, which had sixty-four cannons, a mighty force. Soon after, there came the sixteen-cannon *Active* and the sixteen-cannon *Kingfisher*. They anchored in the bay in such positions that all could train their guns upon the town. The word was that other ships were on their way.

I had little doubt that if the many soldiers already in Boston did not subdue the rebels, these ships would. Clearly their cannons could destroy everything. It was even rumored Admiral Graves wanted to do exactly that. It was also obvious that any Boston ship trying to elude the soon-to-come closing of the port would be smashed into splinters by cannonballs.

I hoped the fear of that fate would hurry up the paying of the tea fine.

Thus, I saw for myself how effectively the British Empire worked, and I felt grand to be a part of it.

Thursday, May 26, 1774

Having to wait before going to army headquarters made me impatient. But meanwhile, I needed to deliver letters my uncle had copied, moving about town to businesses, taverns, and private homes. When

I was done, I went to the Commons to observe the new troops. I swelled with pride as I beheld their impressive increase in numbers.

From the Commons, I walked the full length of Long Wharf. Standing on its end, I admired the new ships, their multiple masts and spars, the complexity of their rigging, as well as the open gun ports with muzzles pointing right at Boston.

Magnificent to behold, the ships were powerful and elegant, and I recalled my boyish whims of going to sea. I tried to imagine such a life, with notions that were all delightful. I could have been the first in my family to visit England or see foreign lands. Perhaps I would have taken a whaling voyage.

In that spirit of adventure, and being alone as usual, I decided to go beyond Boston for the first time since we had arrived. I took the short ferry ride from Boston's north side to Charlestown, which was tucked into the side of a hill.

I roamed about the town with its four hundred or so private houses, plus businesses and wharves. Finding it uninteresting, I went on up to the place called Bunker Hill and the mount beyond, Quarry Hill, which overlooked the Mystic River. All was peaceful.

As I wandered, I came upon an odd structure. Built of stone, it looked like a long loaf of bread standing on its end. Its roof was cone-shaped and covered with tile. On the top was one of those metal rods said to defray lightning. A single entryway, approached by a few stone steps, was closed, held shut by a large lock. Some boys playing about the structure told me — when I asked — that gunpowder was stored there.

Much more interesting to me was the view to the east — the Mystic River and beyond — that lay below. It was sufficiently enticing that I went down a steep path for about a mile, passing clay pits and brick kilns, to the river's edge. I followed the beach for some three miles farther, roundabout to Charlestown again, before returning home to Boston by ferry.

It was a fine outing and made me even more eager for my appointment at Province House. This day had been my best time in Boston.

But no sooner did I return home than Faith rushed up to me — tears streaming down her face — crying, "Mercy is gone!"

"Gone? Where? What happened?"

Mother, full of distress, came into the room. "Mercy has run away," she announced.

"What do you mean?"

"Abner Hosmer."

"What about him?"

"She's gone to marry him," wailed Faith.

"Marry him!" I was dumbfounded.

Mother said, "He came to the door, and she left with him."

"They met secretly in Boston a few times," added Faith, her speech in bits and pieces. "She . . . never . . . told me. Never." She put a hand to her heart to cover her pain and to swear she spoke the truth.

"Lawyer Hosmer gave our house to his son," explained Mother. "Mercy told me that. And when she marries Abner — which she says will happen as soon as she gets back to Tullbury — the house will belong to her, too."

I recalled the moment Mother told us the house would be mine.

I acknowledged (in my thoughts) that I had not acted well toward Mercy, showing smugness that it was I who had inherited it. It made me frustrated and sorry at the same time. But all I said now was "She has betrayed us. And Father. They won't even be married in our church. The Hosmers go to the Congregational church."

"I have to wish her well," said Mother, pressing her hands together to suggest a prayer. Tears trickled from her eyes.

"I'll never speak her name again," I said, even as I acknowledged I could have treated her better.

Faith was inconsolable. Even as Uncle William tried to comfort her, he was bewildered. For my part, I could easily imagine Father's anger at Mercy's actions. As for Mother, in the past she had always agreed with Father. But as I looked at her, standing as still as stone, I realized I didn't truly know what she was thinking now.

I had not foreseen that Mercy would do such a thing, and even if I had, I doubted I could have prevented it. She was too strong-willed. In any case, her leaving was almost like another death in the family and caused me genuine grief, as I became acutely aware how alone I felt.

That night my nightmares returned.

Friday, May 27, 1774

In the morning, to my great relief, it was time for me to go to the army headquarters, Province House, to learn what Mr. Congreve had arranged. Moreover, going there allowed me to put Mercy's elopement out of mind. I told myself that at least *I* would be able to uphold Father's ideals.

Uncle William gave me Mr. Congreve's letter of introduction. It was inscribed to a Captain Brown.

"You must ask for him and give him the letter yourself," said Uncle William. "Be respectful."

Unable to read the folded letter because it was sealed, I set off, reminding myself that some danger might be involved. You may be sure that intrigued even as it worried me, so I had equal degrees of high anticipation and nervousness.

Province House proved to be one of the grandest buildings in Boston. A great, square, redbrick structure, it was three stories high, topped by a cupola. Over the large front door was the royal emblem of Great Britain.

I walked up broad, red stone steps and passed under a balcony. On either side of the main door were red-coated soldiers to whom I presented my letter. When the inscription was read, the note was returned to me and I was waved forward into a large, high, round room. It was crowded with officers and gentlemen coming and going, all of whom filled my ears with constant talk speculating about what would happen next in Boston.

Not knowing where to turn or whom I might approach, I stood against a wall and looked on. My perplexity must have been noted because it wasn't long before an officer came up to me and said, "Why are you loitering here?"

I handed over my letter. The officer read the cover name, looked at me with inquisitive eyes, then said, "I can deliver this."

Wanting to do as I had been told, I said, "Sir, I was instructed to hand it to the captain personally."

The officer considered me for a moment longer before giving the letter back. "This way," he said.

I followed close behind as we moved through a narrow, crowded hall until we reached a closed door. My tension increased. *What if they ask me to do something truly dangerous?* I bolstered myself by thinking it would be a good thing if I could demonstrate my bravery.

The officer knocked on the door.

I heard "Come in" from the other side. The officer opened the door and put his hand to my back so that I was edged forward. I heard the door shut behind me.

I found myself in a small, high-ceilinged room, in which there were two chairs and a long table, the table covered with maps. More maps were on the walls.

Behind the table stood two soldiers, one much older than the other. I judged the older one was Captain Brown and recognized his uniform as being from the Fifth Foot Regiment.

He was a middle-aged man, rather stocky, wearing a scarlet jacket with green lapels, tan trousers, and high black boots. On his table was a round brimmed hat, decorated with black feathers. What impressed me most was the sheathed sword that he wore.

Since it was the way of the English army, I knew he had purchased his rank, which is to say he was a gentleman. Later I discovered that it had cost him fifteen hundred pounds to become a captain. By way of contrast, Father's income had been fifty pounds a year.

The other soldier bore no sword, so I took him to be of lower rank than a captain.

After some moments, during which I stood there, my heart thumping, the captain looked up. His face showed firmness, but nothing forbidding.

"Yes, boy?" he said. "Have you something for me?"

I stepped forward, bowed, and held out Mr. Congreve's letter. "For Captain Brown, sir."

He took it, unfolded it, and began to read. As he did, he looked up, trying to match me with the letter.

I waited, wanting so much to look like a soldier—though I had no idea what that meant other than to stand at attention, head up, hands pressed to my sides.

Captain Brown handed the letter to the other man as he said, "My ensign, DeBérniere." This soldier also read the letter, glancing at me to do his own evaluation.

"You," the captain said to me, "are Noah Cope."

"Yes, sir."

"I was expecting you. Mr. Congreve—whom I know well— told me you wish to show your loyalty to king and country."

"Yes, sir. And to my father."

"I regret what happened to him, but your allegiance is admirable."

"Thank you, sir," I said, my face warm with pride. His voice had taken on a friendly tone, which put me at my ease. Feeling a liking for him, I decided I trusted him.

"Mr. Congreve informs me you've recently come to Boston with your widowed mother."

"Yes, sir."

"Few in town know you."

"No one, sir."

"Age?"

"Thirteen, sir."

When Captain Brown held out his hand, Ensign DeBérniere returned the letter. "You come well recommended. Willing — Mr. Congreve informs me — to do something that involves some hazard."

"Yes, sir."

The captain studied the letter a second time, then put it down and considered me again. I had the pleasing notion he was measuring me for a uniform.

"What," he said, "do you know about the Green Dragon?"

"*Dragon,* sir?" I exclaimed.

It was DeBérniere who said, "The Green Dragon is the name of a tavern on Union Street. It's notorious for being where radical leaders meet and plan their rebellious activities. They are forceful men. I fear you know about tar and feathering. You must also know about the dumping of the tea."

"I do, sir."

"That," continued DeBérniere, "among many other treasonous acts, was planned in the Green Dragon. You may trust us when we tell you these traitors are few and have no real following. They are, for the most part, smugglers, like Mr. Hancock. But they make considerable trouble, and they meet at the Green Dragon. A Mr. Adams is their despicable leader."

"The point being," said Captain Brown, "if we secured your employment there as a dishwasher, waiter, or whatnot, you would go unnoticed."

"Being a boy is the perfect disguise," added DeBérniere.

A dishwasher! This was not the heroic placement I'd hoped for. I struggled not to show my disappointment, but I was not going to refuse. I consoled myself that it would, in fact, not be dangerous. In any case, I needed to have the work and could only hope it paid something. And, in no small part, I was there to demonstrate my loyalty. All I said, then, was "Yes, sir. I'm willing."

"Be clear: it is a precarious duty to undertake," Captain Brown said.

I doubted that but said nothing.

DeBérniere added, "If you are unmasked, there would be little we could do to help you. These men, as you well know, are violent."

"If you were alert," the captain continued, "you could overhear much of what was being said, radical activities and plans, which would be of great interest to us. You could pass the information on. That would be of considerable service to His Majesty's army. But it will have to be done clandestinely."

"I want to show my loyalty, sir."

For the first time, Captain Brown smiled. "Your letter tells me you can read and write."

"I can, sir."

"Excellent. Memory?"

"Very good, sir."

"Fine. Mr. Congreve's note says that your great-uncle—who has, I gather, aside from supporting our king, an esteemed reputation for trustworthiness and integrity—recommends you highly. I shall honor that by assuming you have the same qualities. Therefore, I shall give you a letter of introduction to someone who is already in my employ there. All I need say is he is a friend. Nothing more. No names. You must never mention me to anyone."

"I understand, sir."

"You will hear lots of politics discussed there. Do not share your patriotism. We appreciate it. They won't."

"Yes, sir."

"Now, since you can write, you must compose brief reports and give them to—well, DeBérniere here shall work that out. Once he arranges things, he will send a note to your uncle. Is that all understood?"

"Yes, sir."

"Have you access to paper and ink?"

"My great-uncle, sir. He's a scrivener."

"Ah, yes. Mr. Congreve chose well."

Captain Brown sat down at his table, drew a sheet of paper toward him, took up a quill, wrote with it, sprinkled the writing with sand, shook the letter out, folded it over, and held it out for me.

"My letter will gain you employment at the Green Dragon," said the captain. "Do you want to know about pay?"

"If you wish it, sir."

"Five shillings a week. It will be sent to your Uncle William, who resides"—he glanced at the letter—"on Hog Alley. He alone shall know of your employment."

"Thank you, sir." Five shillings was far more money than I had imagined. The situation was becoming better and better.

The captain went on: "Wait three days before going to the Dragon. Once there, ask for a Mr. Simpson. Give him my note. But, again, you must not speak my name or say what you are doing there to anyone—other than your uncle. Is that understood?"

"Yes, sir."

"Good. I look forward to receiving your reports. Come here only when it's of significant importance." Much softer, he added with a smile, "You remind me of my son. About the same age."

"Thank you, sir. May I ask, where is he?"

"England. Now, good luck."

"Thank you, sir."

"Dismissed," said Captain Brown, treating me like a true soldier.

Clutching the letter in my hand, I left Province House. Moreover, I now understood what I had agreed to do. I was in the British army—employed as a spy.

Let there be no mistake. While it was an odd position, I was thrilled. I was showing my loyalty. I had direction to my life. The money was good. The position, I thought, safe. I even allowed myself to fancy that I might uncover a vast treasonous plot that would save the whole empire. How grand that would be. I would be a hero.

For all that, I was grateful.

———

I went home and told my mother merely that I had secured employment.

Her response was muted. "Where?"

"A tavern."

"How much will you earn?"

"Five shillings a week."

"Doing what?"

"Dishwashing and the like," I said, enjoying the deception.

She took me right to Uncle William and told me to repeat my news.

"Good," proclaimed my great-uncle, giving me the knowing look of an accomplice. To my mother, he said, "You have my word, Clem, as long as Noah brings in such sums, you are more than welcome to remain here."

All this gave me the satisfaction that I had served the family well. My only regret was that my father didn't know what I had done.

I found a private moment to tell Uncle William what I was about to do, though I did not speak Captain Brown's name. "Sir," I said, "do you approve of what I'm doing?"

"In perilous times," he said, "we are often called upon to do perilous things. Anything to assist the Crown government to keep order must be applauded." He put a finger to his lips, which I presumed meant he understood all about my new position.

And Mercy, I wondered — what would she have said about what I had agreed to do? I recalled her saying, "Feelings are a hindrance."

In the end, it didn't matter. I would go forward. That I was trusted to do so in secret delighted me.

Monday, May 30, 1774

Three mornings later, I was no sooner up than Uncle William took me aside and whispered, "Word has been sent: You are to deliver your . . . your reports to the New Bakery on Fish Street. Ask for a Mr. Ludlow. I shall supply you with ink and paper. You are not to sign your name to anything."

I was impressed that Captain Brown acted so fast. It told me that my task was important, which further pleased me.

So it was that, feeling much enthusiasm, I set off for the Green Dragon.

I asked three people for directions, and all knew of the tavern and guided me on.

Before I went there, I looked upon Fish Street to locate that New Bakery, the place to deliver my secret reports. I found it but did not go in.

A few seconds later, I was standing before the Green Dragon. It proved to be a wide, brick structure of two levels, five windows on the first level, six on the second, all facing the street. Massive chimneys stood on both ends of the building. As for its name, I cannot explain it, save that over the front door hung a copper figure of such a beast, which had turned green with age. What came first, the name or the creature, I never learned.

That said, I was sure I was like Saint George, outside a real dragon's cave and about to give battle. As I understood things, it was here that the Sons of Liberty met and planned their treasonous activities.

Of course, I knew there was no true dragon within, but I felt I was going to enter the lair where I would find the men who were responsible for my father's death.

Uneasy in an excited way, happy that my loyalty had gained purpose and direction, I clenched and unclenched my fists, took a deep breath, flipped the hair out of my eyes, and stepped inside the Green Dragon.

PART 3

1774

Since merchants' business was often conducted in taverns, I had been in many when delivering Uncle William's copy work. Now, with Captain Brown's letter in hand, I stood inside the entry and looked about the Green Dragon.

Despite the inevitable large fireplace (the Green Dragon had two), these taverns were, for the most part, illuminated by whale oil lamps, whose pale white light revealed benches, tables, and chairs scattered about under low, smoke-blackened ceilings. With their alcoves, corners, and multiple small rooms, taverns seemed designed for sharing secrets and discreet dealings. They were rather like furnished caves. Yet, when crowded, as was the case most evenings, the commotion was ear-clogging.

Boston beer and rum were served from a closet-like enclosure, so the air was thick with whiffs of such, to which was added the smell of coffee, tea, and tobacco, plus the ever-present bay brine reek. There were also aromas of roasting birds and meats upon the open hearths, along with baking pies. Put all these odors together, and you can imagine the thick, fuggy stench. It being morning, only a few patrons were there, and they were clustered around tables, heads bent in conversation like birds sipping water from puddles.

As I stood there, a young Black man, with a leather apron wrapped round his middle and a pitcher in hand, went by bringing drinks to patrons at a table. Once delivered, he started to pass me by again, only to stop.

"Are you looking for someone?" he asked. He was a head taller than me, and I guessed him to be a few years older as well.

Broad-faced, full-lipped, he had a deep, dark complexion beneath curly black hair. He considered me with interested eyes.

I held up my letter. "For Mr. Simpson."

"Over there," he said, and pointed to a corner somewhat isolated from the rest of the large room. I nodded and moved toward it.

Sitting at a table was a man—I assumed he was Mr. Simpson—reading (by candlelight) a copy of the *Boston Gazette*, which I came to know as a rebel newspaper. On the table was also the *Boston Post-Boy*, which favored the Crown. Before him sat a wooden money box and a battered cocked hat.

"Mr. Simpson, sir?"

Without looking up, he said, "That's me."

"A letter, sir." I held out Captain Brown's note.

Though his eyes remained on his newspaper, he said, "Who from?"

I had been instructed not to mention Captain Brown's name, so I continued to hold out the message to suggest he'd find the answer there.

Mr. Simpson frowned, sighed, put down his paper, but still did not look at me. Instead, he reached for the letter, unfolded it, and held it up. I could see his eyes scan the words. Only when done did he consider me in silence.

Now that I fully saw him, he was a small man with a receding gray hairline on the top of his head and a receding chin below. He was ill-shaved, and he had runny red eyes and a grum, florid face with veiny cheeks that told me he was a drinker.

Trying to keep from fidgeting, I continued to stand before him while he gazed at me with no visible enthusiasm. It was what he did next that surprised me. He tipped the letter into the candle flame and burned it, letting the dusty ash drop to the table, after which he brushed it all away.

I decided Mr. Simpson was Captain Brown's "friend" and that he perfectly understood why I was there, and since the Dragon was a radical place, perhaps he was a secret Loyalist. You may be sure I did not ask.

"Looking for employment, are you?" he said. The question was put in a loud voice so that — I thought — others might hear. Moreover, it was clear he didn't care what I answered, suggesting he knew my response beforehand.

"Yes, sir," I said, deciding this was a game and that I needed to play my part.

"Willing to do what you're told?"

"Yes, sir."

"Don't mind scrubbing? Sweeping? Waiting on men who can be rude? Who will ignore you?"

"No, sir."

"Mind taking orders from a Black?"

"No, sir."

"Five pence a day."

"Yes, sir."

"Now again, your name?"

"Noah Cope."

"All right," he said in an indifferent voice. "Jolla," he called out.

The young Black man I'd briefly met came over. Mr. Simpson

gestured to me and said, "Jolla, this here is Noah Cope. New hire. Set him to work wherever you see fit." With that, he made a hand wave of dismissal, ceased paying attention to me, and returned to his newspaper.

Beckoning, the young man led me off some paces before he turned about and faced me. "I'm Jolla," he said. "Jolla Freeman. The last name? Tells people what I am."

I noted that he felt compelled to tell me he was not enslaved. He went on: "This is a good place to work. The most important in Boston." He gestured toward a far corner. "The Sons of Liberty meet right there. Do their talking."

Feeling bold, and too full of my mission, I blurted out, "Are you their friend?"

The moment I spoke, I regretted my question, because he didn't answer but studied me intently, clearly choosing how to reply. After a few moments he cocked his head to one side, looked at me straight on, and said, "Anytime a man speaks of liberty, I'll stand with him. No one should be enslaved." He had taken my question and returned it as a challenge.

Since the sentiment expressed was much the way Whigs talked, I immediately supposed he was a radical, even as I was surprised that he—being both young and Black—would be so outspoken with his opinions. Remembering Captain Brown's caution not to say where my allegiance lay, I rebuked myself for failing to keep my political thoughts to myself.

When I gave no reply, he asked, "How old are you?"

"Thirteen."

"Young," he said. "Lots to learn," he added while offering up the trace of an amused smile, which irritated me — he couldn't be *that* much older than me. His smile also made me wonder if he guessed why I was there.

"I'm your boss," he let me know, "but I can be friendly, too." He held out his hand. After a moment of hesitation, I shook it. It was the first time I had ever taken the hand of a Black person.

"Come along," he said. "I'll show you your work."

I followed, trying — with little success — to make sense of him. But once I hung my coat on a peg and tied on my apron, I was ready to work.

Jolla introduced me to an older, stoop-shouldered Black man by the name of Ephraim Wilde. I was told he did much as I would be asked to do: take orders, serve, clean tables, and sweep. There was also William Gallagher, a white man, who was both cook and drink dispenser. Over time, other than being alongside them, I would have little to do with these other employees. In any case, I quickly learned that it was Jolla who oversaw the Green Dragon. When I arrived in the morning, he was already there, and when I left at the end of the day, he was still doing tasks. He organized the employees, waited on tables, took orders, delivered requests, and received money. He even ordered the tavern's drink and food.

Yes, Mr. Simpson, the owner, was always at his corner table with one of Boston's five newspapers before him. And all money was given to him and deposited — by him — in his box. From time to time Jolla did consult with him, receiving either nods or shakes of the head. But it was Jolla who ran things, including me. Mr. Simpson's relation to me was, at best, uninterested. From my first moments at the Green Dragon, it was Jolla for whom I worked.

All that first day I watched as Jolla hurried about the tavern, talking to one, now another patron. Everyone knew him, as he seemed to know all. A customer would walk in and Jolla remembered his regular wants and told me what to serve him before the man even sat down. He addressed many by name, while he was called his in return. In his brief chats, there were jests exchanged, insults bandied, along with earnest conversation as he constantly dipped in and out of the tavern talk, the discussions, debates, and arguments among patrons, taking part in whatever was nattered. Nor was he shy about telling people, many of whom were white gentlemen and older than him, his thoughts.

In other words, from the moment I met him, Jolla was unlike any young man I had ever known, Black or white. His professional skill and bold self-assurance impressed me from the start. Since I had already been told he was my boss, it was easy to decide I needed to be on his good side, but it was never far from my mind how I had been betrayed in Tullbury. I reminded myself that I had to be careful and make sure I didn't reveal the real reason for my being in the Green Dragon. I wasn't there to make friends with anyone.

Though my work at the tavern was not complicated, it was unceasing. For the most part, it consisted of delivering food and drink to tables, clearing away dirtied tankards and plates, washing them in a tub of cold water, cleaning tables, sweeping, and sopping up spillage. Then I did the same again. And again. Not interesting work, but engaging, for I was able to listen to endless bits of talk, learning about worlds of which I had but small intelligence: trade, shipping, business, and, of course, Boston politics. And though I had been secretly tasked to listen, I first had to serve patrons with speed and deal with money accurately.

As I went about my chores, no one took notice of me — save Jolla, and he told me what to do. Indeed, not only was he in charge; since I was new as well as young, he took on the role of my instructor and protector. When I dropped something or brought a wrong order, confused money, or made other blunders, he stepped between me and the patron's sharp reprimand, smoothing things. Early on, you may be sure Jolla needed to provide this advice constantly, guiding me with a mix of firmness and patronizing sympathy. Since, at first, I was prone to making many mistakes, I needed to give him numerous thanks. But I had the sense that he liked having someone younger working for him. I even thought he found me amusing. Indeed, his constant corrections reminded me of my sister Mercy, though he wasn't peevish as she had often been.

In good time, I learned my way, remembering orders, how to know which table or person to serve, and how to be correct with money (the coins coming from many countries), so the anxieties I first had were gradually smoothed away.

I soon understood why Captain Brown had posted me at the Green Dragon. The place was crowded with men — very few women — full of loud and constant discourse. Since a boy serving men is ignored, I was able to listen to the chatter, which was often about politics, sometimes quiet and earnest, other times loud and enraged. These conversations were unending, peppered with the usual radical seasonings: "rights," "just laws," "freedom," and always, "liberty."

Discussions were most often about what was happening in Boston on any given day, its trade, and the crisis that would come when the port was shut down. And it *would* be closed, because, during that first day, I learned that the tea fine was not paid, voted down at an unruly town meeting. Or so I heard.

Captain Brown was right: by working at the Green Dragon, I would learn a lot about rebel activities.

It was late when I was dismissed at the end of my first day. Exhausted, I pulled on my old jacket, but my weariness came from work, not boredom. I had felt isolated, even though my hours had been filled by a demanding crowd.

As I started to leave, Jolla said, "Can you do the work?"

"I think so."

"Mr. Simpson doesn't take on many. You must have good connections." His look invited me to say more, and once again I sensed he suspected something. Though I refrained from saying a word, I wondered what he thought of me.

When I got home, I told my mother only that my tasks weren't hard. She asked no more, content to know that I was making good money. Faith was more curious, but when I described how I waited on tables, she soon lost interest. As for Uncle William, he took me aside and asked, "Is everything arranged?"

"I think so," I assured him. "But I need paper and ink."

"That will be yours."

I went to sleep content, my sole uneasiness being Jolla and his watchfulness. I suspected I would have to be on guard to keep my secret from him.

Tuesday, May 31, 1774

I soon learned of one man who was a regular at the Green Dragon. Always sitting at the same Sons of Liberty table, he gathered considerable attention from all kinds of patrons who seemed to want to talk or listen to what he had to say.

Short and plump, he was round-faced to the degree that he had a double chin. Spectacles sat low on his nose. His clothing was neither fashionable nor neat, nor, for that matter, very clean. While there was always a tankard of ale before him, or a meat pie, I never saw him drink or eat much: he was too busy in earnest conversations. Though he looked altogether ordinary, it was clear he was important.

I asked Jolla who he was.

"Samuel Adams" was the reply. "The chief rebel—they say—in all the colonies. The leader of the Sons of Liberty."

Remembering what Ensign DeBérniere had said of this Adams, I knew that I was where I most wanted to be, near my principal enemy. And since his presence both alarmed and excited me, I paid close attention to his table, trying to hear what he, as well as the others about him, said.

There were some men who regularly conferred with Mr. Adams—I admit they did not look ferocious, no more than he did. Jolla told me they were important Sons of Liberty. There was a Mr. Revere, a silversmith. Doctors Warren and Church, medical men. Wealthy, swarthy John Hancock, a merchant, was often there, dressed in fashion, a great contrast to Mr. Adams's attire. Mr. Hancock talked a lot, constantly using the word "liberty." I recalled his mansion overlooking the Commons and that Uncle William said he was the richest man in Massachusetts and a smuggler.

What I overheard at that table was politics, which took time for me to understand. I soon learned that Mr. Adams and his friends wanted to know, beyond all else, the activities of the English army. There was constant talk about soldiers, new arrivals, where they camped, what they were doing. Did they do anything unusual? Where were guns, muskets, and cannons stored? Where was gunpowder? These concerns echoed what I had heard in Tullbury. You may be sure I paid even closer attention.

Jolla noticed my interest. At one point he—with that same slightly mocking smile—said, "You're putting those big ears of yours to good use."

"It's interesting" was my careful reply, nothing more.

That second night when I returned home, I stood at my uncle's desk and, by the light of a candle, wrote out a summary of what I had heard.

There was much talk of the army on the Commons, and that they practiced maneuvers. The Sons of Liberty seem to want to know all about what the army is doing.

Wednesday, June 1, 1774

The next morning, before I went to work at the Green Dragon, I stepped into that New Bakery and asked for Mr. Ludlow. He proved a large, muscular man, quite bald. When I found him, he was elbow deep into a barrel of flour.

"Mr. Ludlow, sir?"

"Yes."

"I was told to give this to you."

I offered up my note for Captain Brown. The baker seemed to know what I was doing, for he took my report into his large, flour-dusted hands—barely considered me—and without a word, not so much as a nod, shoved my report into his apron pocket. With that done, I went off to the Green Dragon.

From then on, two, three times a week, I delivered such reports. In short, I was now a working spy.

At the tavern, I learned that the Boston Port Act had gone into effect. All incoming shipping was halted and declared illegal. In a brief time, the outgoing trade would also be stopped. It meant that the busiest port in the North American colonies would be shut down. The sole Boston boat allowed to move was the ferry between Charlestown and Boston, and even that, not at night. The closest open harbor (much smaller) was the town of Marblehead, twenty miles to the north, which added expense and difficulty to trade.

To mark the day, many of the town's seventeen churches rang their bells the way they did when a great person had died. Whigs proclaimed a day of humiliation and prayer. Tories were unhappy too. No laughter on the streets. No idle chatter. Faces everywhere were severe and full of dour anger. The business blood was about to be sucked out of a living body—the body being Boston. I thought it a proper chastisement for the destruction of the tea.

At the Green Dragon, traders, businessmen, mechanics, and artisans gathered in knots of frustration and wrath. Whig or Tory, all complained. The act made everyone find fault with England's government.

I watched Jolla. I took note that, while listening to many an argument, he committed to no side that day. It made me even more curious about his loyalties.

As the hours passed, the Green Dragon became full of loud, argumentative customers. Disputes were heated. Once, twice, fistfights broke out, Whigs against Tories, Tories against Whigs. At one point, Jolla called on me to help pull two men apart.

More than one person berated Mr. Adams to his face, accusing him of being the one who had organized the dumping of the tea, the cause of the law and the resulting devastation for Boston. He never lost his temper. During one argument, I heard him say, "Liberty once lost is lost forever," which stuck in my mind.

What I witnessed in the Green Dragon more than anything was anger against Great Britain, ferocious anger. I heard no one—Whig or Tory—defend the act. I found such resentment troubling. I understood, as my father had informed me, that destroying the tea was wrong, but hearing the arguments over the course of the day, I had to agree that to punish so many merchants for what so few had done seemed mistaken. Father had said that as well. But I told myself that the English government must've known what was right, that it was not for the likes of me to question it. If it took sacrifice to quell the radicals, so be it.

That said, talk of rebellion was common. I also heard a novel word, "independency," though I didn't know what it meant. At Mr. Adams's table, there was also talk about starting a boycott of British goods to strike back.

Debates whipped about like storm-tossed trees in the middle of a great tempest. Having lived in the country, I well knew that in storms, large trees often crashed, carrying down smaller ones with them. All in all, the frenzied talk was stimulating but alarming, too.

I reported all this to Captain Brown.

As it happened, before the dinner hour, there was a lull of patrons, so Jolla took a short rest in the alley behind the tavern. As he passed me by, he called to me to come out with him.

"Looks like you can use a pause," he said. He was right. It had been a busy day and more to come.

We sat down side by side, backs against the Dragon building. The air was balmy. After the noon hubbub in the tavern, the quiet was welcome calm.

After a few moments during which we did no more than sit and breathe, he turned to me. "Mind my asking? I'm guessing you're new to Boston. Where do you come from?"

"Tullbury. Out west."

"When?"

Instantly suspicious of his questions, all I said was "In April."

"With your family?"

"My mother and sisters."

"Father?"

"Died."

"Sorry to hear that. Did he have an occupation?"

"A pastor." Wanting to push his questions away, I said, "What about your parents?"

"Never knew them. Before your father died, did he take positions in all these arguments?"

I shrugged.

"Huh. Lots of pastors taking sides. The English Church in Boston has pledged allegiance to the Crown."

"Have you?" I felt bold enough to ask.

He shook his head. "All this Whig talk about England trying to enslave Massachusetts. If you listen to what people are saying, there will be new laws taking away liberties in Massachusetts. But that's mostly whites they're talking about. Many of my people are already enslaved, but I don't hear the rebels talking about giving Black people liberty. That John Hancock inside—you've been hanging around the Sons' table. You hear him talk?"

I nodded.

"Always talking liberty, isn't he? Well, he enslaves Black people. And he's not freeing them. And enslaved folk in Massachusetts have petitioned General Gage to give them freedom. He turned them down. Not much help from either party."

Wanting to get on his good side, I said, "My father preached against slavery. Called it an outrage."

Jolla said, "Did anyone listen?"

Stymied, I said, "I heard someone say that General Gage will extend a deal to enslaved people. Something like, 'Join the English army and gain your freedom.'"

"Possible," said Jolla. "We'll have to see — Whigs or Tories, whoever makes the best offer." He gave me an assessing look. "I'd say you have a lot to learn."

"About what?"

Instead of answering, he got up, and, clearly not satisfied by my attempt at sympathy, went back into the tavern.

I sat there thinking over Jolla's statement that I had a lot to learn and his words "whoever makes the best offer." I had thought Jolla a radical. I was no longer sure. What did he believe? I took it as my task to find out.

As I continued to sit there, I realized I had thought little about slavery. Father had said it was wrong, so I considered it wrong. But the only enslaved people in Tullbury were at Lawyer Hosmer's, and my dealings with them had been almost nil. It occurred to me that I didn't even know their names.

I went back to work.

Friday, June 3, 1774
With my long days at the Green Dragon, I wasn't at the Hog Alley house very much. It became rare for me to have conversations with

Mother, Faith, or Great-Uncle William, and I paid less and less attention to what they were doing, though Faith, I was pleased to see, had taken a decided liking to Uncle William. He was even giving her lessons in penmanship, enjoying their exchanges. I did ask him if my first week's pay had come to him, and he assured me it had.

"I passed it on to your mother, who gave some back to me."

That said, I spent little time with Mother or Faith. They settled all too quickly into old household ways, talking too fondly (I thought) about Tullbury. It was almost as if they wished to return. I even overheard Mother quote Luke 6:27 to Faith: "'Love your enemies, do good to those that harm you.'" And there I was at the Green Dragon, engaged every day in secret work that would bring rightful harm to the rebels.

In other words, as my family receded from my immediate concerns, the Green Dragon became my world, with me constantly alert for important news to pass on to Captain Brown.

Saturday, June 4, 1774

It was King George's birthday.

Before I went to work, I stood on the edge of the Commons and watched as regulars practiced their shooting. They snatched rolls of cartridges from their pouches, used their teeth to rip open the paper that held powder and ball. Powder was poured into gun barrels. Paper spat away. Balls rammed down barrels with rods. Firelocks primed. I saw them fire an impressive three times a minute.

Once they were done, the artillery unit offered a thundering celebratory cannonade, which was echoed by the navy in the bay.

Sounding less like elation than a warning, all that shooting rattled Boston's windows. It is one thing to hear the blast of a musket. It is quite another to hear a hundred cannons thunder.

I had never seen or heard such an awe-inspiring display of power. No one, I was sure, could stand against it. It reassured me that no one would ever again bully me the way the rebels had in Tullbury.

But I took note: despite our monarch's birthday, Boston citizens were sullen.

Monday, June 6, 1774

Doctor Warren printed a broadside calling for all citizens to refuse to buy anything that came from Great Britain. The Sons of Liberty promised to shame—or worse—anyone who did. I thought it outrageous. They continued to oppose loyalty by being tyrannical.

Soon enough, other broadsides appeared on the streets. They gave lists of Boston Loyalists. Occupations and businesses were noted. And if these people were not born in the American colonies, stars were placed by their names. Crown officials had special marks next to theirs. I was relieved to see that Uncle William was not listed.

But still, I was appalled. These lists were threats of violence. *If I were any of those men*, I thought, *I'd keep a close watch*. It reinforced how careful I had to be at the Green Dragon so as not to reveal what I was doing there.

The *Boston Gazette* published the full texts of laws that had been passed by Parliament, what the Sons of Liberty called the Coercive Acts. These laws:

1. Closed the port of Boston until that tea was paid for.
2. Disallowed all Massachusetts town meetings, and let the governor appoint all government officials. That is, they ended citizen elections.
3. Stated that British officers, if charged for a crime, would not be tried in Massachusetts but taken to London for trial.
4. Required colonists to house British troops in private homes.

There had long been rumors about such laws coming, but when people read the actual texts, anger in town exploded. Patrons at the Green Dragon were seething. All insisted these laws were far too severe.

I believed it served Boston right. My hope was that these strong laws might bring the Loyalists to assert themselves and push the rebels out of Boston. I shared my thoughts with no one.

Tuesday, June 7, 1774

The next day came further news that the charter King William and Queen Mary had created to establish the Province of Massachusetts Bay colony in 1691 was abolished. It meant that the laws by which my family had lived for generations were swept away. *Good,* I thought. As far as I was concerned, the Massachusetts laws hadn't worked. They allowed for much violence. Now royal law and order would be re-established.

Then, to my further delight, more British troops arrived. The Fourth Regiment. The Forty-Third. The Thirty-Eighth. The

Fifty-Ninth. In their brilliant red uniforms, they marched to the Commons and pitched their tents.

As I watched them parade, I kept thinking: *This is good. England is asserting herself. The rebels must give way.* It would be madness to oppose all these new troops and laws. Order would be restored. Violence would be suppressed.

When Jolla suggested again we take a break behind the tavern, I wondered anew if he was trying to find out about me. Or did he ask only because I was younger than him and an eager listener? For my part, his confidence and autonomy set him off from anyone I had known in Tullbury, and I wanted to know more about him, so I was glad to go with him.

"All these laws," he said. "Things are getting worse. There's going to be fighting."

I allowed myself to say, "Great Britain will triumph."

He gave me a questioning glance, and though I waited for him to speak, he didn't. Nor did I.

No more was said. I had the feeling we were dueling, silently.

Friday, June 10, 1774

My message to Captain Brown was:

> The S of L are trying to find out where there are stores of guns and gunpowder which they might steal and hide away. People are saying fighting will come.

Friday, June 17, 1774

Business at the Green Dragon was unusually slack. When I asked Jolla if he knew why, he told me there was a town meeting at Faneuil Hall to debate how to resolve the port closing crisis.

"Go," said Jolla. "Maybe you'll learn something."

Faneuil Hall, where so many public meetings were held, was set in the open square that faced Merchant's Row, not far from the Green Dragon. A large redbrick building, it was two stories high, with an immense cupola perched on its roof. Rows of hitching posts, all filled, stood on the north side.

The meeting proved to be crowded, with much shouting, yelling, and sometimes even screaming. I heard many a merchant cry out that he was going bankrupt. Others agreed. "Pay the fine," I heard. "We must open the port." As far as I could tell, these people were not necessarily Loyalists, but men of business, as well as mechanics, all of whom claimed they were suffering from a lack of trade.

Though no agreement as to what to do was reached, the meeting did approve a boycott of British goods. I didn't see what that would do. In my report to Captain Brown, I wrote what I thought important.

The rebels are going to have a meeting (they call it a "Continental Congress") in the town of Philadelphia. They are trying to get all the colonies to stand against Great Britain. Five delegates from Boston—including Samuel Adams—are going. They say there are *meetings all over Massachusetts in which people are planning to resist England's new laws.*

Writing "all over Massachusetts" made me think about my sister Mercy, in Tullbury. Was she happy there, living in our house, married to a rebel? Were things better there now? Was life what it had been? Did the neighbors talk to her? Did she ever think of me? I wished that I might speak to her, hear her thoughts.

All of which is to say, I missed her.

Friday, July 1, 1774

The fifty-cannon *Preston* arrived. There were now seven battleships in the bay. Five more would arrive. Powerful and fierce, they bristled with cannons. I was sure they could never be dislodged. Rebellion only made things worse. Why could not the Whigs see that?

Many people, including me, stood on Long Wharf and gawked at the ships. I found it hard to know what was uppermost on the faces that surrounded me: fear, or anger, or joy. Speaking for myself, observing the ships made me feel strong. But at the tavern, I was told that sailors on those ships were deserting in vast numbers. What, I wondered, could lure them away? I heard people say the navy was pressing Boston men to replace them, but I wasn't sure what that meant.

Transports (ships without cannons) continued to arrive, bringing more British soldiers. With them came Lord Percy, who, I was told, was a wealthy officer. I learned that Gage put him in charge of all the troops in Boston. At the Dragon, they were saying there were four thousand soldiers in town. One for every four Bostonians. That told me how much Great Britain wanted to restore law and order in Massachusetts—a desire I continued to applaud.

I remembered what my father had told me: "Patience is always the best course. In time, all British government mistakes will be rectified peacefully."

As far as I was concerned, the rebels were the ones constantly making mistakes. I found myself wishing the British government would move faster to fix things.

Saturday, July 2, 1774
Eight brass cannons from Castle William were set up on the Commons. I stared across the field at them. With their muzzles pointing toward town, they had a dreadful beauty. Cannons have no judgment; they crush whatever they strike. Then it occurred to me: since I was in town, perhaps those cannons pointed at me, too.

Tuesday, July 5, 1774
I was working in the Green Dragon when Jolla rushed up to me, grabbed my arm, and said, "They're going to execute a soldier on the Commons for trying to desert. You need to see it."

I had never known Jolla to leave the Green Dragon. His urgency and insistence were such that I didn't ask why, and the two of us ran out of the tavern.

At the far end of the Commons, a large crowd had gathered. When we worked our way through it, we saw a man rope-tied to a post, arms fastened behind his back. Eight yards in front of him stood six British soldiers in full uniform with muskets. Many other soldiers were lined up to stand witness.

Into my ear, Jolla whispered, "It's a warning to them not to desert."

It was perfectly clear what was about to happen. Even as the man stood there, his face showing anguish, he writhed, trying to break free. He was unable to. Tears were flowing down his cheeks. He kept screaming words impossible to understand. I was not even sure he spoke English.

An officer stood nearby. He shouted orders and lifted his sword. The soldiers brought their guns to bear.

"Fire!"

The guns roared. The man at the post fell against the ropes, bleeding and screaming. It was horrible to see, to hear. Even at close range, the poor man didn't die until the officer finished him with a pistol shot to his head. His brains spilled out.

I was appalled. Sick. I wished I hadn't seen the sight.

As Jolla and I walked back to the Green Dragon, he said, "Guess how many soldiers have deserted?"

Numb, I shook my head.

He said, "I heard it's about two hundred."

"Are . . . are they all shot?"

"Mostly they get away. Noah, I'm telling you," he added, "that man was killed because he wanted to be free."

"How do you know about all this?"

"From the tavern. The two best times to find things out are early morning and late at night. In the morning, people tell me what kept them awake. At night, they say what keeps them from sleeping."

I asked the question I had been holding back. "Why did you want me to see that execution?"

"Told you, you've got a lot to learn. That includes learning the price people are willing to pay for wanting to be free. You said your father preached against slavery. I asked if anyone listened. Maybe you'll be one who does."

That night, I tried to sleep but could not get the execution out of my head. I asked myself: *Is this the way England treats people who want to be free?*

Thursday, July 7, 1774

Walking to work in the morning, I observed a troop of blue-coated soldiers, the uniform of Royal Navy Marines, marching in close formation, muskets in hand. They were surrounding some seven people who looked to be, in the main, laborers. One was a boy. One was a Black man. Another, a white man with gray hair. They were being guarded like prisoners. Unwilling and wretched (the boy was crying), they were pushed forward by the soldiers, who used their gun butts to move them on. I was sure they were criminals. But as this group went along, people on the street were crying out, "Tyrants!" "Free them!" "Weaklings!"

I asked a man what was happening.

He said, "The ships have so many desertions, they are snatching men off streets — pressing them, forcing them into the navy."

I had a sudden, searing memory of being led away by Mr. Poor and Mr. Trak in Tullbury.

"Is the navy allowed to do that?" I asked.

"All I know is that they act so. And do you know what happens to most of those who are taken?"

I shook my head.

"They die."

I recalled my Uncle William telling me that General Gage, when he came to Boston, had promised he would uphold liberties and freedom for all British Americans.

When I arrived at the Green Dragon, Jolla, as always, was already there. He must have seen something on my face, for right away he asked what was troubling me.

"I saw a navy press gang."

He grimaced. "Welcome to Boston," he said. "How do you like being in a place where there are all kinds of slavery?"

I spent much of the day thinking over his remark. The fact was Jolla had a knack for asking questions that made me uncomfortable. I had no replies, much less answers. What if the things the rebels were saying about British tyranny were true? It gave me a moment of panic. I pushed the notion away as being impossible. *Don't ask stupid questions*, I scolded myself. *Stay loyal.*

Saturday, July 9, 1774

With the port closed, the food supply was decreasing. But something surprising was happening. Food was coming into Boston from many other places. Fruit from western Massachusetts. Fish from Rhode Island. I saw a wagon full of rice that came all the way from Carolina, down south. It shocked me that there were people from all the colonies who agreed with the Boston rebels. I even heard my mother say, "Other folks are being kind to Boston. I never thought I'd thank the Whigs. I am doing so now."

I had never imagined Mother would say such a thing. But then, let it be admitted, I rarely asked for her thoughts—she had always agreed with Father, and I had never had reason to think that would change. I refrained from asking her now, as, with Jolla's questions already causing me unease, I wanted no more unsettling notions.

Thursday, August 11, 1774

The summer heat brought heavy, moist air to Boston. Every day was like walking through a swamp. My work at the Dragon continued.

"Did you hear?" Jolla said, pulling me aside one evening. "Sam Adams and his cousin John Adams, along with a couple of others, have taken a carriage to Philadelphia."

"What about it?"

"It's for a meeting with the other colonies to decide how to deal with the British. They're calling it a congress."

"Won't they be arrested?"

"Not likely. They are being protected by two armed guards in front, and four more to cover their back."

"Wise."

"They're going, they say, to find ways to protect their freedom. But when I saw that carriage roll out, who do you think I saw as their four rear guards?"

I shook my head.

"Enslaved Black men," said Jolla. "Someone once said to me, 'Choose your enemy before they choose you.'"

I felt a flash of anger. "What am I supposed to do with that?"

"I'm telling you, sometimes knowing your enemy is easy. But sometimes it's hard."

My frustration burst out. "Am I your enemy?"

"You tell me," he said.

"Hope not."

"Happy to hear it," he said. "What are you, then?"

I was about to say "a Loyalist" but held back. I told myself it was because I knew better than to reveal my beliefs. But witnessing the execution and the press gang had dented my devotion. What I had seen troubled me. Things weren't completely right.

Brooding, I went silently back to work.

Friday, August 12, 1774

In the morning, on my way to the Dragon, I saw a fair number of broadsides scattered about on the streets. I picked one up, and when I saw it was a statement from the Sons of Liberty, I brought it to the Green Dragon.

Jolla saw me studying it and asked, "What are you reading?"

"Have you seen this?"

"What is it?"

"I found it on the street. You'll like it." I read it aloud: "'The country people are determined to protect you and screen you from any attempt to keep you in your present slavery.'"

He considered me for a moment. Then he asked, "Who do you think that's for?"

"Blacks," I answered.

Jolla shook his head. "It's for British soldiers. The rebels are trying to get them to desert. That 'present slavery' is the British army. But if an enslaved Black man runs off, do you think the rebels will protect him?"

He went to Mr. Simpson's table and grabbed a copy of the *Boston Gazette*. "The radical newspaper," he said, and he pointed to a column on the front page. "Look here. See this piece written by someone who calls himself 'Libertas'? It's about how Americans must defend their liberties. All well argued. Same time, here," he said, folding back a page and pointing to an advertisement. He read: "'A healthy Negro girl, about twenty years of age. Good-natured. Fond of children. Price, forty pounds.'" He looked up. "Not much liberty there."

I recalled Jolla saying of John Hancock—one of the Sons of Liberty leaders—"Well, he enslaves Black people." He wasn't the only one.

"They're hypocrites," I said, using my father's word. But I felt I had to say something more. "I'm hoping the English government will give freedom to enslaved Blacks."

"Are you?" he threw back. "Right now, English troops are

putting down Black people trying to get free in Jamaica and other islands."

"Where's that?"

"West Indies islands."

"How do you know?"

"Until they shut the port, think of all that molasses—to make rum—coming to Boston from the islands. Ships spread news. Who do you think grows and cuts the sugar?"

"Slaves?"

He nodded. "Ephraim Wilde," he said, referring to the other man who worked the tables at the Green Dragon.

"What about him?"

"Does what you do here, right?"

"I suppose," I said, realizing Jolla was very angry, which I had not witnessed before.

"But you get paid for what you do, right? He doesn't."

"Why?"

"He's enslaved by Mr. Simpson."

I had not known and was much abashed.

Jolla walked off, leaving me feeling disheartened and adrift.

The truth was Jolla managed to upset me so greatly that I made up my mind not to talk to him so much. But that was a hard resolution to stick to. While our talk often left me rattled and uncomfortable, I sensed he wasn't trying to make me unhappy, but to shake up my thoughts. Indeed, his talk made me understand how little I knew, that there was much I had to learn. And that made me want to find out more.

In days to come, I tried striking up a friendship with Ephraim Wilde. While he was always civil, he wanted nothing to do with me. I could hardly blame him.

Saturday, August 13, 1774

I had a bad nightmare. My dream combined the press gang and the execution. I was on the street when I saw the marines gather up some people and then execute them. I woke up upset and had to convince myself it was a night fancy. *Such a thing could not happen to me,* I had to remind myself before I could return to sleep.

Sunday, August 14, 1774

Heading to church with my family, we passed a squad of marines. Memories of the press gang and wisps of my dream made it hard to concentrate during the service, with all the British officers there.

I kept thinking: *Can I trust them or not?* But I also wondered, *Can I trust Jolla?*

Wednesday, August 24, 1774

At the table occupied by the Sons of Liberty, I kept hearing rebel talk about the need to gather guns and gunpowder, and for places to hide it. The rebels also claimed more and more militia meetings were being held, with constant mustering in the other colonies. Committees and congresses were springing up everywhere. New governments were coming into life. Meanwhile, food and fuel kept arriving in Boston from elsewhere at a fast rate. I heard far less support for Great Britain. It made me uneasy.

Captain Brown said I was to come only when it was important, but I felt the need to report what I had heard to him. In truth, what I wanted was encouragement. Since I had pulled back from talking with Jolla, I was feeling isolated again. After three months of gathering information at the Dragon, all I had achieved was the dulling of my own loyalty.

I went to army headquarters and told Captain Brown that at the Green Dragon I heard fewer and fewer expressions of loyalty.

He replied: "I can assure you, Noah, all this treasonous activity is confined to Boston. The Loyalists—and they are many—are being intimidated. As you might remember, you aren't my sole informant. I have others sending reports. They tell me our troops merely need to move out from Boston and all those militias will melt away. Those who are loyal to the king—as you are—are waiting for us to put down these treasonous leaders."

"But, sir, in my town—"

"Yes, I know," he said, cutting me off. "Your father was killed there. By a mob. How many?"

"Fifteen."

"Trifling. As soon as we arrest Mr. Adams and Mr. Hancock, the rebellion will collapse. Good people will emerge."

"Why don't you do it now, sir?"

"All I can say is that the troops refer to General Thomas Gage as 'Timid Tommy.' But, Noah, do you know why we are here?"

"To protect British liberties."

"I'm glad you understand."

I went away reassured. Captain Brown had to have it right, that there were few rebels and most were in Boston. It was painful to think Tullbury was an exception, but I hoped it was so.

Though I was attempting not to talk so much to Jolla, I was eager to tell him what the captain said. It would be good to show him I was right to be a Loyalist, and that the British wanted to protect liberties.

Besides, I missed speaking with him. Not a friend, exactly, but the only one I could talk to regularly. He knew things I didn't, and I could talk to him about matters I found troubling. How different than with my Tullbury friends. With them, it had been all fun, no challenge other than boyish competition. But Jolla would have us talk of weighty adult matters, and he treated my thoughts as worthy — even when he knew more than me. Father had always told me what to think. Jolla was always trying to get me to think for myself.

Thursday, August 25, 1774

When I saw the opportunity, I spoke to Jolla. Without mentioning Captain Brown's name, I told him I heard someone say that it was simply a few people who supported the Sons of Liberty, that most Massachusetts citizens were loyal.

"Whoever said that is a fool," said Jolla. "That's what he wants to believe."

Offended, I said, "How can you say that?"

"That man you heard, was he someone in the government, the army?"

Of course, he guessed right, which annoyed me, but I refused to answer.

"Strong people on top always think the bottom is weak. What happens next is that things go topsy-turvy."

"What do you mean?"

"Watch: there are lots of soldiers in Boston, but wait until they actually try to do something."

"What'll happen?"

"Just know there are far fewer Loyalists than radicals."

"Not true," I insisted. "That's only what the rebels say."

"Look around you, Noah. And use your big ears to listen."

Smarting from the remark, I tried to convince myself that I didn't like Jolla.

The execution and the press gang continued to trouble me. I'd look at a soldier and wonder if he ever thought of deserting. Or when I saw a blue-coated marine, I'd remember the press gang. There were also those things I knew about the rebels, their violence, their hypocrisy. Jolla's talk kept it front of mind. No wonder I slept ill and had more bad dreams, night visions full of musket-holding tormentors that danced round my head. Sometimes Father was there. Sometimes he was a devil.

I would wake in a sweat.

I felt a great need to talk to someone. Not Faith. Nor my mother. Not Uncle William. That left the one person I had been talking to: Jolla. While I suspected he knew why I was at the Green Dragon, the fact was he had done me no harm. Then, too, we were working together most of the time, interacting constantly. Deciding not to talk so much had made me want to talk more. It was like trying to ignore an itch. The more you tried not to think about it, the more you wanted to scratch it. I admitted to myself that far from disliking him, I wanted to trust him. But I was frustrated that I couldn't tell what side he was on. I kept telling myself it had to be Whig or Tory, and I didn't know enough about him to tell which it was.

As it happened, that afternoon, he asked me to go out back with him. I agreed. We sat for a while, and then he said, "You were serving Mr. Dunphy."

I nodded.

"Did he ask you a lot of questions about your politics?"

"He did."

"You give him answers?"

"Not really."

"Good. He's an agitator. Likes to make trouble."

I said, "Thank you for telling me."

He gave a quick nod.

As I sat there, I thought of all the things Jolla had done to challenge me, and here he was protecting me. After a moment, I said, "You've been helpful to me."

"May sound stupid to say, but if I've learned anything in my life it's that the only way you get by is by helping people."

As I thought about his remark, I realized again how little I knew about that life of his.

I blurted out, "What happened to your parents?"

"How come you're asking?"

"You asked me about mine. I'd like to know about yours."

"I'm not sure any other white person has ever asked me that."

I waited, not sure if he would speak.

It took him a while, sitting in silence, me looking at him, before he said, "I was told I was born right here in Boston. But I don't know anything about my father. My mother? A bit of memory. Brothers? Sisters? No idea. I do remember—maybe I was five or six—being sold to a Mr. Jennings. Up in Salem. He called me Hannibal, after an ancient general. Only later did I understand the name was his idea of a joke. Powerful white man. Powerless Black boy."

I was startled by the deep grief his face showed. He must have sensed it because he looked away. It took some moments for him to continue. "I cleaned up after him. Served him at the table. But he didn't live long. When he died, I was about ten years old and wasn't sure what would happen. To my surprise, his widow decided to go to England and set me free."

"Why?"

"Said she couldn't be bothered with me."

"Did she give you food? Money?"

Jolla shook his head. "All she said was 'Go to Boston,' and pointed the way. You may be sure I ran, and you may be double sure I had enough sense to know I might be grabbed. Held. Be enslaved again. Who would believe a Black kid who said he was free? How would I prove it?

"Salem isn't far, but I was scared and cautious. I walked at night. Took me three days. During the day I slept or hid in fields. No food. I wasn't even sure where I was going."

"It must have been awful," I said.

"Was. When I got to Boston, I went up to the first Black people I saw. Turned out they were enslaved, but they heard my story — told through tears — and brought me to some freemen, who took me to others. Over the next few nights, I was passed on until an old couple — free — were willing to take me in. Good folks. They kept me as their own. Gave me an African name, Jolla. The man, Mr. Freeman — that's where I got the last name — taught me to read. He told me, 'A man who can read knows more than he knows.' Never did learn to write well.

"A year later, I got work here. Decent place. There's food, and I get to know things."

"Mr. Simpson pay you much?"

"Just food."

"No salary?" I said, surprised.

"Tips."

I didn't know what to say. "Do you still live with those old people?"

"They died. I have my place."

"Alone?"

"Alone."

I tried to understand all he had told me. I had to feel for him. Alone. Little money. No family. We talked no more but sat in a silence filled with his story. I was embarrassed by my ignorance.

That night, as I tried to sleep, I kept thinking about Jolla. And what it meant to be enslaved. I tried telling myself that my job was to find out about the Sons of Liberty, not slavery, that I was there to defend England, not to free anyone.

Even so, I wondered if I should tell Jolla my own tale, what had brought us to Boston. After all, he had told me his. But what if Jolla betrayed me as Micah had done in Tullbury? It was impossible to forget the terrible harm Micah did. I told myself that Jolla was completely different. I had seen him in many circumstances, but one thing stood out: he always said what he believed.

The Green Dragon was a place for rebels. I was a Loyalist. I was there to spy. But I reminded myself that Jolla had warned me about that Mr. Dunphy. That was an act of friendship.

Father had said: "The English empire is the greatest in the world. The Church of England and the empire are one. Being invincible, it will protect us. Give all your loyalty to that."

I had believed Father's words when he spoke them. I was not sure I still did. But I felt I was incapable of shaping new notions. I thought how Jolla challenged me to do so, and how uncomfortable it made me feel. But—a nagging thought—maybe it was what I needed to do. I couldn't escape the feeling that I knew less than I thought I did.

Friday, August 26, 1774
I learned something of great importance.

As I served the Sons of Liberty table, I realized Doctor Warren and Mr. Revere were talking about what they claimed was the largest store of gunpowder in Massachusetts. I was eager to know where it was, so I hovered about their table. I had no idea where it might be until I realized they were speaking about Charlestown, right across the Charles River. As they talked, I remembered I'd seen the very structure they were describing when I had wandered through that area. Now the rebels were talking of seizing its contents. Soon.

I recalled what Abner Hosmer had told me, that gunpowder was valuable and scarce, that it came from Europe.

Surely this was something Captain Brown must be informed of. It would be wrong not to pass on the information. So, that night when I got home, I began to write to him about what I had learned. Even as I did, I worried that he needed to know sooner than a message might reach him. What if the rebels seized all that gunpowder, the most in Massachusetts?

It was urgent that I talk to Captain Brown.

Saturday, August 27, 1774

By eight o'clock next morning—as the church bells tolled—I was at Province House, pacing the red stone steps. Doors were still shut. When at last they opened and guards were posted, I tried to enter but was held back until I told one of the soldiers that I must see Captain Brown.

"Why should he speak to you?"

"Sir, he'll want to if you give him my name, Noah Cope. Tell him it's an emergency."

The soldier looked doubtful, but something forceful in my manner made him go inside. He returned shortly. "He'll see you."

I went into the room. Captain Brown was sitting at his table, which, as usual, was covered with maps.

Impatient, I stood in front of him. He took a while before he looked up, no doubt wishing to convey his annoyance that I was back again so soon. "Why are you here?" he finally demanded, irritation in his voice.

Talking fast, I said, "Forgive me, sir, but above Charlestown, on a hill, there's a storage place that holds lots of gunpowder. Said to be most in all Massachusetts. Sir, the rebels are planning to seize it."

If the captain had been intending to rebuke me, the words never came. Rather, his face paled. He stared at me. When he did speak, all he said was "Are you sure?"

"Yes, sir. I heard it at the tavern."

"I should have been informed about that store," he said. "Exactly where is it?"

"Beyond Charlestown. Atop what they call Quarry Hill. Overlooking the Mystic River."

"When are they going to get it?"

"Just . . . soon."

"Do you know how valuable that powder is?"

"Yes, sir. Very."

"And it belongs to the Crown. For anyone but representatives of the king to take it would be a brazen theft. More, a disaster."

He went on: "London is considering banning all shipments of guns and gunpowder to the colonies."

I watched the play of emotions on his face. He appeared much concerned.

He studied his table, found a map, pulled it atop the other maps, and spread it out. "Can you show me where that storage place is?"

I stepped forward and looked at the chart. It took me some moments to make sense of it all. Boston and the waters surrounding it were easy to see, as was the Neck that attached it to Roxbury. North of Boston, I saw the channel upon which Charlestown stood. The Mystic River. I put a finger down where I thought the powder was stored.

"You've seen it. Has it one door?" he asked. "Two? Locks?"

"One door, I think. A big lock."

Captain Brown stared at the spot for a long while. When he looked up, he said, "I'm sure we could find it, but if I got you up the Mystic, do you think you could lead me to that spot? It would save time, and speed is important."

"Yes, sir. I think so."

He patted my back. "Noah Cope, you've done well."

"Do you think so, sir?"

"Of course." He smiled. "Have you any doubts?"

"No, sir."

"I wish I had an army of Loyalists like you. We'd deal with this rebellion very quickly, wouldn't we, you and I?"

"Yes, sir," I said, glowing with pleasure.

"As it is, we'll need to move as fast as possible," said the captain. "I shall report to General Gage. Return to the Green Dragon and listen. If you discover that the rebels are moving to get that powder, come to me immediately."

"Please, sir, one question. Do you think the local people will hinder us in any way?"

"Noah, as I've told you before: the people of Massachusetts are — like you — loyal to the king. It will be safe. But we must secure that powder. If I could give you a medal, I would. You deserve one."

Basking in Captain Brown's words, I left in high spirits, any doubts I had about the British and my loyalty evaporated. *Perhaps*, I mused, *I will get a medal.*

Wednesday, August 31, 1774

The following days at the Green Dragon felt long. I was anxious, fretful, worried about that gunpowder. But excited, too. I tried to stay close to the table where the Sons of Liberty gathered. Since Samuel Adams was in Philadelphia, Doctor Warren was in attendance and seemed to be in charge. He met with Mr. Revere, and I did hear talk of gunpowder, how it must be secured and hidden, but as far as I gathered, the chatter had nothing to do with what was in Charlestown. They were talking about the village of Concord instead. I wasn't interested in that.

At one point Jolla took me aside and said, "The way you're staying close to that table, you look like you're trying to find out something."

Though uneasy, I assured him I was not. I must have given something away, because he gave me a doubtful look and that half smile he had that suggested he knew otherwise. But he asked no more. You may be sure I kept away from him after that.

On Wednesday eve, when I returned home, I found a message from Captain Brown:

Be on Long Wharf at 4:00 a.m.

I did not tell my family what I was about to do.

In any case, as I waited, I was elated. At last! My loyalty was finally bringing about something of importance.

Thursday, September 1, 1774

No doubt the night's summer damp-heavy heat would have kept me awake, but my impatience for the morning was such that I slept ill. Tossing on my bed, I think I heard every quarter-hour peal of the church bells, every cry from the night watch. I had found where my mother kept Father's pocket watch and consulted it often.

It was long before dawn when I crept out of the silent Hog Alley house. The cloudless sky held a thin moon; its pale, milky light enabled me to make my way with ease along deserted Newbury, Marlborough, and Cornhill Streets. My mind went back to my final moonlit walk in Tullbury when I had met Nathaniel. I would have liked for him to see me now, doing something that was truly an adventure.

I reached Long Wharf and hurried toward its end. To my delight, I found some three hundred regular soldiers lined up. They were wearing short red jackets and black leather caps that bore their regimental number, stating that they were the Thirty-Eighth Foot. Each man carried a musket as well as a powder horn and bullet pouch attached to his belt. A few held hooded lanterns. I heard no talk among them, nor, when I considered their faces in the small light, did I see any emotion.

In the water below, longboats were clustered around the wharf with Royal Navy seamen sitting over the oars.

This is all my doing! I allowed myself to think, and felt what I rarely did—*joy.* It was exhilarating. I had to work hard to contain my enthusiasm.

As I was looking on, I heard, "Noah Cope."

I swung about. Captain Brown's ensign, DeBérniere, was standing next to the captain, who had his sword on his hip. Captain Brown beckoned to me.

"Stay close to us," he said. "We'll be in the first boat." Bending down to my ear, he added, "We'll be going to secure the king's gunpowder from that place above Charlestown. I've found out all about it now, and it's exactly what you told me, an important powder storage. Since you've been there, you'll lead us. I'll be going along to make sure all is done right. Have no fear—by acting in secret, no one will be alarmed. I assure you, there's no danger. We'll bring the powder to the fort on Castle Island.

"General Gage also wishes to secure two cannons that he has learned are on Cambridge Common. Once we get the gunpowder, DeBérniere will go there with a few soldiers. It's not far from the Charlestown Neck. I want you to go with him. You won't have to do anything. Others will. But when the cannons are gone, I want you to remain in Cambridge to watch how people react—if they react at all—and report back to me so I can inform General Gage. I'm sure you'll be unnoticed. I have written out a pass. Show it to the guards. It will allow you to seek me out at any time."

He handed me a folded piece of paper, which I put deep into my pocket.

"Yes, sir," I said, happy that I had more tasks. "But what about my duties at the Dragon?"

"I've taken care of that. I'll also get word to your Uncle William. If you're late, your family need not worry." He smiled. "And don't forget to eat." He handed me a new shilling. "If you are like my son, boys like to eat."

"Thank you, sir," I said, full of pride at his confidence in me, gratified that he compared me with his son.

Rope ladders had been affixed to the wharf so we could get into the longboats. Captain Brown went down first. DeBérniere next. I followed. Once below, sailors helped us into a boat. The captain told me to sit next to him, which I did, elated to be in a place of such importance, looking over the bow. DeBérniere sat behind me.

The loading of the soldiers into the boats was done with little noise. The most I heard was the scrape of boots and the bump of gunstocks on gunwales. The weather was perfect, temperature mild, the air still.

Once the soldiers were on board, the longboats eased from the wharf, strung out in a line like a row of ducks. As we went slowly into the bay, the oars made soft plashing sounds. Since cloth had been wrapped about the oarlocks, grating was muffled. As for the water, it did no more than ripple, the slight moonlight shivering on its surface.

We moved out beyond Boston's many wharves, going by Hancock's big dock, before passing the North Battery. Upon reaching the northernmost point of Boston, we shifted to the right and cut our way across the waters to the far side of the Charlestown peninsular, a half mile at most. When we came to the Mystic River, which flowed into the bay, it was still dark. During all that time, I heard no one speak.

We traveled up the river for what I supposed was about three miles. Then we pulled to land alongside a small wharf, which I assumed must be part of a nearby farm. Sure enough, the dawn's first light allowed me to make out a cluster of houses on the land beyond. In the same emerging light, I recognized the hills where I had wandered the time I had gone to Charlestown.

By the wharf, I saw eight wagons with drivers and horses in shaft traces. A big man, not in uniform, was also waiting there. As we touched the shore—the tide was high—I heard him call out, "Captain Brown, sir. Sheriff Phipps here."

I was sure his presence had been arranged.

Captain Brown stepped onto the land along with DeBérniere and me. Boat by boat, the soldiers disembarked. Silence was maintained.

After quietly conferring with Sheriff Phipps, Captain Brown called out, "Soldiers." His voice was hushed.

The men clustered about him. I, too, stood nearby.

"Atop that hill is a powder magazine. Inside is some two hundred and fifty half barrels of the king's gunpowder. Our task is to remove that powder, load it onto these wagons—which are matted with hay—haul it down to the boats, and bring it all to Castle William.

"I don't know if any of you have anything that burns—coals to light pipes and the like. All of that must be thrown away. Douse your lantern flames as well. We are going to a packed powder house, so you must lay down your muskets. I will put aside my sword. Metal will make sparks. The slightest spark will blow the powder and you to hell. We'll wait until there is more daylight to do our work. Is all that understood?"

There were murmurs of "Yes, sir. Of course."

The company commanders went among the soldiers, passing along Captain Brown's words. Lanterns were snuffed out. I saw a couple of glowing embers arc through the air and land in the water with a hiss.

Captain Brown put a hand on my shoulder. "Master Cope, lead the way."

There I was, a boy, leading a stealthy army undertaking as the ruddy dawn began to bloom in the east. Right behind me came the captain and his ensign. Soldiers followed, marching in good, close order. Other soldiers led the horse-drawn wagons. Some helped push the wagons up the hill. Taking up the rear was Sheriff Phipps. I led them all, fairly prickling with delight.

To be sure, I had one worry—would anyone oppose us? I reminded myself of Captain Brown's insistence that it was highly unlikely. I told myself I could trust him to know.

We went up the hill along a wide cow track, passing wheat fields. I heard the steady thump of boots on the ground, the rumblement of wagons, the cheerful chirrup of summer crickets, the rustle of the tall wheat. Now and again a horse blew breath or whinnied.

As we approached the hilltop, there were some trees, but for the most part, it was open space. Daylight grew, and I began to see the powder house on the hill's summit. It was as I remembered it: a tall, stone, loaf-shaped structure.

When we drew close, the captain called a halt. To demonstrate caution, he laid his sword on the ground with elaborate care. What I heard next was a soft *clink, clink* as the redcoat regulars did the same with their muskets.

In the hush that followed, the captain walked slowly to the powder house and climbed its stone steps. From his pocket, he withdrew a large key and, with extreme caution, used it to unlock the door, then pulled it open. From where I stood, all I saw within was darkness.

What came next was an unhurried and careful removal of the gunpowder. Soldiers went into the building four at a time. No one else entered until that party came out, hauling a half-size barrel. Then another four went in. Once a powder barrel was removed, it was carried with much gentleness to a wagon, into which it was stowed with equal care.

Though it took some time, I did no more than look on.

At one point a man came by, stopped, gawked, and went away. From the way he staggered, he might well have been muzzed. *So much*, I thought, *for rebel interference*. The captain was correct. Step away from Boston, and all was peaceful. Once again, it was a comfort to know he was right.

It took four hours to remove all the powder barrels and set them into wagons. By then it had become full daylight.

When all was ready, Captain Brown took up his sword. Muskets were reclaimed. The loaded wagons made a slow descent down the hill. At the shore of the Mystic River, the barrels were loaded into the rowboats.

As the last wagon went down, Captain Brown came to me. He put a hand on my shoulder in friendly fashion. "When you return to Boston from Cambridge — it's an eight-mile walk — come to me at Province House and make your report. Do you still have your pass?"

I touched my pocket. "Yes, sir."

"I doubt there will be anything for you to tell me, but it's always best to be sure. Good work. Safe travels."

With that, he went off in the last of the boats. That left Sheriff Phipps, Ensign DeBérniere, some ten regular soldiers, and me. We stood watching from the hill until the powder-laden longboats, low in the water, pulled away and headed downriver, moving steadily back toward the bay and Castle William.

The operation had been achieved to perfection. Best of all, it was as the captain had foretold: There was no resistance to what we had done. No rebels to oppose the Crown. One drunken sot. All was at peace.

So it was that Sheriff Phipps, DeBérniere, the soldiers, and I started off for Cambridge, which, I was informed, was four miles beyond Charlestown. I considered it a holiday.

———

It was perhaps noon when we started along a path that took us north from the powder house, then down over Bunker Hill. Much like Boston, the Charlestown peninsular had a low and narrow neck, ten yards wide, which at low tide connected it to the mainland. Once over it, we continued along a much wider path that led west. We passed a few people, but no one hailed us or impeded us in any way.

As we traveled on, we walked through open country and hilly farmland, where summer hay was growing. We went by more people, and though we received a few curious glances, for the most part we were met with indifference. The day being less hot, moving along with DeBérniere, Sheriff Phipps, and the soldiers was easy and enjoyable.

We soon reached Cambridge.

Though much bigger than Tullbury, Cambridge proved a modest town, with buildings of brick and wood clustered about. I estimated some thousand people lived there.

When we entered the town, I saw, to the north of the main road, a group of large brick buildings. Sheriff Phipps informed me that it was Harvard College. East of the college was a common. Farther east, facing the common, was a church. To the west was a tavern whose sign proclaimed it was the Red Lion. Close to that structure was a smaller building that looked like a grammar school. Another building appeared to be a courthouse, which Sheriff Phipps confirmed. A few people were about on the common, and while I'm sure we were noticed, no words were exchanged. Under the summer sun, it was a picture of peace.

Sitting in the middle of the common were two cannons mounted on wheeled carriages. No one was attending them. I had no doubt they were the cannons we were meant to take.

While the soldiers and I waited beside the cannons, Sheriff Phipps went to the nearby tavern. He soon returned, guiding a team of horses, which, he informed us, he had borrowed. The horses were attached to the gun carriages, and with DeBérniere in charge, the soldiers led them away on what I was told was the Watertown Road. It would, they said, bend around to the Boston Neck and bring them to town. That left me quite alone, and I was perfectly content with that.

My simple task, as set forth by Captain Brown, was to observe the local population and report anything that might be considered unusual. My immediate observation was that there was nothing to see. Cambridge Common remained empty. All was peaceful.

With little to do, I wandered about among the Harvard buildings. I tried to imagine my father there as a student. I also mused on what it would have been like for me to have attended. I had, after all, been destined to enroll there. What, I wondered, would Father think of me now? Would he be proud? I hoped so. Considering that my father's temperament—so sure of himself—made for an exemplary pastor, I doubted I would be a good minister. Too anxious. In any case, such a notion—me, a minister—seemed to belong to another time. *What*, I asked myself, *should I strive to be? What trade or skill might I follow?* I had to admit I had no idea.

My reflections making me sad, I didn't wish to linger at the college. Instead, I moved on to ramble about the village but saw nothing of interest. Feeling hunger, I clutched the shilling Captain Brown had given me and repaired to the tavern. By then it was late afternoon.

The tavern, situated on the edge of the village common, was like other taverns I'd been in: dim, smelling of rum, crowded with people, and noisy with idle chatter.

I purchased a meat pie and a mug of cider, then sat in a corner wedged between two full tables, where I ate and drank my fill. No one paid me any mind. I listened hard but heard not one whisper about the morning's excursion to the Charlestown powder store. Nothing about the Cambridge cannons that had been taken away either. I had to remind myself of the great tension in Boston. It seemed to be part of another world. Captain Brown was right: leave Boston, and all rebellion melted away. I felt good and, for once, comfortable with myself.

My meal done, I decided that it was time to head back to town. If I left now, I'd reach home by evening, so my mother would not fret. In the morning, I would report to Captain Brown that nothing untoward had happened.

But sitting there much relaxed, my stomach full, my high-backed bench comfortable, the tavern air stale, my lack of sleep from the previous night overtook me: I dozed.

I suspect I slept for about two hours before waking with a start. As I tried to push the torpor from my head, I realized a man had rushed into the tavern, his face flush with excitement. In a loud voice he proclaimed, "Over in Charlestown, this morning, the redcoats attacked and killed our militiamen."

All tavern talk ceased until someone shouted, "Say on!"

The man cried, "A whole regiment of British troops snuck out from Boston early this morning, went to Charlestown, and stole the gunpowder stored there. When some militia tried to stop them, they were shot down."

There was momentary speechless silence as the news sank in. Then the patrons erupted with shouts, curses, and cries of fury, even as people rushed outside.

Not yet fully awake, I sat there trying to make sense of what I had heard. It was — I knew — an utterly false account of what had happened that morning. After all, I was there in Charlestown. No theft occurred. The powder that had been removed belonged to the Crown. No one made any attempt to stop the effort. I had seen the regulars go off in the boats. I had gone along with the remaining few soldiers to Cambridge. They hauled away the cannons. Not so much as one person interfered. No shot was fired. No one was killed.

Baffled and alarmed, I hurried out of the tavern, thinking I should tell people that the news was wrong. To my astonishment, there were hundreds of people gathered on the common, all churning about. Muskets were in evidence, as were sticks and clubs. All these people, it seemed, were talking at once, a constant rumble of furious voices. They were telling one another what I had heard: of the violent seizure of gunpowder in Charlestown by British regulars. That six militiamen had been shot. No, eight. Twelve.

Knowing for a certainty that what I was hearing was not true, I had no doubt that among the mass of people, which was increasing every moment, I was the sole person who knew what had truly occurred at the powder house. But the intense rage I observed made me fearful to say anything that might reveal my role. People might turn on me.

As I moved through the crowd, I began to hear more bewildering news: General Gage was going to disarm every radical in Boston. That if rebels didn't give up their guns, the Royal Navy fleet would bombard the town.

Even that wasn't all. I heard people telling one another that English troops were about to march out of Boston. To Cambridge. Which is to say, the war that people had so feared had begun—because of what had *not* happened in Charlestown. Because of what I had started.

While I had no knowledge if any of those reports—that British troops were on the move—were true, if the news I'd heard about the powder was so false, as I knew it was, the rest seemed as unlikely. That said, I wasn't sure what to do. Even as I tried to think, more and more people were arriving on the common. Hundreds! At one point I even thought I caught a glimpse of Jolla, then realized that of course it wasn't him. But there were other Black people, as outraged as everyone else. Were they free? Were they enslaved? I had no idea. Regardless, they were there. Also, many a grayhead, as well as those quite young—young (it seemed) as me. I even believed I saw Tullbury folks, though the crowds were so dense I couldn't be sure, and I did not want to draw close.

It didn't matter who these people were: the general rage was like boiling water, hot and steaming. I began to fear—absurd as it might have been—that people would see me for what I was, someone loyal to the king. An enemy. I felt myself in danger.

Fearing for my safety, I decided I must get back to Boston—eight miles away—to report to Captain Brown and to tell my family I was all right. But as to which was foremost in my mind—my well-being or the well-being of the British army—I cannot in all honesty say.

By the time I decided to leave Cambridge, there must have been a thousand people on the common, with more arriving all the time. The alarm—I kept telling myself it was nothing more than that, a false rumor—that British regulars had shot down militiamen, that they were coming out of Boston, seemed to have swept the whole countryside.

Why would people believe the rumors? I kept asking myself. How had they heard them in the first place? And where had all the people come from? Had not Captain Brown told me there were only a few rebels?

By then I was running south, out of Cambridge along the Watertown Road, passing some fine buildings. Whereas the road I had taken into Cambridge from Charlestown had been for the most part empty, the Watertown Road was crowded. More than crowded. A torrent of people was heading toward Cambridge on foot and horseback. It didn't matter that it was early evening, the moon low in the eastern sky. As I went along, moving fast, I was pushing—quite alone—against a massive flow coming the other way. These new people were sure that the rumors I had heard were accurate. Any number of men called out to me, "Go back to Cambridge, boy." "The English are attacking," they yelled. "Stop. We need everyone in Cambridge!"

I rushed toward Boston in deep confusion: All these people were incensed about something that had not happened. Yet it was quite evident they truly believed the British army had acted with terrible violence. I told myself that the rebels always thought the worst of the British. All the same, I kept asking myself: *How could so many be so wrong?*

The familiar feeling of anger around me and the taste of my own fear were such that as I fled, all that had happened in Tullbury flooded back into my mind. Father being dragged out of our house. The stripping off of his clothes. The tar and feathering. His agony and death. I recalled with painful clarity how I was taken away, beaten. My collapse. My humiliation. I lived it all again, so that, even as I ran, I was running to save my life.

By the time I reached the small town of Roxbury, it was dark, but moonlight allowed me to continue. From Roxbury, I made a sharp turn east and headed for the Neck, and the entrance to Boston. As I approached, I saw the tide was rising. I began to run faster, sloshing through ankle-deep bay water. Drawing closer to town, I heard the clamor of church bells. Clearly, Boston was sounding an alarm that something of great import was happening. I ran faster still.

When I rushed out upon the Neck and drier land, I saw many lit lanterns before me and a large contingent of British soldiers, far more than I had seen stationed there before. I surmised they were strengthening the defenses at the Neck to ward off an attack.

Sure enough, at the Neck gate, I was forced to stop by British army regulars who pointed their guns at me and demanded to know what I was doing there. In haste, I drew out Captain Brown's pass. It was read by lantern light, given back, and I was allowed to go on, but I did ask, "What is happening, sir?"

"A rebel attack. Thirteen thousand are coming from Cambridge."

Thirteen thousand. I shook my head. "Forgive me, sir, but I came from Cambridge. People are going there, not here."

"You're wrong," I was told with great authority. "Now move on before you get hurt."

I had no choice but to rush forward. As I did, I couldn't help but recognize that radicals and redcoats both believed untrue things about the other. But the notion that I alone knew the truth seemed impossible.

Once beyond the fortifications, I went as fast as I could through Boston's true entryway. In town, on the streets, armed soldiers were everywhere. Distressed citizens, lanterns in hand, were rushing about. Despite the lateness of the hour, many windows showed flaring candles within. The town was in turmoil.

I reached Hog Alley and Uncle William's house and burst inside. My mother was up. So was Faith. Uncle William was there too.

"Where were you?" Faith demanded.

"We were worried," added Mother.

"I tried to tell her all was well," Uncle William offered. "That you were at work. But people are saying the rebels are about to attack the town."

"It's not true," I said.

"How do you know?" asked Faith.

"Because I was in Cambridge, and they think they'll be attacked by the army. Is there something I can drink? I have to go."

Faith hurried from the room.

"Go where?" Mother asked.

"Army headquarters."

"Army headquarters?" Mother cried. "Why? And what were you doing in Cambridge?"

Faith returned with a jug of cider.

Not wishing to take the time to explain, I took a deep drink, then dashed out into the street, ignoring my mother's calls, and headed for Province House.

Friday, September 2, 1774

As I approached army headquarters, I saw that almost every window of its three floors was lit up. Soldiers were crowded about, with many rushing in and out of the front doors. Officers were everywhere. All was in such chaos that without anyone stopping me, I passed right on in, down the hall, and into the room where I always met with Captain Brown.

The room was full, with officers clustered around the captain's table, which was still covered with maps. Captain Brown was there, but it took me a moment to realize that General Gage himself was holding court.

Flustered, not sure I should be there but wanting to speak to Captain Brown, I hung back and watched.

The general looked pale and disconcerted, his uniform in unusual disarray. As for the many officers in the room, they seemed frazzled. As I stood looking on, I heard the general say, "I've issued orders that the Neck fortifications be built up. I want six field cannons sent there. Place cannons at the town entryway as well. I've sent a message to the admiral that his ships must move in closer to shore. I want a ship anchored between Hudson's Point and Charlestown to cut off the ferry."

There was much murmuring and saluting. "Yes, sir. Right away, sir." Officers hurried in and out of the room.

Even as I stood there I heard, "Noah."

It was Captain Brown. Next to him was DeBérniere.

"Come here!" cried the captain.

I went forward. Strange as it seems, the military men made way for me until I stood before the captain's table. I was aware that all eyes were on me.

"Report," the captain barked.

General Gage said, "Who is this boy? Why is he here?"

"Sir," said Captain Brown, "he was with me at the powder house, and I sent him on to Cambridge."

"Were you there?" asked the general.

"Yes, sir."

It was Captain Brown who said, "What did you see?"

"Please, sir," I said, preferring to keep my eyes on the familiar captain to steady myself, "in Cambridge, there are many people gathered. They all believe that when we got the powder, we shot down rebel militiamen."

"Why would they think that?"

"Forgive me, sir, I believe they think it's what the army would do."

"How many are in Cambridge?" asked the general.

"When I left maybe a . . . a thousand. Or more. I don't know, sir. But others were coming every moment. They're outraged, sir."

"Armed?"

"Yes, sir."

No one spoke until I heard General Gage mutter, "I need more troops," and he rushed out of the room. Officers streamed out after him until only Captain Brown, DeBérniere, and I remained.

Captain Brown said, "Noah, have you any idea why those people in Cambridge believe there was a shooting?"

"Sir," I said, "it's what I said: I think they believe it's something the army would do."

The captain, staring before him, stood without speaking. I waited. Then he said, "Tomorrow, as usual, go to the Green Dragon. I need to know what you hear."

"Yes, sir."

"Be off with you, now. Go home."

I stood there. "Sir?"

"Yes?"

"Did I do anything wrong?"

"Of course not. You did precisely what I asked."

"Thank you, sir."

I started out.

"Noah!"

"Yes, sir."

"Did you hear anyone speak up to defend the army?"

"No, sir. Not one."

I walked out of Province House, unable to make sense of things. Either nothing was happening, or everything. Or that *nothing* was becoming *something*. Were the rebels a small group, as Captain Brown and DeBérniere believed, or—as I had seen myself—were they a huge number? That the British officers were worried, clearly fearful of what might happen next, upset me.

A memory made me come to an abrupt stop. Captain Brown had said, "All this treasonous activity is confined to Boston."

He had been wrong, very wrong.

When I got home, my mother was waiting up for me. "I need to know," she demanded as soon as I walked in. "Why were you in Cambridge? And at army headquarters? What were you doing there?"

I was so tired and upset, I didn't care what I said. "At that tavern, the Green Dragon, I work for the army. They sent me there."

Mother was taken aback. "For the army? Doing what?"

"Learning what the rebels are about."

"Noah, I told you, I don't want you working for the army."

"I have to," I cried. "I have to do my part."

"Part? What part?"

"For England!" I shouted at her, something I'd never done before. I immediately felt ashamed. "I'm . . . I'm trying to be . . ." I stammered, ". . . like Father."

She stood up, her face pale, hands pressed together as she stared at me. I could tell she was trying to find what to say. "Noah . . . your father listened to no one. He thought he was right about everything. Don't . . . don't be like that. Think for yourself."

Shocked by her words, I stood there. "Did . . . did you ever say anything like that to Father?"

She was quiet for a moment and then said, "It's not for a wife to contradict her husband."

Then, as if regretting what she'd said, she spun about and left the room.

Astonished, I stood unmoving, wishing I might hear her again to be certain of her words. I even started to go after her but stopped.

Don't be like that. Think for yourself. Did she really mean it?

I was afraid to follow and ask.

Mother's words agitated me, made me feel indignant, and finally left me exhausted. I could not take in all — or perhaps any — of the implications. I pushed my thoughts away, only to have my head fill with images of what I had seen in Cambridge. So many people. Old. Young. Black. White.

I went back to Mother's words: "Your father listened to no one. He thought he was right about everything. Don't . . . don't be like that. Think for yourself."

I recalled that right after Father's burial, with the family gathered around the table, Mother had said to me, "Be true to yourself."

At the time, I assumed she meant I should be true to Father.

I had been wrong.

She meant I mustn't believe all that Father had said.

No more than I could trust what Captain Brown claimed.

Something Mercy had once said came to me: "Don't bother so much about what Father says. Make your own decisions."

I crept to my bed. As I lay there, all I could see were those people on Cambridge Common. I recalled the joy I had felt that morning, my pride in what I had done. Did I still wish to take credit for what had happened? What I now felt was nothing but confusion.

I *had* to think things out for myself. Mother's words. Jolla's talk about slavery and the price of freedom. The execution. The press gang. Everything that had happened. My vow to be loyal. I tried to put it all together. To my dismay, I realized I didn't know how to. Instead, my only thought was: *What am I being loyal to?*

PART 4

1774

Friday, September 2, 1774, continued

In the morning, having slept poorly, I woke tired and distressed. All those people in Cambridge, had they done anything? Had war begun? I listened for gunshots. Cannon fire. All I heard were church bells, which rang the way they always did, slowly, gravely.

The bells reminded me of Father, which led, with greater force, to what my mother had said about him. Why had she never said anything like that before? I could not help but remember what Father often said: "It was pride that turned angels into devils and humility that made men angels." She said he believed he was right about everything. Was she suggesting Father was full of pride?

It was too hard for me to consider. Instead, I made myself get up, only to realize I'd overslept. I rushed out—ignoring my mother's pleas to stay. The truth is I was afraid to speak to her.

The streets appeared normal and calm. People were going about their regular Boston busyness. I went straight to the Green Dragon. When I got there, Jolla demanded: "Where have you been?"

I'd forgotten he wouldn't know. "Long story. Can I explain?"

"Get to work first. Tell me later."

I threw myself into my tasks, cleaning tables, gathering dirty dishes. What I wanted to gather was news.

I soon learned that the patrons all knew about the taking of the Charlestown powder. They said nothing about shooting deaths, though they knew the wild rumors. They also knew that something like four thousand wrathful rebels had assembled in Cambridge from all over New England because they believed there had been a massacre by the British army.

I discovered that it was Doctor Warren—with other rebel leaders—who had gone to Cambridge and told the great crowd that there had been no killing in Charlestown, that the British were not about to attack, that all of it was false rumors. Doctor Warren and his friends were somehow able to break the fever and get those vast numbers of people to disperse. I was glad that some rebels had sense. People were already referring to what happened as no more than a "powder alarm."

By afternoon, my feelings grew so disturbed by the combination of what I had witnessed in Cambridge and what my mother had said that I could no longer contain myself. I needed to talk, and Jolla was the only person I could talk to. I felt an almost desperate need to tell him what I had seen in Cambridge and to figure out what it meant—and to do that, I was convinced, I would have to start with what had happened in Tullbury. It all seemed connected, though I hardly knew why or how to put all the pieces together.

I waited for a lull in the tavern, and when one occurred, I found Jolla and said, "I need to tell you where I was yesterday." We went out back, sat down, and right off—having practiced in my mind—I made myself say, "I can't tell you about yesterday until you know how my father died."

Taken by surprise, Jolla swung around toward me. "What?"

"They're tied together."

He stared at me. "How?"

Though I had forced myself to begin, I sat for a long moment before going on. It was so painful, I even turned away. "My father was killed by the Sons of Liberty." Having got that out, I stopped.

"Go on," said Jolla. "I'm listening."

Slowly, I told him what had happened to Father in Tullbury. How my family had to flee and come to Boston. It was still so hard to talk about that I could not get myself to say I had been beaten.

"His death made me decide I must be loyal."

"To what?"

His question stopped me again. After a moment I said, "I wanted to oppose all those rebels who killed him."

Jolla remain silent, his eyes fixed on me.

"When we first came to Boston," I went on, "I tried to join the army. Thought I'd get revenge that way. It wasn't possible. Still, I needed to find work. A friend of my Uncle William's arranged for me to go to Province House. I was hired by a Captain Brown to come here and listen for the army—"

Jolla looked at me quizzically.

"He pays my salary. Enough for my family to live."

Jolla was silent for what felt like a long time. Then he said, "So, you're here because you're what they call a lurcher."

"What's that?"

"A spy."

Uncomfortable, I said, "You angry with me?"

"It's only what I guessed." He looked at me. "You might say I'm a spy too."

"What do you mean?"

"I'm always trying to find out what's happening, what will happen. Trying to decide what to do."

"For yourself?"

"For me. And my Black friends."

I said, "Do you know about the Charlestown powder house? What happened?"

"Everybody does."

"Jolla, I was with English troops when they went to Charlestown yesterday. I led them there. Then Captain Brown sent a few troops to Cambridge to get some cannons. He told me to go and see what happened. Nothing did. Not at first. But then people began to gather. They all believed the redcoats shot down some rebels. Jolla, it never happened."

Jolla gave me a look that suggested he didn't believe me.

"It's true," I cried. "I was there. I really led them."

He was silent again. Then, "Long as you're working in this place, you'd better keep all that to yourself. The British Coffee House, on King Street, that's where British officers gather. Maybe you should work there."

"When I was in Tullbury," I said, "the Sons of Liberty weren't that many. Even so, they bullied the town. They were hateful. But my father said there was the British Empire. He said it would defend us. That's what he was loyal to. What I wanted to be loyal to. That's what Captain Brown says as well. But what if England can't defend me or my family?"

"Good questions."

"Jolla," I said, all but pleading, "when I talk to British officers, they always tell me there are just a few rebels. The ones meeting here at the Green Dragon. But in Cambridge, I saw more than a thousand. They weren't only Boston people either. They were coming from everywhere. I even imagined I saw you."

"Wasn't me. But I told you, I know Black folks, free, not free, who want to believe what that Mr. Adams and Doctor Warren and all their friends say. They're ready to fight for freedom. Trouble is, nobody is offering it to them. All that liberty talk, for me, it's like finding a feather. You know it's from a bird. A liberty bird. But the bird isn't there. It was just flying by. You'll think I'm crazy, but sometimes I wish that bird would pluck me up and take me to a place that's all free. Can you understand that?"

"Hope so," I said.

We were silent again.

"What's going to happen?" I asked.

"With what?"

"Everything."

His answer was to stand up, his signal that we had to get back to work. He started off, stopped, and said, "All these people around Boston, they're gathering guns. Gunpowder. Marching. The English army is doing the same. One of these days, the two sides are going to meet." He brought his hands together with a loud slap. "I don't want to be between them. You know what I want to be loyal to?"

"What?"

"What gets my people free. What do you want?"

"Not sure."

"Not sure isn't much." With that, he walked into the tavern.

That evening, at quitting time, Jolla said, "I want to show you something."

"What?"

"The White Horse Tavern."

"What's that?"

"On Beach Street. It's the Black people's tavern. Let's go."

The White Horse Tavern was near at hand to the Fort Hill neighborhood, where many of the free Blacks lived. Though the tavern itself was like most other Boston taverns, it was the patrons who were different: all Black men. When Jolla led me in, I was the sole white person. The moment we entered, the crowded room became still.

"He works for me at the Dragon," Jolla announced at the door. The mood shifted. The talk resumed, though I sensed many a curious glance.

I soon realized Jolla was known there, welcomed with greetings and handshakes. He took a seat at a table, had me sit by his side, introduced me, explained how we worked in the same place, that he was my boss.

I listened to the talk. It was about Boston, and largely what I knew. But I soon understood the difference. Some of the Black men were free; others were not. But they all talked about what they wished they might do in the present crisis.

One man said he was going to slip out and join the rebel militia. "Just tell them I'm free. See what happens. They talk freedom

"We should form our own regiment. Offer it to the rebels and see what they say and do."

Another said it was better to wait for war to break out. "It's coming. Then anything can happen."

"Nothing will happen," said someone. "Because there's slavery everywhere."

"But the British might do something."

The debate that followed was long and by turns intense, excited, and angry, sometimes full of anguish. It wasn't an argument but talk about the best thing to do.

Later, when Jolla and I walked out, I said, "You've got a whole extra life."

"You have it backwards," he said. "You're my extra life. You're mixed up some. But at least you admit to it. Most folks can't do that. Makes me think there might be something to you, Noah Cope. If you can just learn to think for yourself."

Feeling stung, I continued on with Jolla, neither of us talking. I worked on accepting the idea that Jolla had a whole existence I didn't know and probably never would. Acknowledging that he moved in a world so separate from mine was jarring. I tried to console myself by reflecting that he didn't know everything that had happened to me in Tullbury either.

Then Jolla said, "I'm going fishing Sunday. Want to come?"

Not sure if it was a test or an offer of friendship, but glad to do something that got me away from Boston, I agreed.

He named a place and time.

It was Sunday, which meant the Green Dragon was closed. I knew I should have gone to church with my family, but wanting some escape from heavy thoughts, I was happy to meet Jolla instead. We were to join up at Scarlet's Wharf (off Ship Street), where Jolla said he had a friend who would let him borrow a boat.

I got there first. It was a crisp, bright day, but warm enough that I left my coat at home and had only my shirt, trousers, and boots. As I sat there on the wharf, feet dangling, I gazed upon the British warships riding anchor in the bay. Their gun ports were open, so I saw the black cannons poking out. Once again, I had the unsettling feeling that the guns were pointed at me. I wanted to consider those ships my friends, my protectors, but there was something grim about them. Like a floating wall, they were blocking the way to and from Boston, keeping everything within. And that, I knew, included me.

My mind jumped back to those rebels in Cambridge. There had been so many. As I sat staring at the ships, I had the sensation that the British were on one side and rebels were on the other.

It was like something Jolla had said: I was in between.

Jolla showed up, fishing string and hooks in hand. He led me out along the wharf and approached a watchman. Old friends, the two exchanged greetings. When Jolla told him what we wanted to do, the watchman pointed out an old rowboat.

"That one has been abandoned," he said. "The owner left town. But better keep away from those ships. They don't like people getting close. Truth is, they don't want anyone out there."

We found the boat tied to the wharf. Oars had been left in it. We climbed in, sat side by side, each took up an oar, and began to row into the bay.

"Where are we heading?" I asked.

"Best fishing is in the channel between Noddle's Island and the Charlestown peninsular," Jolla said. He gestured in the direction he wanted to go.

"You fish a lot?"

"When I'm out there, if someone gives me an order, it's me doing the telling. No one to bother me."

"Am I bothering you?"

He laughed. "Sometimes you're a bother. But maybe a friend, too," he added.

"Thanks," I muttered, pleased.

We rowed on. "We'll go to Morton's Point first," said Jolla. "East side of the Charlestown peninsular. Has a wet, sandy beach. Good for getting bait. Clams. I brought a small knife."

"What are we going to catch?"

"Flounder, maybe. Sweet-tasting. Your mother a good cook?"

"I think so. You should come around sometime."

"She know about me?"

"No."

"Because I'm Black?"

"She just learned what my work is."

"The spying, you mean?"

"She doesn't want me to have anything to do with the army."

We rowed on. Jolla nodded toward the British ships. "They look powerful."

"They are. Protecting us," I added.

"Protecting themselves," said Jolla.

With the passage between Noddle's Island and the Charlestown peninsular so narrow, we had to cross near the twenty-cannon *Lively,* so close that I saw men on the deck, looking at us. I waved but received no response.

It wasn't long before we reached Morton's Point. We shook off our boots and waded through the warm, shallow water, engaging in a splashing war. Laughing, wet, we hauled the rowboat onto the sandy shore.

Then Jolla picked up a small stone and, with a flip of his wrist, sent it skipping over the water. It bounced nine times before sinking.

"How'd you do that?"

He showed me again, and his second stone skipped twelve times.

I found a stone and threw it, but it immediately sank with a *plunk*.

Jolla doubled over in laughter. "You need practice," he sputtered. "Come on. Ever go for littlenecks?" he asked as we moved along the beach.

"What's that?"

"Kind of clam. Good bait. I'll walk along the sand and stamp my feet. If there's a squirt, dig right there."

"Really?"

"Watch."

Jolla set off across the beach, stamping his feet down hard. As he promised, a jet of water shot up. I knelt and scooped away the sand with both hands. About five inches deep, I came upon one of those littleneck clams. Oblong, it had a whitish shell and was about four inches long, clamped tight.

"How come they squirt?" I asked.

"I guess when they get stomped on, they fight back with whatever they have."

It wasn't long before we had two dozen or so clams. We gathered them in a pile farther up on the beach and sat down where the warm sun helped dry us off.

Jolla said, "Ever eat one?"

I shook my head.

"They're good." He plucked a clam from our pile, pulled his small knife from his pocket, and worked his hands so fast I was not able to see what he did, but the clam split apart. He scooped out the orange insides and offered it to me on the tip of his knife. "Try it," he said.

I grimaced. It looked slabbery.

He laughed. "Go on."

Feeling it was a dare, I popped it into my mouth. It was sweet and salty at the same time.

"What do you think?"

"All right," I said, trying to swallow.

"You being loyal to me?" he said with a grin. I had never seen him so relaxed.

I laughed. It was good to be with a friend—or maybe even someone a little like an older brother.

We continued to sit and eat some more. It was good to be doing nothing, thinking nothing.

The sky was clear, with only a few puffy white clouds that reminded me of meandering sheep. The sea smell was tangy. The bay was calm, the water lapping the shore like a cat's tongue at a saucer. Squawking gulls swooped low.

"They want our clams," said Jolla. He gutted one and threw it into the air. On the fly, a gull dove, caught the clam in its bill, and then sped away.

"That's freedom," he said.

The peacefulness of it all put me in mind as to how frazzled Boston was. Even as I sat there, worry crept in. "You really think there's going to be a war?" I asked Jolla.

"Do."

"The alarm about the powder?"

He nodded. "The last couple of days, a brass cannon was stolen from the Commons."

"Who did it?"

"No question: rebels. Same time, Gage got more troops to come from New York and Quebec. He's put field guns on the Neck." He gestured to the ships. "No trade in or out. Nothing. Boston is getting smaller. Tighter. Angrier."

"What'll you do?"

"Don't have a lot of choices," he said. "In Boston, I'm pretty safe, because a lot of people know me. Know I'm free. But if I go somewhere else, they might try to force me back into slavery. If someone came up to you and said, 'Prove that you're free,' how would you do it?"

"I'm . . . white."

"Exactly. So, no one will ask. I'm Black. Different. Always will be. You going to make up your mind?"

"About what?"

"What you're loyal to."

I remained silent.

"Come on, try to answer the question. What are you loyal to?"

"As I said, when I came to Boston, I wanted to join the army. I don't anymore."

"Join the navy." His tone was sarcastic.

I immediately remembered the press gang. "I don't think so," I said, turning to look at the ships in the bay. That's when I saw a long-boat, six oars flashing in unison, moving in our direction. It must have come from the *Lively,* the ship we had passed.

Ignoring it, we remained sitting, content with eating clams. But then I realized that the longboat was still approaching. I said, "Jolla . . . is that boat coming here?"

He stared at it for a while. "Is." He put down his knife.

I said, "For us?"

Still studying the longboat, Jolla let another moment go before saying, "Afraid so. Their Sunday outing."

"I shouldn't have waved. What if it's a press gang?"

"It might be," he said, getting up.

I stood up and stared out over the water at the boat.

There were six men at the oars, clearly working hard to get to our beach. But there were more: five British blue-coated soldiers, each one holding a musket. They resembled the press gang I'd seen in Boston.

"Marines," said Jolla, saying what I was thinking.

I looked behind us. Rising from the beach was a hill. "What's on the other side?" I asked, pointing.

"Morton's Hill, then Breed's Hill," said Jolla. "Get over that, and after about a mile or so, you're in Charlestown." He glanced back around at the longboat. "They're getting closer. We better leave."

"What about our boat?" I said. "Boots?"

"Come back later."

"Let's go," I said.

We ran up the hummock behind the beach. As we went, we glanced back. One of the marines — still in the boat — had lifted his musket and was pointing it in our direction.

"Get down!" Jolla shouted.

We threw ourselves onto the stiff, sharp grass, pressing faces into sand even as there came the *boom* of a gunshot. The next second, I thought I heard a musket ball zipping over our heads.

I eased myself up on an elbow, looked back, and saw another marine lift his musket. I dropped down again. Another *boom*. A ball went shooting by, closer.

The two of us leaped up and sprinted toward the top of the rise, flung ourselves over, and rolled down the incline on the other side. We struck the bottom and lay there, panting. There was a wall of sand between us and the marines.

"You get hit?" I asked.

"No. You?"

"No."

He pushed himself up. "Stay here." He crawled back to the dune crest and peeked over. "Their boat has reached the beach," he let me know. "The marines are getting out."

"What are they doing?"

"They have hatchets. Hey, they're chopping up our boat. All five marines are on shore. They're coming after us. Come on!"

He whirled around and began to run. I was right with him, bounding up what he had called Morton's Hill. When we reached the summit, there was another musket explosion, though I didn't hear the ball. But when another shot came, I felt a sharp sting on my left arm. Not that we stopped running. Legs churning, arms pumping, we tore on as fast as possible until, panting, we reached another hilltop. Only then did we stop and look back. The marines were no longer coming after us but had returned to their boat. Our rowboat lay in pieces.

"They busted our boat," I said.

As we stood there, I felt a burning in my arm. When I peered at it, I saw that my shirt was torn and my skin bleeding, the blood soaking into the cloth. Only then did I realize that the musket ball had grazed my arm. I wasn't in much pain, so I knew a bone hadn't been broken. Even so, trying to make sense of events, I stared at the seeping wound.

"Better keep going," Jolla said, not realizing what had happened.

When he started running again, I stayed with him, pressing a hand to my bleeding arm.

We came down the second hill and headed for the next, Breed's. When we reached its top, we turned to look back at the beach, maybe a half mile away. The marines were being rowed back to their ship.

Knowing we were now safe, we stood there, breathless, hearts hammering, watching as their boat pulled farther from the beach.

Jolla turned toward me, started to say something but stopped. Though my hand was covering the wound, blood dripped down my arm.

"You got hit!" he cried.

"Not bad. Stings."

"Let me see." He pulled my hand away and inspected the wound. "You're lucky. It barely scraped you. Get your shirt off."

He stepped behind me and helped me pull off my shirt, the motion causing me to wince.

"Scars," he abruptly said in a different voice. "Who beat you?"

Shame flooded me. I mumbled something like, "A long time ago."

"Not that long," he said, but added nothing more. Instead, he wrapped the shirt around my arm. The bleeding stopped.

"Could have been a lot worse," he said. "But you'll get another scar."

I knew he was asking me to say more, but I replied only, "Be all right."

He stepped back and studied me. "Noah, people die from wounds more than anything."

I made no response. Instead, we stood there, watching the

longboat pull back across the bay. My stinging arm made me understand how close I'd come to being killed. Or being caught and put in
the navy. If that had happened, I'd never have gotten free.

Jolla said, "You missed your chance. Can't be more Loyalist
than being in the Royal Navy."

I gazed at the longboat, its oars shifting in unison. As I watched,
I suddenly felt shaky. I said, "The British say their army is here to
protect liberty."

Jolla said, "Have you seen their regimental drummers?"

"I met them. I remember their yellow jackets. They told me they
were from a place called Barbados."

"They're enslaved."

"They are?" I said, surprised. "To the army?"

"Right."

I was truly shocked. *The British army enslaves people.* Somehow
my arm hurt more. I was trembling.

"You all right?" Jolla asked. "Better sit down."

I did, head bowed to my knees. I was dizzy. Jolla stood before
me, looking down.

"Could have been you that was hit," I said, trying to make light
of it.

"But it wasn't." Jolla continued to stand in front of me, now looking out across the bay. "Don't move until you're steady."

"I'm fine," I finally said, though I wasn't. The dizziness was gone
but I was deeply rattled. *The army has slaves.*

Jolla said, "Can you walk back to Boston?"

"Our boots," I said.

Jolla snorted. "Gone." He held out a hand. I took hold of it and stood up, feeling another moment of weakness. It passed.

"Thanks," I said.

"For what?"

"The clams."

He grinned. No more was said, but I was glad I had a friend.

Barefooted, we started back. I kept thinking about what had happened, and what Jolla had told me about the drummers. After a while I said, "How come you know so much?"

"When your life depends on knowing, you better know."

What do I know? I asked myself. I wasn't sure.

As we came down from Breed's Hill, Charlestown was beneath us. Across the river lay Boston.

We passed through Charlestown, then took the ferry back to Boston. We didn't talk much. I was still thinking about what might have happened if we'd been caught. Or if either of us had been shot.

Once we got off the ferry and stepped into Boston, Jolla said, "I have to tell my wharf friend what happened to the rowboat."

"What'll you say?"

He lifted a shoulder. "People know how the navy acts. Good thing it was abandoned, though. You going to get home all right?"

"Be fine."

He started off. "Jolla," I called, "do you think the rebels are right?"

"They're right about England. Wrong about me."

"And the English?"

"Wrong about Massachusetts. But wrong about me too."

"Is anybody right?"

"You want to be loyal. Fine. But no point in being loyal to what keeps you in a cage." It was the way he looked that stuck in my mind: he was challenging me, pushing me to find my own answers to my questions. But when I didn't reply, he merely said, "See you at work tomorrow," and headed off to the wharf.

I went in another direction, thinking over what Jolla said about "being loyal to what keeps you in a cage." Being shirtless, and my wound badly covered, I hastened home.

If the British were our protectors, I thought, why had they tried to kill us? Why did we have to run away from them? If the rebels are for freedom, why did they kill my father? If both sides proclaim liberty, why do both sides enslave people?

My mind went back to Tullbury. Before Father's murder, things seemed simple. Except, if all had been simple, his death and everything that followed wouldn't have happened. And now I could never go back there. Which meant, I admitted to myself, things weren't simple at all.

I made my way to Hog Alley. No one was at home. Still at church, I guessed. I knew my joining them there would please Mother, but thinking about press gangs and what Jolla had told me about the drummers being enslaved, plus what I knew about press gangs, I didn't want to sit with British officers.

I had admired them, had wanted to be among them. No more.

My arm had long stopped bleeding. I got a different shirt and put on some old shoes, though they were tight. Then I headed down Orange Street, toward the Neck, the place where we had first entered Boston back in April.

The Neck had changed. The army had turned the barricades into a true fort with many men. A guard station, painted white, had also been built. A large contingent of soldiers was standing by in readiness, cannons in place. It was clear: the army believed Boston would be attacked.

As for the flow of ordinary people who were moving out of town—and it was a steady stream—the soldiers were stopping them and questioning each one. I watched the troops take muskets, powder, and ammunition from any person who had them.

At the same time, people were coming into town. It was easy to tell they were Loyalists fleeing the rebels, hauling wagons loaded with furniture.

It was like two armies moving into position.

I remembered asking Jolla, "You really think there's going to be a war?" And his answer, "Do."

If it happened, I wondered, what would I do? What would my family do? "Think for yourself," my mother had said. I was struggling.

It was easier to think about Mercy. I supposed she was married and living in our old house. I was glad she wasn't in Boston. But her husband was in the rebel militia. Maybe he had gone to Cambridge. Had she accepted his views? Mother had said, "It's not for a wife to contradict her husband." I could not see Mercy being so mild.

When I returned to Hog Alley, Faith was sitting on the steps before the house.

"Where were you?" she demanded. "You should have been at church."

"Went fishing with a friend."

She made a disapproving face. "You going to tell Mother?"

I shook my head. "Don't say anything to her."

As I entered, Uncle William pulled me into a corner. "A message to you from Captain Brown. You are to see him first thing in the morning. Province House."

"Does he say why?"

"No, but it must be serious."

A week ago, the summons would have stirred me. Now I was reluctant to go. But I had no choice. I worked for Captain Brown. His pay allowed us to live. I'd have to see him.

I shared nothing about my day with my family and even hid the slight wound in my arm.

Monday, September 5, 1774

Morning found me at the doors of Province House when they opened. Over time, I'd become familiar enough that when I waved my pass, I was allowed right through. I knocked on Captain Brown's door. "Noah Cope, sir," I called.

He bade me come in. When I did, I found him with another soldier.

"Cannon was stolen from the Commons" was the first thing

Captain Brown said to me. "Was there any talk at the Green Dragon as to who did it?"

I knew what Jolla had told me, but I found myself reluctant to report what I had heard. "No one spoke about it, sir," I lied.

Captain Brown went on. "Guns and munitions are being stolen, taken from everywhere. When people leave Boston, we're checking them. If they have guns, we're removing them."

"Yes, sir, I saw."

"A worse problem is that guns and gunpowder are being hidden. We must know where. How well do you know the area beyond Boston?"

"Very little."

The captain turned to the other man. "This is Lieutenant Nathaniel Bascom," he told me. "The King's Own Regiment. A mapmaker."

Lieutenant Bascom was a small, blond-haired man. There was something amiable about his face, with its pink cheeks and blue eyes. But he looked at me without much interest.

"This is Noah Cope," Captain Brown told the lieutenant. "My special assistant.

"I want you," the captain said to me, "to go about the countryside with Lieutenant Bascom. He needs to see what's there and remain unnoticed. We can't send troops. That might stir up more alarms. But a man with a boy won't raise suspicion. While he makes notes for his maps, you can look out for gun hiding places. The government in London is pressing General Gage to take strong action. Over the summer, some eleven regiments have been sent."

"What about the Green Dragon?" I said.

"I'll make arrangements."

I stood there, thinking about the day before, feeling the ache in my arm from where the musket ball grazed me when I had to run from the marines. "Sir, I'd rather not do this," I blurted out.

"Why?"

I wanted to say, "How can I work for an army that shot me? That enslaves people? That's ready to blow up the whole town?" But facing Captain Brown, I was tongue-tacked and mute.

He frowned. "Consider it an order."

When I got to the tavern, I told Jolla what Captain Brown had ordered me to do. "I don't want to work for him anymore."

"Then don't."

"I have to. My salary."

"In that case, keep a lookout for press gangs," he said, dryly.

Tuesday, November 15, 1774

Over the next two months—as arranged by Captain Brown—I was given time off from the Green Dragon to meet with Lieutenant Bascom and walk out from Boston to meander about country roads, towns, and paths. I carried the lieutenant's equipment—pens, inks, paper, blank books—so that I appeared (and indeed was) his servant. I never told my family what I was doing. As far as they were concerned—or knew—I continued at the tavern in a regular fashion. Happily, my mother asked no questions.

On the days we rambled, the lieutenant took notes and made

sketches of the land. After a day's roving, he would return to Province House to work on his maps. If we got back early, I went to the Dragon.

The lieutenant and I rarely talked. Though I sought to be friendly, he would have none of it. He was not harsh, but clearly he had no interest in who I was or how I came to work for Captain Brown. But once, I did ask him what he intended to do with his charts.

"They're for the army. You can't fight a war without maps."

"What war?"

"The one that's coming."

"Is it planned?" I asked.

"It's what London wants."

Jolla had said the same thing, that war was coming. So had the people at the White Horse Tavern. My sense that I was helping to bring it on made me like what I was doing even less. The only satisfaction I gained from all the walking was to increase my endurance. When we had run from that press gang, I had been all puffy. The next time, I might have to run faster.

As Lieutenant Bascom and I went around, we had multiple occasions to go into taverns. While the lieutenant sorted out his notes and sketches at a table, I tucked myself into corners and listened to the ever-constant talk. What I learned was that guns and munitions were indeed being hidden in any number of places. One of the places I heard mentioned was Concord, near Tullbury. That troubled me.

I never told Captain Brown what I heard.

I hoped we would get close to my old home so I could see Mercy, talk to her and find out how she was, and warn her she was probably better off avoiding Concord. But we never went that far.

I was always glad to get back to the Green Dragon and Jolla—my safe place. When there, I heard more stories about how guns and gunpowder were being taken out of Boston. That was also where I first heard of "minutemen," members of the rebel militia who were to be ready at a moment's notice to react to any excursions by British troops.

The messages I sent to Captain Brown were fewer, and those I did send were repetitious, containing only what everybody seemed to know.

Constant talk of a coming war.

In mid-November, the soldiers who had been camped on the Commons marched into winter barracks, leaving their wet tents to get into dry quarters. Empty warehouses were being occupied, places where rum had been made, now unused because the Port Act cut off the molasses supply.

As for officers, new laws allowed them to be placed in civilian houses. Homeowners were turned into servants, cleaning up after the officers and even feeding them. When officers moved into homes owned by those who had left Boston, they often brought about breakage or outright pillage. All this caused further anger. I had to wonder what we'd do if they took over Uncle William's house. Perhaps his friendship with Mr. Congreve would protect him, and us.

General Gage issued orders that no soldier should appear on the streets with side arms. He was fearful of outbursts between troops and civilians. If any soldier was found to be part of any disturbance, they were held for investigation. That made the regular soldiers unhappy. They wanted nothing more than to strike back at the insults Boston people hurled at them.

In other words, contending lines were drawing ever closer. Jolla was right: it was only a matter of time before they met and crashed.

My rambles with Lieutenant Bascom came to an end. "We have enough information for now," he informed me.

"Information for what?" I asked.

His answer: "To suppress the rebellion."

I went back to work full-time at the Green Dragon. I was happier there. But the truth is I no longer wished to be a spy.

The messages I sent to Captain Brown had nothing of importance in them.

Friday, November 18, 1774

When Jolla and I stepped out of the Green Dragon after closing, the night was cold and snowy, the first real blow of winter.

As we stood there, shoulders hunched up, feet stamping, he asked, "You have to go right home?"

"No. Why?"

"The Charles River sometimes freezes over," he told me. "You can walk across to Cambridge."

"Really?"

"Know where Hollis Street is?"

"Near my house."

"That's the best place. The water gets so low, it freezes fast."

Glad to do something different, we set off, heading down New-bury Street, quite alone. The falling snow and lowering clouds made everything murky. At the same time, there was enough light from candlelit windows reflected on the snow to let us walk fast, which was good because it warmed us. The snow was falling heavier and colder and brought a deep silence.

"Where do you live?" I asked Jolla. I never knew how much to ask about his personal life.

"North," he said. "The old part of town." He said nothing more.

We trudged on, colder and colder. Finally, I volunteered, "Even if the river is frozen, I'd as soon stay home. Too cold."

"We can walk to the water's edge and turn around."

Jolla found Hollis Street. It was much darker. He stopped suddenly.

"What?"

"Look." He was pointing ahead.

There was the glow of a lantern, its light blurry in the streaking snow.

"What is it?" I asked. "The night watch?"

"Too many for that," he said. Not talking, he moved us closer to the light.

It did not take long to see what was happening. A group of men were unloading a horse-drawn wagon, putting what they took out onto a longboat, which was half in the water and half on land. Clearly the river had not frozen.

We stood there, unnoticed in the snow-clotted darkness. The men were taking half barrels from the wagon, the same kind of tubs removed from the Charlestown powder storage. That they were moving them out of Boston at such an hour and in such a fashion told me that these were rebels working.

By the time we drew near, they were shifting the last of the barrels. Next, they began to transfer muskets from the wagon to their boat.

After a while, I reached over and pulled on Jolla's jacket. He understood. We backed away and didn't speak until we got to the far end of the street.

Jolla spoke my thought: "Rebels stealing guns and powder out of Boston."

The snow was coming down harder. It was icier, too. When we reached Hog Alley, I said, "Want to stay at my house? It'll be warm."

"That be all right?"

"Sure."

"Fine."

We reached the house. There was no light within.

"Everybody's asleep," I whispered.

We stepped into the vestibule, grateful for the heat that emanated from a few winking embers in the hearth. We sat, holding our cold hands out to the warmth.

"You going to tell your Captain Brown what we saw?" he asked.

"Told you. I don't want to be a spy."

"Good," he said. I expected him to add more, but all he said was "Thanks for the heat," and he rolled over, head resting in the crook of an arm. In moments, I heard his sleep breathing.

I stayed awake, thinking: *Should I or should I not tell Captain Brown what I saw?* I remembered the sacred oath I'd taken on the family Bible that I would always be a Loyalist. My next question was the one I had been asking myself since Jolla put it in my head: *What am I being loyal to?* "No point in being loyal to what keeps you in a cage" echoed in my memory. Then came Mother's words: "Think for yourself." I was still pondering all that when I fell asleep. In the morning, when I woke, Jolla was gone.

I did not report what we had seen to Captain Brown.

Which side am I on? I asked myself as I crunched through the snow to the Green Dragon. I didn't know.

Sunday, November 20, 1774

General Gage asked that Faneuil Hall be opened for a church service for the troops. The town officials — Whigs — refused. That seemed petty and stupid to me.

Monday, November 21, 1774

Troops went to the Commons and marched about and fired muskets. They were practicing maneuvers. There was little doubt: they were getting ready for battle.

I kept asking myself, *What will I do when that battle comes?*

Saturday, November 26, 1774

The fortification on the Neck was finished. It was massive. A true fort.

The gossip in the Green Dragon was that General Gage asked London for twenty thousand troops.

For the war, I was sure.

Thursday, December 1, 1774

On this day, I turned fourteen years of age. Mother saluted me. The past year had been like no other.

Friday, December 16, 1774

Captain Brown asked me to come see him. I assumed something important had happened.

When I walked in, he said, "General Gage's request for more troops was turned down. He asked for twenty thousand." In a voice full of exasperation, he said, "Do you know how many were sent?"

"No, sir."

"Five hundred. London doesn't think the rebels require more to put down. But in Rhode Island, forty-five cannons were taken by the rebels. In Portsmouth, they stole a hundred barrels of gunpowder. Noah, it's more important than ever that we know everything those Sons of Liberty are planning. We have many spies. But listen hard, Noah. Things are getting worse. Your reports have slackened off. Not much information. Do better."

Monday, December 19, 1774

The *Boyne,* sixty-four cannons, and the *Asia,* sixty cannons, came into the bay. The *Somerset* followed with another sixty-four cannons. They anchored within musket shot of the town.

Saturday, December 31, 1774

On the last day of the year, Jolla and I went out on Long Wharf to watch the new ships, which were all lit up. The sky was cloudy, the air cold, but the ships' lights were reflected on the water, so that it seemed that all the stars had come down to earth.

"Guess what?" said Jolla. "The *Gazette* said Parliament voted to call what is happening in Massachusetts a rebellion and to suppress it. As part of that, they also made a law that bans all sales of guns or ammunition to the Americas. All that is new."

"War," I said.

"Wars always start in the spring," Jolla said. "You have a few months to make up your mind what to do."

"What are my choices?" I said.

He took my question seriously. "Choose which side you're on. Or find a third way."

We tried to pick the date when the war would begin.

PART 5

1775

Sunday, January 1, 1775

When Uncle William proclaimed that the New Year had begun, Faith announced that I had gotten taller, even as my voice had become lower. "Are you going to change every year?" she asked.

"Don't know," I said, but I liked the idea of being bigger.

As it happened, the winter began mild, which meant the Charles River never froze. But shops and businesses were closing. Food was harder to get and more expensive. If you wanted to get out of Boston, and more people did, the army required you to go by way of the Neck. So many people were leaving that General Gage issued an order: you needed a pass to get out. At the Green Dragon, it was said that Gage did this because he wanted Boston rebels to be held hostage. If all the Whigs left Boston, he feared that the rebels would attack.

Curious as well as anxious, I went and watched the goings. As people left, soldiers checked passes. Wagons, carts, and saddlebags were stuffed with possessions — furniture, clothing, and pots. Everything was inspected. No guns or munitions were allowed out.

I also watched as a stream of Loyalists continued to come into town, and I tried to listen as they gave reasons for their arrival. Many said they were officials appointed by General Gage, such as magistrates and judges, and had been threatened by radicals. Others had tales like ours: they were victims of rebel violence. Some said they feared such attacks or the approaching war.

I watched to see if any Tullbury people arrived. I saw none. I confess I was disappointed.

The passing of people was mostly like a great shuffling of cards: this Loyalist card into Boston, this rebel card beyond.

When would the game be played?

Monday, January 9, 1775

There was an unusual gathering at the Green Dragon. Some twenty or so men joined in, but instead of meeting on the first floor as usual, they went up to the second and sat about a long table, Mr. Revere presiding.

Jolla and I served food and drink. That meant we were going up and down the steps and heard only bits and pieces of the talk.

Realizing it was a secret meeting, but wanting to know more, we agreed to alternate our serving so we might best learn what was said. When the people left, Jolla and I tried to put together the pieces of what we'd heard.

We determined that these men had formed themselves into a special committee charged with keeping a closer watch on British army movements. They were sure something important was going to happen soon, and their surveillance was to be achieved by going out on two-man patrols day and night, no matter the weather. Then they would share what they had observed, reporting to Doctor Warren, Doctor Church, or Mr. Hancock.

"They must think," I told Jolla, "that the army is planning on something big."

"They're watching so they can stop it." Then he added, "If they can."

Tuesday, January 10, 1775

As I walked to work in the morning, I saw a tar and feathering in the middle of Boston. It happened near what was called the Old South Meeting House on Milk Street.

Someone—a man told me it was a rebel named Tom Ditson—had tried to buy a gun from a British soldier. He was caught by redcoats, and as I watched (part of a large crowd of onlookers), he was tarred and feathered, abused for being a rebel.

This tar and feathering was done by English soldiers, not radicals. It gave me a thought I'd never had before: *The more people believe a thing, the crueler they are defending it.*

Wednesday, January 18, 1775

The queen's birthday. The fleet batteries fired a royal salute. I saw no one else celebrate. It meant nothing to me.

In the past, Father had brought such occasions as royal birthdays to our attention. He had always called himself an Englishman, never an American.

Which am I? I still had no ready answer.

When I arrived that morning at the Green Dragon, I saw right away that Jolla was troubled. "I need to talk to you," he said.

We went out back. "The place I've been living in is an old house on Gravel Street," he said. I had asked where he lived before, but he had always avoided giving specifics.

"There's a basement where I've had room to sleep for a couple of years. The owners have fled town. Now the empty house has been taken over by British officers. They've told me to get out. Said, 'We don't want Blacks in our house.'"

"What are you going to do?"

"No choice. I have to move."

"Where?"

"Think I could stay at your place? Just a corner for sleep. I have a straw mattress."

"I'll ask my Uncle William," I said.

"Could you do it fast? I have to get out by tomorrow."

That night when I walked in, Mother and Uncle William were sitting up by candlelight before a low fire, she on a high-backed settle working on her embroidery, he in a chair reading the *Post-Boy* newspaper.

We exchanged a few words about the day, after which I said, "I have a good friend at the Green Dragon. We work together. He's a bit older than me and lives alone. But he's been pushed out of his place because British officers have taken over the house. Can he move in here?"

There was a moment of silence.

"Please, sir, he has no place to go."

"Where are his parents?" Mother asked.

"He has none."

Uncle William said, "What's his name?"

"Jolla, sir. Jolla Freeman."

"An African?"

"Born in Boston."

"A slave?" asked Mother.

"He's free."

Uncle William was rolling his hands, pulling at his fingers.

"How good a friend is he?" was Mother's question.

"The best I have in Boston. I trust him," I found myself saying. And I knew it was true.

"You are a loyal one," said Uncle William.

No one spoke further until Uncle William said, "If he's working at the Green Dragon, I suppose he can pay some rent."

"I think so," I returned, though I wasn't sure. I added, "He and I can share my space."

The two adults looked at each other across the room. Uncle William went through his alphabet of gestures.

"It's fine with me," said Mother.

"And me," agreed Uncle William. "But," he added, "he needs to pay rent. And he must sleep in the basement."

"Why?"

"Because" was all Uncle William said, though he might as well have said, "Black."

Thursday, January 19, 1775

The next morning when I entered the Green Dragon, I saw Jolla's eyes — full of a question — turn to me.

I threw out a smile and called, "All fine."

He returned my grin.

"But the basement," I added.

He shrugged. "That's where I am now."

After work, we went to Jolla's living place on Gravel Street, close to the Mill Pond. It was, in fact, a large, elegant brick house, with a fine entrance. We went around to the back and got in by way of a cellar door and stone steps that led down.

The air was cold, and by the light of a small candle Jolla had brought, I saw that the dirt floor was damp, the ceiling low. There were no windows. It smelled of mold. In one corner, Jolla had tried to make a decent place. A straw sack mattress was on the ground. Two folded blankets. There was a small wooden box in which the things he owned were stowed.

I looked around. "Where did you eat?" I asked.

"At the tavern. This is my sleeping spot."

"How did you find it?"

"A friend of mine was enslaved to the people who owned the house. He arranged for me to live here. I paid a small amount."

"Where is your friend now?"

"I don't know. When the householders left, they took him with them."

"No idea where?"

"None. Then the officers moved in."

We carried his box and mattress to the Hog Alley house, where I introduced Jolla to the family. They were welcoming enough, though Faith somewhat standoffish.

The entryway to our basement was at the back of the house. I had never gone down there before. It was fusty-smelling, the floor hard-packed earth. Ceiling beams were so low that Jolla had to bend when he was standing.

He looked around, said nothing, and set his box of things down on the ground. I laid out the mattress. "Like my other place," he said.

"It is," I said, feeling embarrassed. Then I said, "I'll be back."

I returned to my own space and gathered my things, including my straw mattress. I brought it all to the basement.

"What are you doing?" asked Jolla.

"Moving in. That all right with you?"

He offered up a smile.

From that time on, Jolla lived in our house.

Wanting to be sure Uncle William didn't change his mind, I took the tip monies I earned at the Dragon and added them to what Jolla paid for rent.

"Good money makes a good contract," said Uncle William as he pocketed the extra coins.

His words bound me that much tighter to the tavern and what I was paid by Captain Brown to do there.

Friday, January 20, 1775

The Green Dragon was abuzz with news that the rebels had hauled away some hundred barrels of army gunpowder. No one was sure how they got it.

"Doesn't matter how," said Jolla. "What matters is when they use it."

Monday, January 23, 1775

There were more and more fistfights and multi-person brawls on the streets. The English soldiers — their numbers increasing — seemed to always find their way into these clashes. From what I could see, they often began them. General Gage tried to dampen the outbursts by warning his soldiers he would punish them if they engaged in public disputes. I doubted he would succeed. So did Jolla.

It was the same at the Green Dragon. Arguments among patrons had never been louder, angrier. People were tense, waiting for something to explode. I was weary of adults arguing, throwing constant insults back and forth. Each side accused the other of being traitors to an Englishman's rights and liberties. Both accused the other side of tyranny. Their words were so similar, if I hadn't known the people speaking, it would have been hard to say who was Whig, who was Tory.

As far as I was concerned, both were right and wrong. It made my head hurt.

Tuesday, January 24, 1775

Jolla said, "Here's news that might please you."

"What?"

"The township of Marshfield—"

"Where's that?"

"Maybe twenty miles south of Boston. I guess there are lots of Loyalists there. Must be the only place in Massachusetts. They asked General Gage to defend them. He's sent troops. Maybe you should go," he said with a grin.

Irritated, I said, "I'd rather stay here."

"And do what? What do you want?" He was pushing me again, almost taunting me to make up my mind and declare myself.

Instead, I answered, "To find out what I am."

Friday, January 27, 1775

Smallpox was discovered at the house of someone named John Bartlet. A tailor on Cold Lane. The illness brought on high fevers, red rashes, vomiting, and great fatigue. Then came eruptions—almost like pebbles on the skin—which burst and became scabbed. Those that survived the disease were permanently scarred.

I had already felt I was surrounded by enemies. Now a new and unseen one was added: the disease. Since it was easy to catch, sick soldiers were confined. Sick citizens were forced out of town. Many died. There was said to be a way to avoid it—inoculation—but many were afraid of that. You had to be cautious as to where you went, never truly knowing where contagion lurked or who carried the sickness. It increased the feeling that there were enemies both without and within the town.

Thursday, February 2, 1775

The Green Dragon was in a state of seething excitement. The official announcement had come across the sea: the London Parliament declared Massachusetts to be in a state of rebellion.

"How does that make things different than they already are?" I asked Jolla.

"Don't know," he replied.

When we got home, we asked Uncle William.

"I suppose it means that from now on if anyone in Massachusetts—like Mr. Hancock or Mr. Adams—goes against the king and government, they will be arrested for being traitors, taken to England, given a trial, and found guilty."

"What'll happen next?" I asked.

"They'll be hanged."

I could only imagine such a terrible event. Boston would explode. Riots. Burnings. Violent clashes with the army. We would have to leave.

And go where? We had no other home.

But for all my visions of chaos, since nothing happened, we stayed where we were.

Tuesday, February 21, 1775

At the Green Dragon, I overheard a troubling conversation wherein I learned that the Massachusetts congress, which was claiming to be the new government of the province, had decided to create an army of fifteen thousand.

I felt obliged to report to Captain Brown.

I took along that note that Captain Brown had given me when we were getting the powder in Charlestown—the pass that gave me permission to see him—and went to Province House. When I presented it, I was waved on through.

After I told the captain my news, he said, "We've already heard that information from other sources. It's important, but I doubt the rebels can raise such an army."

"But, sir, what about all the people during the Powder Alarm who—"

"Noah, I assure you, it doesn't matter if they do raise an army. When we act, we shall brush the rebels away with ease. Still, I'm glad you came. I was going to call you in. Tomorrow I want you to join me and DeBérniere at the Neck for more marches through the country. I need to inspect the roads going west."

"Please, sir, may I ask why?"

He smiled and said, "Armies always need to know the terrain. Be here in the morning. Dress warmly. It may be cold."

Knowing it was more planning for war, I was reluctant to go. But again, I felt I had no choice if I wanted to collect my salary. Then I realized I'd lose my tips, the extra money I gave to Uncle William.

"Sir," I said, "I'm happy to go, but I'll lose some money."

"How so?"

"Patrons leave me extras. My house depends on it."

"How much?"

"As much as five shillings a week."

"I'll see that it's paid," said the captain.

And it was.

Wednesday, February 22, 1775

The next morning when I met Captain Brown and DeBérniere, they were dressed in plain brown clothing, wide-brimmed hats, and old boots. True spies.

We left town by way of Roxbury and continued beyond it. I

walked behind the two, carrying their packs. We wandered the main roads, paths, even cow lanes. Along the way, Brown and DeBérniere were always conferring and writing things down in a little book the ensign carried.

All that week, Captain Brown, DeBérniere, and I went about, in and out of Boston, going on the main road as far west as Concord. I had hopes we would go a little farther, to Tullbury, that I might see Mercy. It didn't happen.

I wondered if my sister ever thought of me. If she was well. For my part, I was finally able to acknowledge to myself how fond of her I was. Did she feel the same toward me? I missed her. I didn't enjoy talking to Faith. She was too young. In any case, she preferred chattering with Uncle William. As for Mother, ever since she had said what she did about Father, we were shy with each other.

"Think for yourself," Mother had said.

I kept trying.

Wednesday, March 1, 1775

The Boston Sons of Liberty had urged citizens not to buy British goods. Now the new Massachusetts rebel government issued an *order* that all engage in a boycott. My sense was that many people followed those instructions. The closing of the port had meant that British goods, from books to boots, grew scarce. The shops that featured such English products suffered much decline in sales and closed. Scarcity was everywhere. The fewer shops there were, the higher prices went up.

Saturday, March 4, 1775

The *Boston Gazette* reported that rebel leaders met with General Gage at Province House. The newspaper claimed that he told them that if so much as one British soldier was killed by rebel militiamen, he would have the Royal Navy bombard coastal towns and burn them down. Admiral Graves, he said, was eager to do it. I saw for myself that the Royal Navy ships were placed to do great damage.

I asked Jolla what he would do if a bombardment began.

"Hide," he said.

"Where?"

He shrugged.

From then on, as I went about Boston, I began to view it in a new way: Where was the best place to hide? To look upon the world is one thing. To look upon the world in search of a hiding place requires different eyes.

Saturday, March 18, 1775

A rumor flew about Boston that a huge quantity of cartridges and musket balls had been stolen from the English army. No one offered facts, but most people believed it.

When I asked Jolla about it, all he did was make that gesture, a loud clapping of hands. I understood his meaning all too well. War was coming.

Monday, March 20, 1775

Captain Brown called upon me to join him and DeBérniere for yet another survey of the country west of Boston.

Before we left, Captain Brown said, "General Gage has asked me to determine all possible routes, fast routes, to Concord."

"Fast for whom, sir?" I asked.

DeBérniere said, "Our army regulars."

We set off through the towns of Roxbury, Brookline, Weston, Lincoln, and Lexington, DeBérniere always taking notes.

At our farthest foray, Concord, we stopped at an elegant home, which belonged to a man named Mr. Richard Bliss. He welcomed Captain Brown and provided him with all kinds of information about the rebels in town. He said that the local militia was well organized. He also told Captain Brown where cannons, gunpowder, and shot were hidden in Concord.

That made me think of Abner Hosmer, Mercy's husband. I recalled he had been part of the Concord militia. Should I warn her—and therefore him—that Captain Brown knew about hidden military stores? What if the army seized them as they had in Charlestown? Would Abner be called up? I remembered thinking how he and I might meet in a battle. I wanted nothing to do with that now. Rather, I kept wondering if I should warn Mercy about what could happen.

Mr. Bliss gave a fine dinner to Brown and DeBérniere. Of course, I ate in the kitchen. When we returned to Boston, Mr. Bliss came with us. From his talk, it appeared he was leaving Concord forever. I heard him say, "It's become too perilous for me."

"He was smart to leave town," Jolla said to me when I reported all that happened. "Sounds like there's going to be troubles there."

I kept thinking of how close Tullbury was to Concord. Would Mercy be safer in Boston too?

Thursday, March 23, 1775

Lord Percy—who commanded all the soldiers in Boston—took some thousand troops out of town through the Neck. I watched them march from the Commons, drums beating and fifes twittering, birdlike. There was great excitement in town. Where were they going? For what purpose?

In fact, nothing happened. At the end of the day, they marched back. People at the Green Dragon said it was merely a display of force.

Jolla and I tried to put into words our feelings about what we had seen and heard. We decided there was a great storm of war drawing closer. The sensation was akin to dark, churning clouds, sudden gusts of wind, flashes of lightning, bringing a different smell to the air.

Does war, I wondered, *have a smell?*

When I asked that aloud, Jolla told me about how ravens follow armies into battle.

"Why?"

"They seem to predict that there will be dead bodies. And they eat them. Starting with the eyes."

Walking to the Dragon in the morning, I spied a raven sitting on a pole. It let out a loud caw. Was it watching me? My eyes? I tried to tell myself that seeing the raven was a coincidence. Nonetheless, it made me queasy.

Tuesday, April 4, 1775

One year after Father was killed. His death at the hands of rebels still filled me with bitter sadness.

Monday, April 10, 1775

At the Green Dragon, I heard Doctor Warren tell Mr. Revere that Mr. Adams and Mr. Hancock had left town and were hiding in either Concord or Lexington.

"Wonder what made them go now," mused Jolla when I told him.

I said, "Someone said they feared arrest."

"You going to tell Captain Brown where they are?" Jolla asked me.

Before I could reply, he said, "If you were to tell him, and he was unaware, and those two got caught, and rebels knew it was you that informed him, how long do you think you'd live?"

"Not long."

"Well . . . ?"

"Captain Brown told me that if those two were arrested, the whole rebellion would end."

"You really believe that? How many people went to Cambridge because of that powder business?"

"Thousands."

"Think all those people would stop being rebels because of those *two* men?"

He began to walk away from me.

"What would you do?" I called after him.

"It's your war. Not mine."

The whereabouts of Mr. Adams and Mr. Hancock was important information. I recalled thinking Mr. Adams had been my chief enemy. But I had come to know the truth: many opposed Great Britain, and they did so for many reasons.

I was afraid not to tell Captain Brown about Hancock and Adams but equally scared to tell him. What if I informed him and his reaction led to something like what happened when I spoke about the Charlestown powder? Not wanting to cause another crisis, I decided I wouldn't share what I knew. I further reminded myself he had said he used other spies.

You've stopped being loyal, I told myself.

When we got home, Mother told me with great delight that she had received a letter from Mercy. She gave it to me to read. It was a long letter, but in summary it said:

Mercy was with child. She hoped she'd have a girl. She asked Mother to come and be with her during her groaning time, when she would have her child. She was happy with Abner. He was now a minuteman, mustering with the Concord militia, which had grown much bigger. Mercy further wrote that if the family wanted to come back to Tullbury, she would welcome us in the old house, which had been a wedding gift to Abner from his father. It was fine with Abner if we returned.

Reading Mercy's words, I could almost hear my sister's voice, and it made me wish I could see her again. But I recalled Faith's birth, how frightening that time was, how Mother almost died. Learning that Mercy was with child threw me into fraught worry.

"Will you go to her?" I asked Mother.

"I'll think on it," she said. "I confess I miss our house and the comforts of Tullbury, but my feelings about her husband are complicated."

I said, "How do you think Lawyer Hosmer feels about Mercy?"

Mother had no answer.

That night, in the basement, Jolla asked me if I had made up my mind about talking to Captain Brown about Concord.

I told him I had decided not to but then said, "Remember I told you about my older sister?"

"The one named Mercy?"

"That's her. She married a rebel. He's in the militia in my old town. Close to Concord."

"And?"

"If the troops march to Concord and try to catch Mr. Adams and Mr. Hancock, the militia, with my brother-in-law, might be there to protect them. I don't like him, but my sister is with child. I wonder if I should go to her and tell her it would be better if she could persuade him not to leave home. Or get them to come to Boston."

"Might be good," agreed Jolla.

I kept thinking of going but always found an excuse not to. If I went, I might lose my pay at the Green Dragon. Should I tell Mother what I was considering? Once out of the town, would I be able to get back in? Should I take the chance? What if something happened to me? What if something happened to Mercy?

While I debated these questions, I held back.

Tuesday, April 11, 1775

There was more and more talk at the tavern that a big event was about to occur. The British navy ship *Somerset* positioned herself to block the ferry to Charlestown. That was new. Should I warn Mother that something was about to take place? It was clear that if she was going to Mercy, she needed to go soon. Should I go with her?

Friday, April 14, 1775

A man rushed into the Green Dragon and announced that the *Nautilus,* a Royal Navy warship, was entering the bay. Her speed of entry suggested she bore important news. Perhaps she carried new orders from London.

I hurried over to tell Jolla.

"Go find out if she has news," he said.

I ran out along Long Wharf in time to see the *Nautilus* splash down her anchor. The news of her arrival had spread so fast that I joined a large crowd that had gathered to learn what was unfolding. British officers, some of whom I recognized as part of General Gage's staff, were in attendance — clearly the ship's coming was significant.

As I looked on, a longboat was lowered. The six men at the oars pulled hard for the wharf. Once the boat reached it, a soldier in the uniform of lieutenant came ashore quickly. He held a large packet in his hands — the same kind that Uncle William used for carrying letters. I saw a big red seal on it.

The lieutenant was surrounded by General Gage's officers and hurried away. I, with many others, followed. They brought the man straight to Province House and he disappeared inside. I was tempted to follow, but having left Captain Brown's pass at home, I was unable to. Instead, I returned to the tavern to tell Jolla what I had seen.

"Some new orders or laws from London," suggested Jolla. "It won't be good."

That was the general notion at the Green Dragon. It might well have been new instructions, but no one at the tavern was sure what they were.

Saturday, April 15, 1775
I heard Mr. Revere tell Doctor Warren that two companies of British soldiers were taken off regular duty. "They must be planning an action," he said. He promised that his committee would increase its patrols. I also heard him say they needed to keep Mr. Adams and Mr. Hancock safe.

Monday, April 17, 1775
In the morning, Jolla and I went down to the Commons. We saw two Royal Navy ships anchored in the Charles River with some twenty longboats clustered around them. That was unusual.

When we got to the Green Dragon, it was being claimed that British troops were about to march to Concord, sixteen miles west, to seize powder, as well as Misters Hancock and Adams. It was said like a known fact. This information, so people claimed, had been provided by a Mr. Jasper, a gunsmith, who said he heard it from a British officer (a sergeant) who had brought in his gun for repair.

Then a stableman who worked at Province House came to the

tavern and announced he had heard the same thing: troops were going to Concord. Since the man had been drinking, no one knew if it was true. Still, most people believed it.

All I could think about was Mercy.

Tuesday, April 18, 1775

Throughout the day, the tavern churned with talk about what the British were doing or not doing. Most people believed they were going to march to Concord, seek out hidden guns and powder, and arrest Hancock and Adams and send them to London for trial. In short, all kinds of dire things were predicted. For my part, I kept fretting about what troops in Concord would mean. Would Abner be there? Would there be fighting? Would it reach Tullbury? Would Mercy be safe?

That night, under a thick moon, Jolla and I walked home from the Green Dragon. We passed the night watch twice, which was unusual, but knowing us, they let us be.

As we turned onto Hog Alley, looking toward the Commons, we saw many lit lamps along the far side. They appeared to be on the banks of the Charles River.

Curious, and without needing to say anything to each other, we started across the Commons, but pulled up short when we realized we were seeing a large troop of milling redcoats. In the moonlight, their upright bayonets reminded me of picket fences.

When we drew as close as we dared, we saw soldiers getting into longboats. Their uniforms told me they were grenadiers and light infantry, the army's best.

A few of those boats, loaded with standing soldiers, had already pushed away from shore and were being rowed across the river to the Cambridge side, a mile away. There was little noise beyond the shuffling of feet, the swishing of oars in water.

"They *are* going to Concord," Jolla said.

Seeing all those troops in motion brought a jarring halt to my seesawing thoughts about Mercy and Abner and whether I should alert them about the British army marching on Concord.

"My sister," I said. "I have to warn her. Tell her to keep her husband home and stay safe." Jolla and I ran back across the Commons.

As we rushed along, I noticed that the Christ Church had two lights in its tall steeple. *That,* I thought, *is odd.*

Reaching the house, Jolla said, "How are you going to get to your sister?"

"I'll try to cross the river with those troops. I can move along with them. Should be safe."

"They'll never let you."

"I thought of a way," I said as we hurried inside.

"How?"

"Show you."

We went to our basement. I sparked a candle, fished around my rumpled clothing, and found that pass Captain Brown had given me months before. I handed it to Jolla. He read it, then gave it back.

I said, "I'll show it to the soldiers and say I'm going to join Captain Brown. They'll let me."

"What if he isn't there?"

"Doesn't matter. Once I sneak over the river with the troops, I can get to Tullbury on my own."

"Risky. Want me to go with you?"

"I wish. But the pass is just for me. Don't tell my mother where I've gone."

Jolla said, "Be careful. Good luck."

Clutching Captain Brown's pass in my hand, I tore out of the house and headed back to the Commons.

It was about ten thirty when I approached the riverside, and the crowd of troops had not yet all boarded longboats. Awaiting orders to get on, the men, standing with their companies, were quiet. Officers were giving few commands. Off to one side were their horses. I heard the animals' blow-breathing, the stamp of their hooves, and now and again a nicker. A light breeze flowed out of the southwest and carried the smell of sweat, gun iron, and the horses. In the sky, the brightest light came from the moon. I was able to make out dark clouds drifting by, indifferent to what was happening below.

Once among the soldiers, I, anxious and fearful, wasn't so sure of myself. But to get to Tullbury, I had to cross the river, and I saw no way to do so quickly other than with the troops. A few soldiers gave me questioning looks, but no one said anything.

As far as I could see, there were two officers in charge. They were on horseback. "Who are they?" I asked the soldier I happened to be standing next to.

"Major Pitcairn. Lieutenant Colonel Smith."

I knew their names. They were important men.

Making myself move, I slipped forward, pass in hand, until I stood on the riverbank with some soldiers. Longboats were being rowed across, while others approached. I tried to appear casual, though I was anything but. I avoided looking into faces, fearing I'd give myself away.

When orders were shouted out, a group of soldiers moved forward, stepped into the shallow water, then climbed into a boat. Tense, I shuffled along, praying I'd not be uncovered and sent away. Then, just as I was about to get into a boat, a sergeant holding a lamp up stretched out his arm and blocked my way.

"What are you doing here, boy?"

I had my speech ready: "Please, sir, I'm supposed to join Captain Brown. I have a pass." I held it out. The sergeant put his lantern over the paper and quickly scanned the words.

"Where's this Captain Brown?" he demanded.

I pointed out over the river. "On that boat that just left."

The sergeant darted a quick look. In a hurry, he thrust the pass back into my hand. "All right. Step fast. Come on. Come on," he called to the soldiers behind me. "Move along. Quick."

I climbed into the boat, sailors lending a hand.

(I would learn later that General Gage forbade anyone who was not a soldier to leave town.)

When about twelve soldiers were in the boat, all standing, holding their muskets upright, we were pushed into deeper water. Sailors gathered up the oars and began to row. Their splash was steady, the water calm, as we skirted the mid-river British warships.

Reaching the other side, the boat lay so deep from the soldiers' weight, it was unable to draw close to the shore. That meant the men (and I) had to jump out and wade knee-deep in the water to get to the land.

I had gotten across.

Wednesday, April 19, 1775

But once I was on the Cambridge side — one of the officers called the place Lechmere Point — I realized it was so dark that I'd be unable to find my way on my own. I needed to stay with the troops until daylight came, when I could dash ahead. I remained, then, among the waiting soldiers, trying to make myself as inconspicuous as possible, listening as men, who were as wet and as cold as I, muttered and cursed.

The soldiers, crowded close together, stood on a dark, muddy road. It seemed to take forever for all the longboats to go back across and return with the rest of the troops. Each boat made two trips to bring the regulars, plus a third trip to fetch the officers' horses and supplies.

While we lingered, there were more questioning looks in my direction, but there was enough crowding and confusion that no one bothered with me. On my part, I kept moving between the soldiers and held my face blank, my pass in my shirt pocket ready for inspection. I could only hope I'd meet with no difficulty.

It was cold and frustrating to wait, but as I stood there, I had the thought: *When I get to Tullbury, what if I meet the men who killed my father and beat me?* I worked to push such fears away, telling myself I must concentrate only on reaching Mercy.

When all the soldiers and supplies were ferried over the river, new orders were called. Everyone moved forward, crossing a deep inlet. This time the water was waist-high, which meant the soldiers had to hold their muskets above their heads. I went along. *Are you sure you want to do this?* I kept asking myself. My constant answer: *I must warn Mercy. Make sure she's safe. Keep Abner home.*

Once we passed that inlet, supplies were distributed to the soldiers. Each redcoat received ammunition. Some of the men counted their cartridges. Others stuffed them in their pouches. Hunks of bread and pieces of salt pork, a day's ration, were also distributed. When they saw what had been given to them, many soldiers threw the food away in disgust.

It must have been near two a.m. when the troops formed into a huge column and began to head west. The Black drummers in their yellow jackets led the way, beating their drums just loudly enough to help the soldiers march in unison. I counted the thumps, perhaps a hundred a minute. I supposed the soldiers, moving to that beat, would be able to cover about four miles an hour on that dirt road, making a steady *tramp-tramp, tramp-tramp.*

I put myself at the tail end of the column, mingling with the supply haulers—who were not in uniform—and trying, as before, to keep out of the way. No one seemed to care that I was there. My thoughts kept going to Mercy. I began to think about and enjoy what she would say when she saw me at her door. What I hoped for most was that seeing me would make her happy and that we could speak freely to each other.

I so wanted to talk to her about what Mother said about Father. It had continued to bother me. Had Mother ever said anything of the same to Mercy? Did Mercy agree? I had little doubt she would give me some advice. I was in need of it.

As the soldiers marched, no one spoke. All I heard were tramping feet, horses nickering, and the soft, steady beat of the drums. Now there was enough moonlight to notice trees on both sides of the road. And I could make out low stone walls and behind them what I supposed were farm fields. Houses. We must have made enough noise, because as we passed by, lights flared within buildings. And on the dark hills beyond, I noticed what appeared to be beacon fires. It became clear to me, as it must have been to the soldiers, that people knew about our passing. It didn't seem to matter. We kept going. I looked back to see if any ravens were following. If any were, it was too dark to see them, though once, I was sure I heard flapping wings close by. It sent a shiver down my back.

Some of the soldiers began to sing:

"Yankee Doodle came to town
For to buy a firelock.
We will tar and feather him
And so we will John Hancock."

"Quiet," barked an officer.

The singing ceased. The sole sounds were the steady tramp of feet and the low *rat-ta-tat, rat-ta-tat* of the drums. The monotonous beat gave me the peculiar sensation that I was walking in my sleep, that this was a dream. But I knew it wasn't.

An hour's march brought us to a cluster of houses.

"Menotomy," I heard someone murmur. The name of a town.

Once, twice, I saw people emerge from houses. The light behind them made the figures appear black. They stood still, perhaps to gaze at us, then disappeared, no doubt alarmed by what they saw, a parade of shadows. I wondered if they guessed what was happening.

The march pressed on, along with the tramp of feet and the constant beat of the drums.

I wished Jolla were with me.

The first glow of dawn brought a sound from far ahead: the beating of other drums. I heard a soldier mutter, "They know we're coming."

I told myself this was the moment to dash ahead, but after bolting out ten steps, I knew I could not maintain the pace. It was less effort to keep pace with the soldiers, as if I were tied to them. Then, too, especially with other drums drawing nearer, it might be safer to stay close to the army. What if the soldiers thought I was going ahead to warn the rebel militia?

With the sound of those approaching drums, there was a change in the rhythm of the redcoats' marching. It became quicker, sharper. The English drums seemed to rattle faster and louder. I think the soldiers wanted to get to whatever was about to happen.

My heart beat more rapidly too.

Rat-ta-tat. Rat-ta-tat.

Invisible birds began to chirp. They seemed to come from another world.

From farther ahead came the sharp ringing of what I supposed were church bells, sounding an alarm. That clanging was soon followed by gunshots. I hoped they were *only* alarms.

Dawn came slowly. Though the light was muted and hazy, the countryside seemed to be teeming with unseen people who knew what was happening. I heard the sound of someone running, and now and again a shout. I also sensed a rising tension among the soldiers, along with whispers—perhaps prayers, perhaps curses—and swifter breathing.

Rat-ta-tat. Rat-ta-tat.

The bells continued their harsh clanging.

Wanting to see what was happening and frustrated by the slow, if steady, movement of the troops, I jumped to the side of the road and pushed forward until I was near the head of the column. No one seemed to notice or care what I did so long as I traveled with them.

Rat-ta-tat. Rat-ta-tat.

A blue-gray dawn spread across the eastern sky. From the warm earth a white mist eddied up. The growing light revealed a town, its few buildings scattered. I recognized it as one of the places we had passed through on our way to Boston: Lexington.

Quite suddenly, the church bells stopped ringing, bringing an eerie hush. The only noise I heard was the trudging of boots as the column of soldiers continued to steadily advance.

Rat-ta-tat. Rat-ta-tat.

Fifes began to play, a shrill, squeaky sound like swords scraping one against another, causing a cold shiver to slide down my spine.

The road split in two, the forks going around what looked to be a three-story meetinghouse, from which resumed the clanging of bells, harsh, metallic, and angry.

The dawn grew brighter.

Behind that meetinghouse, I could see a green, the common. On it, I began to make out a ragged line of some seventy men. Even in the dull light, I could tell they were not in uniforms but were wearing dark coats, loose shirts, floppy-brimmed hats, and boots. Powder horns were slung by cords over shoulders. Every one of them held a musket or rifle. They were rebel militiamen.

Off to one side of the common, a clutch of people was standing, watching what was happening. For the most part, they were women and a few children. No one was talking.

The British officers shouted orders, after which the troops halted to load their guns. I had seen them practice on the Boston Commons, so I knew how fast they could do it. I heard clicks and snaps, the pounding of balls into gun barrels.

No sooner were muskets primed than there were more shouted orders, causing the soldiers to split into three groups, one going to the right fork, one to the left. The third moved forward onto the green in double-quick time, heading straight for the militiamen. Their guns, with bayonets, were thrust forward.

I stood at some distance watching, almost afraid to breathe.

As the British soldiers advanced, the militiamen began to back away. To my eyes, they appeared to be dispersing. It made no difference to the British. They continued to press steadily forward until they were about two hundred feet from the militia.

At that moment, a single shot boomed.

Where it came from, where it was aimed, I had no idea. But no sooner did it fly than the British troops lurched forward a few more yards, halted, put guns to shoulders, and began to fire at the militia, a thunderously rapid and repeating *bang-bang*. Billowing clouds floated up, filling the air with an acrid stench. The smoke drifted to where I and the Lexington citizens were watching from the side. It made my eyes smart. I heard someone moan as well as a whispered *"Dear God."*

It was then that Major Pitcairn appeared on his horse and shouted orders so that his troops formed into a battle line. He whirled about and shouted at the militia: "Lay down your arms and disperse, you damned rebels!"

I thought they *were* moving back.

The next moment, there was another volley of shots from the British. Then, as one, the regulars gave a loud shout, lowered their bayonets, and charged straight at the militia. A couple of the militiamen fired, but most scrambled to get out of the way of the redcoats' charge, an assault that included haphazard shooting and wild stabbing with bayonets.

It was terrible to see. People around me groaned. Sobbed.

The smoke cleared. The rebels—who had stopped shooting—were fleeing to higher land.

Militiamen, perhaps seven or eight, lay upon the common, dead. Other men were on the ground, writhing in the agony of their wounds. I saw no redcoats down. Cartridge paper littered the common, like a field of small spring flowers.

The British officers shouted more orders. A drumroll sounded. The regulars halted, reassembled into lines, and let forth a victory cheer: "Huzzah! Huzzah! Huzzah!" they cried, pointing their guns into the air and firing off a ragged volley.

Even as I stood there, numb with fright, the British troops, summoned by drumrolls and shouted orders, re-formed into a column and continued to march on toward Concord, their drums beating, their fifes shrieking. As they moved away, the meetinghouse bell began to ring again. Now, I was sure, it was tolling deaths. I was afraid to move.

The sounds of British drums and fifes began to fade. Knowing the Lexington militia had been called out, I feared the same thing would happen to the Concord minutemen, of which Abner might be one. My head filled with a single thought: *I must reach Mercy!* With that, I tore down the road, catching up with the English regulars as they moved toward Concord.

The English soldiers continued marching, moving faster than before. Though it was an effort to keep up, I managed to stay alongside, but it was hard to do so. With my side aching, I knew I would not be able to reach Concord before they did.

Daylight increased. The air was warm, sweet. We passed more stone fences. Farm fields. Houses. Behind us, bells kept ringing, sounding desperate. Birds flew by, high and fast.

I saw Lieutenant Colonel Smith on his large horse, leading

the way. By his side, also on a horse, was another soldier. It was DeBérniere. All that wandering and mapping we had done: he was guiding the whole movement. It gave me a peculiar feeling, that I was somehow connected to all that was happening. *Captain Brown must be here*. I didn't see him.

Short of breath, I struggled to match the soldiers' pace. My head hurt, fogged with shock and exhaustion. No longer thinking rationally, I clung to the notion that I must get to Tullbury. To Mercy. I was not sure I could.

It took more than an hour to march from Lexington to Concord. By then it was full daylight. I had pushed myself as hard as I could, but I knew I was too late. As the British reached the town, which lay between two hills, some two hundred rebel militiamen emerged out of the village, their own drums and fifes playing. They came from the west and were heading right for the redcoats. They all carried guns.

Belatedly realizing how many British soldiers were coming toward them, the militiamen halted, wheeled about, and started going back in the direction from which they had come.

It was bizarre. For a while, the two opposing armies were marching in the same direction, one in front of the other, their music-making a squawking muddle midst the jagged thumps of jarring drums.

We had reached Concord.

As I watched, detachments of British troops went off into Concord itself, perhaps looking for Adams and Hancock. Or guns and powder. Another group, maybe a hundred soldiers, continued forward, following the militiamen. Since that was the direction I needed to go, I went along.

I realized where they were all heading: the North Bridge that spanned the Concord River. On the far side of it was a hill, the summit crowded with militiamen. The marching rebels, the ones that had come out of the town, now crossed the bridge and went to the higher ground where the other rebels stood. The two groups melded and were joined by more. Overall, there were perhaps four hundred militiamen.

The hundred or so redcoats meanwhile reached the bridge, crossed it, and then halted. They must have seen what I did — the militia, now in far greater numbers than the soldiers, was moving down toward the bridge, toward them.

I stood where I was, realizing that the only way for me to go forward to Tullbury was over that bridge. But it was blocked by the British and, coming at them, the advancing militia.

The British began to back off the bridge. Some of the soldiers started to pull up bridge planks but quickly abandoned the effort and hurried to catch up with the retreating troops.

On the far side, the militia drew closer.

A British officer leaped on a horse and went off in a gallop toward town. I wondered if he was going to get more troops, but when I looked back, I didn't see any coming. What I did see was smoke rising from Concord. *Is the town burning?*

At their end of the bridge, the redcoats halted and lined up in four columns; the front rows knelt, while others stood at their backs, guns to shoulders. I heard the words "Fire! Fire!"

The redcoats fired several volleys at the advancing militia.

In return, from the militia side, someone shouted, "Fire, fellow soldiers, for God's sake, fire!" The militiamen began to shoot at the British. Flashes of flame poked out of billowing puffs of stenchy smoke. The continuous *crash-crash* of shooting guns was deafening.

To my astonishment, the redcoats spun about and began to retreat in great disorder, running back toward the town, leaving two dead soldiers by the bridge.

Though the militia followed, the shooting stopped.

All that I witnessed happened in a matter of minutes. When it was over, and the smoke eddied away, I saw that I would now be able to get over the bridge. The British were retreating fast. The militiamen pursued them.

Still determined to reach Mercy, I ran to the empty bridge, went by the dead British soldiers, and raced over. Only then did I realize two militiamen lay on the ground, partially blocking my way. They were unmoving, bleeding. I would have to pass right by them. Frightened, I halted and drew closer. That's when I saw that one of the men was Abner Hosmer, Mercy's husband.

Horrified, I stopped and looked down at him.

Young and big, Abner lay there, face contorted in a grimace, mouth agape, eyes wide open but blank, no sense of strength about him at all. Though he was not moving, blood leaked through his torn jacket, making its walnut color turn darker. From a jagged hole in his chest, blood trickled down and pooled onto the earth next to a musket that must have been his. As I stood there, scared, not knowing what to do, his blood sank into the earth and disappeared.

On shaky knees, I knelt, shoved the hair away from my eyes, and sought some sense of life in Abner. I found none. No movement of his chest. No sound of breath.

I gazed into his face. The most frightening thing was that he did not look back. His face gave nothing nor asked anything. I had no doubt his soul had fled. It was terrifying.

As I looked on, knowing he was dead, the fingers on his left hand twitched. I reached out and touched them. The hand was warm. I plucked at those fingers. They lifted. Dropped.

I had hated Abner. Had considered him an enemy. All the same, I was filled with chest-squeezing grief. What had happened was awful. To him. To Mercy. *I must tell her,* I thought. I was right to come. I was too late to save Abner, but I could still bring Mercy to safety, to Mother's help in Boston.

Incapable of moving, I continued to kneel where I was, the weight of the grief pressing me down. Then I sensed other people had crossed the bridge and were standing around me.

A woman's voice said, "Do you know him, boy?"

I nodded.

"Who is it?"

"Abner . . . Abner Hosmer."

"Hosmer? Connected to Mr. Hosmer, the lawyer?"

I nodded again.

"From Tullbury?"

I don't recall if I answered. I may have nodded.

"He anything to you?"

"Brother-in-law."

Someone said, "Awful soldiers."

A light hand touched my shoulder to give comfort. From a distance, I could hear guns shooting. The thought came into my head: *They're still fighting.*

Giving voice to my thought, a woman said, "The battle is continuing."

"God help us," said another.

My mouth was dry. My eyes stung. That thought kept coming. *I must tell Mercy. I must get her to safety.*

I looked up. Any number of people were standing around me. The adults were gazing at me. The children were looking at Abner. Others were standing around the second fallen man.

I felt a hand under my left arm, pulling. With help, I came to my feet. I never stopped looking down at Abner.

A woman leaned close to my ear and said, "Did you say you came from Tullbury?"

I answered something. I don't know what.

"Have a horse?" asked another.

I shook my head.

"You'll want to take him home, I suppose."

"Yes," I managed to say.

"To your sister?"

A nod.

"Any way to get him there?"

I shook my head again.

Another voice said, "I've got a wagon. Horse. You can borrow them. Bring them back."

The world seemed to be twisting around me. Dizzy, I dropped to kneel on the ground next to Abner's body. I don't know why, but I reached out and touched his blood. It was wet, sticky, and warm. I turned away and vomited.

Feeling weak, I wiped my mouth, then tried to spit out the bitter taste. My breath came in gulps. I wanted to move but was unable to. I was frightened. After a moment, I somehow said, "I need help."

Another touch to my shoulder. "Stay right here. I'll bring my wagon around."

I did as told, remaining where I was, wiping bile from my lips. From a great distance, I heard shooting. I wondered what was happening. More people were being killed.

I don't know how long I stayed there, waiting, wondering: *What can I say to Mercy?*

At some point, I heard the jangle of harness and the thump of horse hooves on the wooden bridge. I looked around. A wagon and horse had come over. A woman and a boy sat in the seat. When the woman jumped down from the wagon, the boy remained, the reins held in his small hands. A too-big brimmed hat sat on his head. His legs were short, so he was unable to reach the toe board with his muddy bare feet.

Someone helped me stand.

"Let's get him in," the woman said to me.

A few of the women and I lifted Abner up. His arms dangled. Struggling, we maneuvered his heavy body into the wagon so that he lay on some old hay. I kept wishing his staring eyes were closed. *He's dead*, I kept thinking, but I found it hard to believe.

The woman turned to me. "What's your name?"

"Noah."

"Noah what?"

"Cope."

"The pastor? The one who was killed?"

I nodded, waiting for a further remark. It didn't come. Instead, the woman helped me climb into the seat next to the boy.

"Now, Noah," the woman said to me, "this is my son. Peter. Peter Grotten. His father went off with the militia. May God keep him. After you get to Tullbury, Peter will return the wagon to me. Are you hearing me, Noah?"

"Yes, ma'am. Thank you."

"I'm sorry for your loss. Tell your sister it will be avenged."

"Thank you," I said again.

A voice said, "Wait. His gun."

Someone put Abner's musket in the wagon alongside his body.

Peter, the boy, said nothing. He was very pale, his jaw clenched. I'm not sure he even looked at me.

"Now go on, Peter," his mother said. "Tullbury. Straight on." The boy jiggled the reins. Horse and wagon began to move forward with a jerk. If I hadn't been holding on, I might have fallen off. Head bowed, eyes stinging, I wasn't seeing the road, only what I had witnessed: the shooting, the shouting, the confusion, and Abner, dead.

I felt sick. *What will I say to Mercy?*

In all the time it took us to go to Tullbury, the boy never said one word to me. Nor did I speak to him. I kept watching the road or turning around to look at Abner's body. I felt a sadness, deep grief mingled with confused thoughts. Even as I knew I had hated Abner, I regretted wishing him dead. *God keep his soul. He did me no harm. I wronged him. And what will Mercy do?*

Going toward Concord — the opposite direction we were heading — were many armed militiamen.

"What news?" they kept calling. "What's happened?"

"A battle. A lot killed," I returned. "Others wounded."

"We'll get them."

By "them," I knew they meant the British.

Does that include me?

As we approached Tullbury, a cut of fear passed through me. Would I be seen, noticed? Attacked? That woman in Concord knew my father's name, knew what happened, but said nothing ill. All the same, Mr. Harwood's words filled my head: "Come see how we deal with Loyalists, boy."

We moved forward. I didn't see any Tullbury Sons of Liberty on the road. Maybe they all — like Abner — had gone to Concord. I gripped my seat board tighter. *Stop thinking of yourself. Get to Mercy. She needs you.*

We entered Tullbury, traveling on its sole road, passing its modest houses. Though it all appeared familiar and unaltered, it also seemed smaller, emptier. I saw a couple of people but didn't recognize them, nor did they pay any mind to me.

We reached my old home. "Here," I said to the boy.

The boy pulled up on the reins. Horse and wagon stopped. It was very quiet, though I heard some twittering birds. I sat there, gazing at the house in which I had been raised. Had lived. It looked old and drab. I noticed that the front steps had been repaired. By Abner, I assumed.

I continued to sit on the wagon. The boy waited patiently, silently. I kept thinking, *What will I say to Mercy? The redcoats killed her husband. The rebels killed her father.*

Before I did anything, the door opened. Mercy stood there, one hand resting on her large belly. Her face seemed much older, and her dark eyes looked at me with disbelief.

"Noah?" she said, as if unsure it was me. It was odd how she spoke. One word, "Noah," but of two parts. The first part spoken up, hopeful, the second half drooped, sensing something bad.

"What is it?" she said. "What's happened?"

I lifted a hand in a weak, empty gesture. All I could say was "Abner."

"What about him?"

My lack of words or my look must have conveyed something, because she put a hand to the door frame to steady herself.

"Tell me," she insisted.

"Abner," I said again.

She came down the two wooden steps, then stopped. "Is . . . is he hurt?"

I couldn't speak.

"How bad?" she asked, not coming closer.

"He was killed," I forced myself to say. "Over at Concord."

She stood there, staring at me. "Abner?" she said, as if not comprehending my words.

I think I nodded.

Her body sagged.

After a moment of awful silence, she straightened somewhat, then moved toward the wagon. Once there, she paused, put her hand on the sideboard to keep herself standing, looked over and in. Her face seemed frozen.

As she continued to look at Abner, she whispered, "What happened?"

"There was a fight in Concord. At the North Bridge," I said. "The redcoats . . . shot him."

She remained standing there, her eyes on Abner's corpse. After a long moment, I heard her say, "Noah, I need your help."

Women neighbors appeared.

We carried Abner into the house. The moment I stepped inside, I recognized the distinct, familiar smell of home, a woody sweetness I'm sure I had never consciously noticed before. It was like the visitation of a spirit, gone almost before it came.

Mercy laid Abner out where Father's body had lain before him. Someone — I don't know who — told me to go to Lawyer Hosmer's house to say what happened, which I did, running the whole way. When I knocked on the door, out of breath, the same woman who had let us in when Mother and I had gone there appeared at the door now. I wished I knew her name.

"Yes?" she said.

I gave her the news. She stared at me, her mouth open in shock.

"Master Abner? Killed?" she asked.

I bobbed my head.

She continued to gaze at me until, without another word, she softly shut the door. I heard the latch click. It seemed very loud.

I headed back toward home. As I did, I passed Father's church. After a moment's hesitation, I went into the graveyard. Since no stone had been erected on Father's grave, I was uncertain where he lay. When I thought I found the spot, grass and weeds had grown over it. It had been a year since his death.

I stood over what I hoped was his place for I don't know how long, trying to find what to say, trying to untangle my emotions. What came into my head was *Forgive me*, but it took moments to know what it was I wanted him to forgive. Then I knew, and the notion frightened me: it was that I no longer believed in his ways or his words, no longer shared his faith in England.

I continued on to my old home. The wagon and the boy were still there. When I got inside the house, I found neighborhood women surrounding Mercy. I was glad they were there. How different than when Father died. One, two of them even nodded to me. No smiles.

Mercy was sitting in a chair, hands clasped over her belly. Her face seemed to show — I hardly knew the word — *desolation*, but also deep quietude. The only thing that moved were her glistening, blinking eyes, as if trying to heed her statement of a year ago: "I don't intend to cry anymore. Feelings are a hindrance."

"Noah," she said.

The surrounding women moved away. I went forward and knelt. Mercy leaned close to my face. "Go back to Boston and tell Mother to come." Then she took my hand and placed it on her stomach. There was movement.

Flustered, I said, "Come back with me. You'll be safer in Boston."

She shook her head. "That's nonsense. Mother needs to come here."

"Will Mr. Hosmer let you stay?"

"Noah, I'm Abner's widow," she said with her old sharpness. "This is my house. I'm not leaving. This is where I live. Now, please. Do as I ask. I can manage until she comes. Just bring Mother here as fast as you can."

"Mercy, I —"

She pushed me away. "Noah, you must do as I say. Go. Hurry."

As her words sank in, I stood up and moved further off. My hopes for a reunion and being as we had been before were as dead as Mercy's husband. "All right," I managed to mutter, upset with myself for being incapable of saying and doing more.

I left the house. The boy in the wagon barely looked at me. I climbed up to the seat and said, "We can go back to Concord."

The boy said nothing. Clucking at his horse, he turned the

creaky wagon around. As we started off, I looked back at the house, Mercy's house. Though it was me that was leaving, I felt abandoned.

On the way back, the boy spoke to me no more than when we had come. Once, twice, I sensed he stole glances at me, but nothing more. I was unable to talk to him. Look at him. One moment I was mad at Mercy for sending me away. Next, I wished that I had told her how much I cared and didn't want her to suffer.

I thought of the neighbors gathered around Mercy. I had been glad to see them, but why had they been so kind to Mercy now, but not when Father was killed? Was it because Abner was a rebel? Was not a life a life?

I hated Tullbury.

All the while, I felt the need to go home. With that sensation, I understood Boston had become my home. *Or maybe,* I thought with anger, *I have no home.*

There were many minutemen on the road, all heading in the same direction we were. *They left their homes to fight,* I thought. *I left my home not to fight.*

It was afternoon when we reached Concord. The boy brought the wagon to a stop. "I live there," he said, pointing. It was the first thing he had said to me.

I climbed out. "Thank you," I said, and took a step away.

"Sir," he called out, "you forgot your gun."

Abner's musket. I should have left it with Mercy, but now I had to take it up.

"Thank you," I said again, and added, "I hope your father is all right."

He looked at me, and I think he nodded. Only then did I notice tear stains on his cheeks.

"I'm sure he will be fine," I said, wishing it to be true.

I started off, musket in hand. Belatedly, I realized that no one had ever called me "sir" before. It made me feel odd.

Concord was full of militiamen. As more continued to arrive, others were going off toward Boston. I went along with them, in their steady, solemn march. I had come to Concord with one army. I would go back to Boston with another. I tried to determine how much time I had been on the road. It seemed forever.

I looked up. Gray storm clouds were high in the western sky, driving a tree-flicking breeze. The smell of rain was ripe. I kept thinking of Mercy, and of how many women died during childbirth.

"Please, God," I murmured, "let her live."

It was the first prayer I had said in a long time.

I continued in the direction of Boston, the same road my family had taken a year ago. It had been empty then. Now it was crowded with men, almost all of them carrying muskets, as I was.

I passed houses pockmarked with bullet holes. Another house was charred, a curl of smoke rising slowly. It wasn't long before I saw bodies on the side of the road. For the most part, they were British soldiers, looking lifeless the way Abner had. I saw far fewer dead militiamen. I recalled the gunshots I had heard after I left Concord. The fighting must have gone on, and it appeared the redcoats had suffered greatly. It was ghastly. I felt despondent. Deeply weary. My eyes stung. My side ached. I was hungry. All I wanted was to get to Boston.

There were some people attending the bodies that lay along the road. Family, friends, or foes were carting away corpses; I wasn't sure who was who. Many things had astonished me that day, but that the British troops had been so mauled by the American militias was among the most stunning.

I lumbered on. My shoulders ached. So did my legs. I kept seeing the dead, even as more and more militiamen were moving east. Into my head came a prayer that Father had taught us, made us memorize. It came as no ancient text, no voice from some other world or book, but rather as a description of the place and moment where I was: "As I walk through the valley of the shadow of death, I will fear no evil: for thou art with me; thy rod and thy staff, they comfort me." Psalm 23:4.

I was sure I *was* walking through that valley of death, but I did fear evil. Nor was I comforted. Instead, I felt alone. I kept thinking, *I want Mercy to live.* And I continued to tell myself: *You have one thing to do—tell Mother that Mercy needs her.*

My labored pace reminded me of how I had walked after Father's funeral.

To reach Boston, I had to walk sixteen miles in semidarkness, the dark broken by the lanterns militiamen carried. It was like a march of fireflies. Though I had been awake for two days, I kept on. I am sure that at some point, even as I walked, I fell asleep. When I woke with a start, I had no idea how long I'd slept or where I was, save that I was still on the road, still walking. No doubt it helped me that I was never truly on my own. And the sleepwalking revived my strength somewhat.

As during the Charlestown Powder Alarm, news of Lexington and Concord had spread a great distance. Countless militiamen were going in the same direction as I was, toward Boston. I heard them talk to one another. Most were from places in Massachusetts. But they also came from Connecticut and Rhode Island. In days to come — so it was said — they would arrive from all over New England.

As I walked along, the men were constantly discussing what had happened, speaking of it as a massacre, the butchery of the militia by English troops. Sometimes they described what I had seen, sometimes not. The number of troops was increased or decreased depending on what moment was described. All agreed that the British had started it and must be brought down. Boston taken. No one asked me what I thought. They all assumed I was joining them.

"Good for you for being here," one of them said to me, as did others when they learned I'd been at the battle. "With boys like you, we'll beat them back."

As the saying goes, I bit my tongue.

It began to rain, a meager dribble. I kept walking, unable to go fast, unable to stop, feeling a damp and cold fatigue. My legs seemed to work on their own.

Abner's musket grew heavy in my hands. More than once, I thought to throw it away but somehow felt I had a duty to keep it.

In any case, I didn't think the men with whom I walked would have allowed me to get rid of it.

I kept hearing the words "With boys like you, we'll beat them back." I kept asking myself, *Who is* them? *Is it me? Which side am I on?*

At one point, without thinking, I put my free hand in my pocket and felt my pass from Captain Brown. I realized that if these militiamen found it on me, they might consider me a spy and shoot me. I was about to destroy it when I realized that I'd need it to get through the Boston Neck fortifications. That's to say, depending on who saw it, it would bring my safe passage or my death. How could one paper hold such opposite things?

I squashed it down to the bottom of my pocket and tried to walk faster, but I managed only to plod on.

Thursday, April 20, 1775

It must have been three in the morning when I reached Roxbury, where I found an encampment of a few hundred militiamen. They were guarding the road to the Neck in case the British came out. As I attempted to walk through, I was stopped, surrounded, and questioned. "Who are you? Where do you come from? Where are you going?"

I told them I had been in Tullbury to see my sister and that I was going home to fetch my mother when I came upon Lexington and Concord.

"In the battle?"

Not knowing what else to do, and wanting to get through, I

nodded. As soon as I did, I was required to relate what I saw. The men listened with rapt attention and treated me with respect, as though I had achieved distinction.

Someone pointed at the musket I carried, asking, "That gun of yours fire at the British?"

Suspecting that Abner had fired it, I shrugged, which they took as great modesty.

One man touched the wooden stock. "For luck," he said.

"You're a Massachusetts hero," a man said. He made a pretend punch to my chest.

I was not going to argue. It was too complicated—and likely unwise to do so.

Another said, "We've got a whole army camped in Cambridge. Going to get Boston."

When they released me, I had to sneak away to walk alone over the Neck toward Boston. With the bay to either side of me, I was crossing a bridge from one world to another.

As I approached the enlarged British defenses that guarded Boston, I was aware that I had Abner's gun in my hand. I didn't want the redcoats at the fortification to misjudge me. Despite its heavy weight, I held the gun up over my head with both hands so there would be no thought that I intended to use it.

"Halt."

I had come to the Neck defenses.

The questions shouted out to me were the same as I had been asked before: "Who are you? Where do you come from? Where are you going?"

I told them I had gone out of Boston with the troops.

"Who were you with?"

"Captain Brown. Fifth Foot."

"Can you prove it?"

I reached into my pocket and pulled out the much-wrinkled pass that Captain Brown had given me.

"My pass," I called out, burnishing it aloft.

"Bring it here. Slowly."

I did as told. A lieutenant holding a lamp snatched the note out of my hand and studied it. It must have satisfied him because he waved me on. No sooner did I cross through than I was surrounded by soldiers who wanted to know what had happened at Lexington and Concord.

Once more I recited what I had seen.

When I was done, someone said, "You're an English hero."

They let me by.

I went straight to Hog Alley. When I got there, instead of going inside our house, I felt compelled to go on to the Commons, where I had first embarked. There were four redcoats standing guard at the edge of the Charles River.

I looked across to the Cambridge side. What I saw was a vast number of low-burning campfires.

"Who are they?" I asked one of the soldiers.

"The Americans."

I returned to Uncle William's house. It was without light, so I supposed all were asleep. I crept into the basement. Jolla was slumbering.

I placed Abner's gun upright in a corner and lay down, my thoughts crowded by images of all I had seen, everything that had happened. What I saw most were faces. Abner's face. Mercy's face. Faces of the marching soldiers. The face of the boy who drove the wagon to Tullbury and back. The faces of the dead who lay on the road. Midst them all, I saw Father's face as he stood among his Sons of Liberty tormentors. There were so many enraged, fearful, and dead faces. I felt numb.

Though I thought I would never sleep, I did. But then, sleep is death's rehearsal, and I had seen enough of it to imitate it well.

When I woke later in the morning, Jolla was sitting against the wall, waiting for me to open my eyes. I no sooner did than he asked, "What happened?"

Muzzy with deep fatigue and full of aches from my forty-mile walk, I told him about the march through Lexington and Concord, the fighting.

He listened in silence and then said, "Did you see your sister?"

I nodded. "Her husband was killed. My brother-in-law. He was with the militia at Concord."

"Who killed him?"

"Redcoats."

"How?"

I told him what I knew, including that I had gone on to my sister in Tullbury and what she said. "She's going to have her baby. She needs my mother to come."

I recounted the many dead I saw when I walked back. "I think the redcoats were beaten badly."

"What about rebel losses?"

"I saw a few bodies by the road. Less than the British. Jolla, when I came in last night, I saw a huge number of campfires out across the river."

"Rebels," he said.

"How many are there?" I asked.

"Don't know. On the street, I heard someone say there are thousands."

"Are they planning to attack?"

"Probably. Have you spoken to your mother? About your sister?"

"Not yet. When I tell her Mercy asked for her, I'm sure she'll want to go to Tullbury. If she asks me to come with her, I'll need to go."

Jolla said nothing.

I went to find Mother.

As I walked into the front room, Mother was squatting before the hearth, cooking. At the sound of my step, she stood and spun around. "Where have you been?"

"Tullbury."

"Tullbury!" she cried. "Did you see Mercy?"

Fearful of speaking, I stood there.

She must have read the misery in my face. "Tell me," she demanded.

"Abner was killed."

"Abner?" she gasped. "What happened?"

I told her.

"Does Mercy know?"

"I brought Abner's body to her. To Tullbury."

She stared at me, hands clasped tightly over her chest. "Dear Lord . . ." she whispered. "Is she all right?"

"She's shortly to have her child. Said to tell you she needs you to go to her. Soon as you can."

Mother closed her eyes and remained motionless, saying nothing. Faith came into the room. And Jolla. So did Uncle William. No one spoke. Everyone watched Mother. Opening her eyes, she found a chair and backed down into it. She was staring at nothing.

"What's the matter?" said Faith.

I said, "Abner was killed."

"Killed! When?"

"Yesterday."

"How?"

"Faith," called Mother, "come here."

Faith went to Mother. Though she embraced my sister, Mother gazed at me. Was she thinking about how she almost died when Faith was born? Father's death? Looking over Faith's head, she said to me, "Tell them what happened."

Once more, I related the events of Lexington and Concord, telling them how I went to Tullbury and how Abner must have been shot. Mother listened, her face full of pain. Faith clung tightly to her. Uncle William, quite pale, stood by and worked his hands. Jolla, silent, looked on but said nothing.

When I had finished talking, I remained standing before Mother. No one spoke. Then Mother said, "I have to go to Mercy."

"I'll go with you," I said, because I knew I should.

Mother said, "I'll need a cart. Or a horse."

"I'll get one," I said, glad to do something.

"I have a friend at a stable," Jolla offered.

"Please," Mother managed to say. "Go, now."

Then Uncle William asked, "What is the rebel army doing?"

"Sitting in Cambridge," Jolla said.

"A siege?" asked Uncle William. "An attack?"

"No one knows."

Jolla and I walked from the house together.

"What about the Dragon?" I said.

"It can wait."

Boston was in turmoil, a kicked-over beehive. A parade of people headed for the Neck, leaving Boston as fast as possible. They were in carriages, carts, on horses, or walking. I saw someone push a barrow filled with furniture. Infants were in arms. Older children — some crying — were being dragged along by elders' hands.

Such departures had been going on for so long I'd thought everyone who wanted to go had already left. It was startling to see so many more fleeing. The reason was clear enough. The news on the street was that the British army had suffered a calamitous defeat as thousands of rebels had chased them from Concord to Boston. Now, it was said, the rebel militias had surrounded Boston and would attack at any moment.

From what Jolla and I gathered, as the British had retreated from Concord, they had been attacked by the rebels all along the sixteen-mile route. The carnage had been halted only when Lord Percy came out of Boston with troops and cannons.

We heard the numbers: 73 redcoats killed, 173 wounded, 26 missing. We had no idea if this was accurate. Nothing was said about how many rebels were killed or wounded. No one knew. People were saying that the American troops surrounding Boston numbered fifteen, twenty thousand. And they would not disperse. We also learned that as soon as the news came into town, British troops had been rushed to all of Boston's vital points to strengthen defenses.

Jolla and I heard the talk, exchanging looks when someone said something important.

"Not good," he said when we had heard enough. "We better get to the stable."

The stable was on Flounder Lane. Jolla's friend—an elderly freeman who worked there—was quick to say, "A horse? You won't find any for hire or sale in town. Too many people herding out."

We tried a few more places, but what Jolla's friend had said proved true. The only way to get out of town was on foot.

Thwarted, we agreed that Jolla would go on to the Green Dragon and learn what was happening. I'd go home, tell my mother what we had discovered, then join him at the tavern.

"Don't leave town without telling me," he said.

"Promise."

In the time it took me to gather news and return home, I don't think my mother moved from her seat in that chair. Faith was still with her, as was Uncle William.

I stood before them. "Everyone is fearful that the rebels will attack soon," I said. "I don't know if it's true, but you need to get out fast. People are leaving in droves. You'll have to walk to Tullbury."

Mother remained silent.

It was Uncle William who asked, "No other way?"

"Nothing, sir."

"Can you ask your friends at Province House?"

I hadn't thought of that. "I'll go right now," I said, and started off. Halfway there, I reached into my pocket, only to realize that when I had returned the night before, my pass to see Captain Brown hadn't been given back to me. But I told myself that since I'd been to Province House so often to see the captain, I'd be recognized and let in.

As I approached army headquarters, I saw a crowd of soldiers, both regulars and officers, gathered about the front doors. Their dejection was obvious. When I mingled among them, the talk was of how many men the British had lost. Though it was much the same numbers I had heard before, there was also talk about how poorly the expedition had been planned. How inept General Gage was. The slothfulness of Lieutenant Colonel Smith. The fortunate arrival of Lord Percy.

I also heard officers talking about how the militiamen attacked the British in what they said was a cowardly fashion, from behind trees, walls, and fences, how they refused to fight in a civilized manner, which is to say, in lines. "They fight the way savages do." It was said with contempt, suggesting the militiamen had cheated.

At the same time, I overheard phrases such as "I never thought they'd fight." And "They're not the weaklings we thought they'd be." Someone said, "Let's pray General Gage has sent for more troops."

But what I discovered beyond all else was disbelief that the rout came at the hands of such a simple-minded people. "The Americans" was said with scorn. Nonetheless, there was one fact that was clear: the unbeatable British army had been beaten. Though I had seen it myself, it was hard to take in all that it implied.

I went up to the front doors, which, as usual, were guarded by two red-coated regulars, one of whom I had seen many times.

"Please, sir," I said to him. "I think you know me. I have to see Captain Brown, but I've lost my pass."

"Ah, boy, I'm afraid I have to tell you: right before Menotomy, on the retreat, as Lord Percy reached the troops, Captain Brown was killed."

The news came upon me with dreadful force. Finding it hard to stand, I sat on the stone steps outside Province House. In my thoughts, I could see the captain as he had been, stocky, in his trim uniform with green lapels, his look serious. I remembered his kindnesses to me. Sitting there, I started to cry softly, wiping away tears. I felt ill. No one paid me any mind.

Surrounded by regulars and officers, I wondered if they had

known Captain Brown. Did they care what happened to him? I remembered he had a son in England. When would he learn of his father's death? When would his wife? What if they never learned? Where would Captain Brown be buried? Here or in England? What would happen to his sword? Where was DeBérniere? He had been, I knew, in Concord. Was he, too, killed? I thought of the boy who had taken me to Tullbury. What had happened to his father? How many had died?

Only after a while did I begin to wonder what Captain Brown's death meant for me. Did I still have a job at the Green Dragon? A wage?

I looked about. The eyes of the soldiers around me were full of unease. Something Father had told me jumped into my head: "The English empire," he had said, "is the greatest in the world. Being invincible, it will protect us. You can be loyal to that."

It had not protected my father. Or Abner. Or Captain Brown. I knew it could not protect me. Deeply shaken, I found it was hard to accept it all, and could comprehend only that everything had changed.

But even as I sat there, I told myself: *It's me who has to protect my family. Mercy needs help. Perhaps Tullbury is safer than Boston after all.*

I made my way to the Dragon.

The tavern was crowded. Of course, Mr. Adams, Mr. Hancock, and Doctors Warren and Church weren't there. Had they been caught? I wondered. As for tavern talk, it was all about what was called the massacre at Lexington and the British army's devastating retreat from Concord. Many spoke of leaving town. They were also sharing a sense of triumph over the English army. In time, I would learn that Hancock and Adams had not been captured.

Jolla came up to me. "You look sick."

"Captain Brown was killed."

"When?"

"On the retreat. Jolla, I have to find a way to get my mother and sister out of Boston."

He said, "The army is issuing passes in Faneul Hall that will let you go. They want ordinary citizens out of the way."

I hurried off.

At Faneuil Hall, before its narrow end, a large trestle table had been set up. A British captain was standing behind it, while two seated lieutenants were filling in the forms — exit passes — for a lengthy line of people. Regulars were standing on guard.

The line was made up of all sorts of people, working men, gentlemen, and women, as well as people looking like beggars. Sullen, impatient, and tense, what they had in common was distress and frustration.

It took an hour for me to reach the table.

"What is your name? Who are you, and what do you wish to do?"

"Sir, my name is Noah Cope. I'm fourteen. I wish to make an application for my mother, my sister, and me. We want to go back to our home in Tullbury."

"Where's that?"

"West of Concord."

The soldier grimaced at the name but drew up a sheet of paper from his pile. It was a printed form with blank spaces. Then he paused. "Why are you going?"

"My other sister, in Tullbury, is with child. She needs my mother to be with her."

He picked up a quill pen, dipped it into a bottle of ink, and said, "What's your mother's name?"

"Clemency Cope, sir."

He filled in the form, sprinkled sand on it, shook it out, and handed the paper to me.

Boston April 20, 1775, Permit *Clemency Cope*,
together with her family, consisting altogether
of *Three persons*, and effects, to pass out
of Boston between sunrise and sunset by order
of His Excellency the Governor. No arms nor
ammunition can pass.

Paper in hand, I headed back to Hog Alley. Boston's narrow, crooked streets were filled with people rushing around in distress. There was a constant banging of hammers as windows were boarded up. In fear of looters, people were also padlocking doors. A gross stench filled the air as house garbage and night soil were dumped onto the streets.

There were more redcoats on the streets than I had ever seen before. They were dashing around doing who knew what. Others, in columns, were marching in quick time with guns and bayonets, going, I supposed, to points of defense.

When I stepped into the house, Mother, Faith, and Uncle William were doing no more than sitting close together, waiting for me.

"Did you make it to Province House?" Uncle William demanded as soon as I walked in.

"Yes, sir," I said, choosing not to mention Captain Brown. "But I had to go to Faneuil Hall. The army is issuing passes for those who wish to leave."

"Were you able to get one?" asked Mother.

I held up the pass.

"For the whole family?" Uncle William said. He reached out and snatched the paper from my hand, studied it, and looked at me. His lower lip was trembling. "It says . . . it says it's for *three* persons."

"My family, sir."

"But . . . but . . . what about me?" he whimpered, looking old and frail. "These are perilous times. Am I not family?"

"Yes, you are!" cried Faith.

My heart sank: I had left out Uncle William. But what burst upon my mind was that I didn't want to go back to Tullbury. Mercy had made it clear: she needed Mother, not me. And those neighbors who had flocked about Abner but who'd had not one word to say about Father. What kind of reception would they give me? Tullbury as I knew it was full of bad memories. Simultaneously, Uncle William, who had no connection to the town, save us, *wanted* to go. Would not his presence afford Mother and Faith any protection on the road they needed?

In any case, as all this tumbled through my mind, I was sure I could get my own pass in a few days and follow if I chose to.

So it was that I answered Uncle William by saying, "The three includes you, sir. I'll come later."

Contradicting his own pleas, Uncle William said, "But I've received word that deserted houses will be turned into barracks for regulars or officers' homes. How can I leave? They'll destroy my home."

Again, wishing to ease his fears, I said, "Jolla and I will look after your house until I can get away, sir. Which will be soon," I added with what I hoped was a reassuring look toward Mother. I was trying to take care of them all.

"Bless you," Uncle William murmured. Much relieved, he shuffled off to his desk.

"Are the Sons of Liberty coming here?" Faith asked in a trembling voice.

"No," I said.

To me, Mother said, "Will you really follow after us?"

"As soon as I can get another pass," I said with as much confidence as I could muster. "At most, one or two days."

Mother said, "I sent Faith out for food. Noah, she didn't find any."

"The tavern will feed me," I said to placate her. "Please, Mercy needs you to come now."

We filled two cloth bags with such things as they required and might carry, clothing, and the family Bible. As we worked, Uncle

William filled my ears with what I must do to take care of his house: closing shutters, locking doors. A long list. I barely listened. Then he handed me the key and showed me where to hide it behind a loose board at one side of the house. "I'm depending on you." I also saw him slyly gather money into a small bag and stuff it into his coat pocket.

All that done—hardly an hour's work—we left the house. I went with them to the fortifications on the Neck, carrying one of the sacks.

Once there, we joined a lengthy line of people clutching passes. Faces were tense as everyone constantly checked back and forward, worried they were about to be attacked. They carried all manner of things, bags, boxes, bundles. That said, by the side of the street, objects had already been discarded as too heavy, awkward, or perhaps not wanted.

Though there were many soldiers examining passes and scrutinizing what people were taking, the line moved forward slowly. Some people, their expressions distraught, were turned back. It was impossible to know why, but it added to the distress and tension of those waiting in line. As I stood there, I saw guns seized. The next day we heard that more than two thousand weapons were collected.

"How long will it take us to get home?" Faith asked as we inched forward.

I noticed she said "home."

She was clutching one of the bulky bags in her arms, even as she held Uncle William's hand, though I was not sure who was leading whom.

"With my bad walking," said Uncle William, "it will take three or four days unless I get a ride."

"Can we get one?" pleaded Faith. He gave no answer.

Mother turned to me. "Noah, promise me again that you'll come as soon as you can."

"I'll be there in two days. Maybe I'll catch up with you." Then, remembering, I said to her: "When I was in Tullbury, I visited Father's grave."

"Is it all right?"

"It's overgrown."

"If there's no stone, it will vanish."

Everything has already vanished, I thought to say but didn't.

Having run out of words, we waited in silence.

It took some two hours to reach the front of the line. All the while I stayed with my family, working hard not to show my impatience with the slow leave-taking.

Faith grew irritable. I held her sack. "Why is it taking so long?" she kept asking Uncle William.

He sighed. "These are perilous times," he told her.

"What is 'perilous'?"

"Frightful."

When we reached the soldiers at the fortification gate, Mother showed the pass. After all that waiting, the soldiers barely examined it, and their search through what my family carried was cursory. Then the three of them, Mother, Faith, and Uncle William, were pushed forward. At the last moment, Faith turned around, dropped her bag, ran to me, and gave me a hug, then scurried back to Uncle William.

Mother called to me: "Come as fast as you can."

I waved.

For as long as possible, I watched as the three of them moved through the fortifications. Mother gave a final glance back. Then she turned and disappeared midst the crowd. Faith, too, was gone. So was Uncle William.

I stood there for a moment and then headed into town.

Now that they were safely out of Boston, my tension greatly eased. I recalled having had the same feelings of relief when we had come *into* town. But as I walked along the jammed, filthy streets, I realized that for the first time in my life, I was truly alone.

PART 6

1775

When I reached the Dragon, there were few patrons, and those much subdued. The rumors being passed about made the claim that there were some six thousand British troops in town, and more were coming, and that the Americans — said to be twenty thousand — had surrounded Boston in a great semicircle from Charlestown to Roxbury. Were the numbers true? Defeat makes an enemy grow large. A rebel attack seemed likely soon. Or at the least a siege. The British army was strengthening defensive positions at the North End and the Neck. If I intended to leave Boston, I must do so speedily.

I told Jolla that my mother, Faith, and Uncle William had gone.

"When are you going to join them?"

I found myself unwilling to share my contradictory thoughts: that the idea of going back to Tullbury deadened my spirits, though the notion of staying in Boston seemed equally untenable.

"I'll go soon" was all I said, showing little enthusiasm. "I have to," I added, almost as an apology. "I promised." .

With his look of challenge, Jolla said, "All those *have to*s are bars in your cage."

I shrugged. "What will you do?"

"No choice," he said. "Right now, Boston may be the only place I can stay free. Anywhere I'm not well known, it'll be hard to prove I'm free."

As we went back to our work about the tavern, I kept thinking, *How does a person prove they are free?*

That afternoon, Jolla and I took our usual pause to talk behind the tavern.

I said, "Uncle William asked me to do some things around the house."

"A lot?"

"No. But when I'm gone, there's no reason you can't stay there."

"If you're going, better move fast," he advised. "I heard that the town's Loyalists have objected to General Gage letting so many people go."

"Why?"

"Same as before: They want Whigs to be here. As hostages."

Everything was getting worse.

"Still a Loyalist?" he said. I knew he wasn't really asking. He was trying to spur me into thinking things through.

I said, "The rebels killed my father. The British killed Abner. Captain Brown was killed. So many, killed. Jolla, I don't want to kill anyone."

"You didn't answer my question. Loyalist? Yes? No?"

"Not sure."

"Then what?"

I sat there, unable to give an answer. Maybe that's why I put off going to get my pass.

Friday, April 21, 1775

Jolla and I moved out of the basement and into the empty house. Not having wood to make a fire, we sat in the dark.

Jolla said, "What are you going to do with your brother-in-law's musket?"

"Sorry I took it. Anyway, I have no cartridges. You can have it."

"A Black man with a gun? I'd be shot on sight."

"I could sell it."

"Don't even try. They'll hang you."

I had no response.

After a while, Jolla said, "The army is taking over more empty houses. Making barracks for regulars. Homes for officers."

"That's what Uncle William worried about. But you'll be here," I said.

Jolla said, "They won't consider me a person."

Once again, I didn't know what to say.

"Do you know what I heard?" Jolla said, breaking the intense silence. "The Massachusetts congress is raising a bigger army. But guess what? They're willing to fight for liberty, but not liberty for runaway slaves — they won't have them in their army."

"Jolla, they're all hypocrites."

"So you've said, but there's something else," added Jolla.

"What?"

"Some rich people here in town are telling their slaves to go away."

"Why?"

"Afraid they'll turn against them."

"Will they?"

"Keep telling you: people are going to be loyal to what keeps them free. But in case you hadn't noticed, it's hard to know what that is.

"You and me," he went on, "we've become friends — that's

not bad. But what happens if I get into a spot that isn't easy to get out of?"

"I'll help you."

The look he gave told me he was unconvinced. Then he said, "I don't want to have to put that loyalty to the test."

Saturday, April 22, 1775

During the long day, we learned that the British army had left Charlestown and that the soldiers previously stationed there had come into Boston to be part of the defense. As for Charlestown residents, the reports were that they had mostly fled. We also learned that the British navy was attempting to seize every boat in town, no matter the size. Whether they were trying to keep people from leaving town or from coming in, no one knew. It told us how anxious the British were.

Sunday, April 23, 1775

In the morning, Jolla said, "My guess is that the best way you can get out of Boston is by a small boat."

"Jolla, they won't permit it."

"You promised your mother you'd go," he said, sounding like an older brother. "Come on."

We went to a wharf near Hog Alley, the one called Walner's, which poked into the bay. As we approached it, we saw two redcoats on guard, blocking the way.

"Can we get a boat to go fishing?" Jolla called out when we drew near.

One of the soldiers shook his head no.

We tried a few other nearby wharves, even old and rotten ones. Redcoats were everywhere. No boats were to be had.

We climbed to the top of Copp's Hill, where the army was installing a battery of navy cannons. All were aimed across the river. From that spot, a view of the Charlestown peninsular was afforded. We talked to the soldiers stationed there. They were sure when the rebels attacked they would come from that direction.

"Not the Neck?"

"Too strong."

Another soldier said, "Don't worry. No one is getting in or out."

That included me, too.

It was perfectly clear what it all meant: Boston was being truly besieged.

Monday, April 24, 1775

Though I knew I had to get my exit pass, I started the day with Jolla, doing the things Uncle William had asked of us to put the house in proper order. Arranged furniture. Hung up cooking pots. Put his desk to one side. When Jolla went to the Green Dragon, I walked over to Faneuil Hall to get a pass for myself. But when I got there, I found no trestle table. No stacks of pass papers. No one in line. At the main door, there were two regulars on guard.

Puzzled, I went up to one of them. "Sir, what about passes to leave town?"

"General Gage has ended all that. No one can leave town."

"No one?"

"No one."

"When did this happen?"

"Last night."

I stood there trying to understand what it meant. It wasn't difficult: I would not be allowed out of Boston.

Being told I couldn't go made me want to leave, which led to frustration and confusion. I had promised my mother I'd go to Tullbury, though it wasn't a pledge I was eager to keep. The thought of being there with people who had killed Father and turned their backs on us repulsed me. In Boston, not that many people knew me. I preferred that. In the end, I knew I didn't want to go. But what upset me now was that I hadn't made the decision to stay. It had been made for me.

I went to the Dragon and told Jolla what had happened.

He said, "Here you are in Boston: the world's largest prison."

That night, the weather being mild, we sat on the steps before the house. Hog Alley was deserted. The town had become quiet, save for church bells, some of which still rang the quarter hours. Now and again, we heard the tramp of marching soldiers.

I said, "I keep picturing Mother, Faith, and Uncle William on the road, heading for Mercy and Tullbury. Wonder how far they got. And you know what else I wonder?"

"What?"

"If I'll ever see them again." I turned to Jolla. "Maybe you're my only family now."

He snorted. "Not family. Friends." Then, after a moment, he added, "Good friends."

I can't explain it, but for the first time in a long time, we laughed.

Tuesday, April 25, 1775
When we got to the Green Dragon, Mr. Simpson, the owner, beckoned me toward him.

In all the time I had worked at the tavern, I had had little to do with him. Jolla was in charge of me the way he was of most everything there.

I went over to Mr. Simpson's corner. He motioned me to a seat opposite him. When I sat, he leaned forward over his table, his face as red as ever. In a small voice, he said, "Speak softly."

"Yes, sir."

"Captain Brown was killed."

"Yes, sir. I know."

"He was paying your wages."

"Yes, sir."

His hand made a gesture of dismissal. "That's gone. Have you heard anything from the army?"

"No, sir."

"No more salary?"

"I doubt it."

"Do you have family here?"

"They left."

"Jolla says you work well. I've seen that for myself. You do fine."

"Thank you, sir."

"You can stay. But here's the thing. I've no money to pay you. Do as ever, and you can eat." Then he added, "As long as we have food."

"Can I keep tips?"

"If you get them."

"Thank you, sir."

I went back to work.

Later, Jolla told me that Mr. Simpson informed him that in case of a battle with the rebels, the British army intended to use the Green Dragon as a medical station. In other words, if that happened, the tavern would cease to be, and my source of food and money, such as it was, would end.

Wednesday, April 26, 1775

Fewer and fewer customers were coming to the tavern. Hardly a wonder. Given the Green Dragon's reputation as a radical place, no soldiers gave it their patronage. The talk was about people who had left Boston. In truth, there were more troops on the streets than citizens. And with food increasingly hard to come by, I was glad for what little we got at the tavern. Jolla told me he went to a wharf and tried to fish, but the redcoats chased him away.

Thursday, April 27, 1775

Jolla wanted to make another attempt at fishing, so we waited until dark and then left the house. He led the way to what he called Byle's Wharf. "Not used much," he said. "If any place is open, it will be."

Our destination was close to Hog Alley, and the streets were, for the most part, empty. We did spy a troop of redcoats on patrol, but they were easily avoided.

"There it is," Jolla said, pointing ahead to the wharf.

We went forward. As we approached, we saw soldiers pacing up and down, blocking any attempt to get on the wharf.

We went back home. Except it wasn't home. It was, I thought, merely the place where we were waiting.

"What are we waiting for?" I asked Jolla.

"Don't know, but something has to happen."

Monday, May 1, 1775

At the Green Dragon, word came that many rebel troops had arrived in Charlestown. Jolla and I went to Copp's Hill to see for ourselves. We watched as the lines of militiamen marched about, headed for the Charlestown Neck, and then disappeared.

No one had an explanation. The puzzling maneuvers increased the unease in Boston. Everybody knew it: an attack was coming.

Saturday, May 13, 1775

It rained overnight. Streets were muddy. Food remained scarce. Meals at the Green Dragon, what there was of them, left us hungry.

Hearing another rumor of American troop movements, we rushed back to Copp's Hill. When we got there, we could see a line of militiamen march onto what Jolla said was Bunker Hill. We watched as they moved down to that other hill, Breed's, but they soon went away. We never learned what they were doing. But once again, everybody said that something big must occur soon. The British soldiers, who had once seemed cocky, full of smiles and laughter, were sullen, tense.

The army stopped firing the evening gun.

Boston was waiting to be attacked.

Jolla summed it up: "The British are stuck."

"So are we," I reminded him.

Wednesday, May 17, 1775

There was a huge fire on Treat's Wharf. There were little means for fighting it, so army uniforms and weapons, along with goods for the poor, were destroyed. No one knew how it came to be lit, whether it was carelessness or, as rumor had it, at the hands of American spies.

After work, we went directly back to the Hog Alley house, keeping away from main streets to avoid the night watch.

"You scared?" I asked Jolla.

"Sure. You?"

"Same."

Thursday, May 18, 1775

That night when we returned to Hog Alley, we found a note that had been left at the door.

I looked at the inscription. "It's from Tullbury!"

"I heard some letters come in with the Charlestown ferry," Jolla said. "Guess it's true."

It was a brief note from Mother. Mercy had survived giving birth to a baby boy. She had named him Abner. They were all comfortable in the house, but Uncle William hired someone to take him to his brother in Worcester. There was no mention of me being expected.

I was relieved that all were safe.

I shared the news with Jolla.

"Sounds like they'll be fine."

I agreed, though the thought made me uncomfortable. My family had been heartbroken by Father's awful death, and yet they were back among people who had been so cruel to us. Could what we'd been through truly mean so little? I made myself admit that though it had been dreadful — and barely more than a year ago — the events that had led to leaving Tullbury seemed to belong to a different age. Though I still had the scars on my back, the pain was in my memory, not my flesh.

Saturday, May 27, 1775

A ship from England brought Boston three British generals: Howe, Clinton, and Burgoyne. The word was General Gage would be removed from command and General Howe would be placed in charge.

Jolla and I talked about it, wondering if the new generals would make a difference. Since we knew nothing of these men, our talk was little more than talk.

Monday, June 12, 1775

General Gage abruptly proclaimed martial law. No more civilian law. Elected officials in Boston had no more power. Simultaneously, Gage offered pardons for all rebels in Massachusetts except for Samuel Adams and John Hancock. They were said to be hiding.

We also learned that the rebels were holding another of their congresses in Philadelphia. Maybe Hancock and Adams were there.

Church bells were tolling deaths all the time as citizens succumbed to sickness or starvation. I wondered what Boston would be like if all the bell ringers died. Their passing would be announced by silence.

Tuesday, June 13, 1775

It was claimed that American spies were going to the North Ferry area to send messages to the soldiers across the way using signal flags. Jolla and I went to try to see them. We saw nothing.

At the other end of town, I noticed that British cannon gunners at the Neck always kept their cannon matches lit in case of an American strike there. I was told the order came from General Gage.

Once home again, I took up Abner's musket and attempted to go through the motions of loading it. I was sure I wasn't doing it right.

I kept trying, telling myself I might have to use it.

Thursday, June 15, 1775

At the Green Dragon, we heard that the Philadelphia congress named someone called George Washington to the head of the American army. We asked about him, but no one knew anything about the man or from where he came.

Saturday, June 17, 1775

Well before dawn, Jolla and I were awoken—as no doubt all Boston was—by a thunderous cannonading.

We were sure the assault on Boston had begun.

We ran outside. Wanting to know from what direction the rebels were coming, we rushed to the Commons, then realized that the noise was emanating from somewhere north of town. We ran up Copp's Hill in hopes it was high enough to allow us to see what was happening. As we approached, we were joined by a crowd of citizens who also wanted to see. None of them knew what was going on either.

When we reached the hill's summit, we were pushed aside by army gunners who were working in a frenzy to finish setting up the new battery. That's when we saw what the shooting was about. It was not taking place in Boston. Instead, below where we stood, in the Charles River channel between Boston and Charlestown, a ship was aiming its cannons in the direction of Breed's Hill on the Charlestown peninsular. There being only partial moonlight, and no dawn, it was too dark to see what the British were aiming at. Even so, the firing cannons from the ship lit up the sky with their sudden, darting spikes of flame.

We asked people what it was all about and were informed that the rebels were building fortifications above Charlestown. It was said they were trying to tighten the siege around Boston. The British ship was trying to dislodge them.

Only when dawn grew did we see what was unfolding.

Above Charlestown, on Breed's Hill, a great number of men were digging and building walls. By the way they were dressed — no one in a red uniform — it was clear they were rebels. Nor did they pay much attention to the cannonballs lofted in their direction by the ship, which we learned was the *Lively*. Her cannon fire fell short of where the men were working, though we saw an occasional ball plow into the earth and sear a scar. Regardless, the Americans kept working, and the *Lively* kept shooting. Soon more British ships would join in: *Symetry* and *Falcon*.

By midmorning, the Copp's Hill cannons went into action, blasting away at the Charlestown peninsular. They would continue to do so all day. Though it made my ears ring, we remained there because it enabled us to see everything happening.

We observed the Royal Navy ships on the Charles River begin to maneuver into new positions, closer to Bunker Hill. That was at the far northern end of the peninsular, port side. But it wasn't until early afternoon that we saw a double column of longboats emerge from around Boston's north side. These boats were full of redcoats, and it was apparent they were heading for the southeast beach of the Charlestown peninsular, Morton's Point, where Jolla and I had been clamming.

Once the longboats reached the point, the British troops climbed out and waded through the river water onto the beach. A massive line of them formed and started up Morton's Hill. We saw flags unfurl, heard the rattle of drums and the thin, high-pitched, shrieking fifes. As the first line of troops began to move, other British soldiers swung around and started up Breed's Hill. No one was opposing them.

The British troops were well advanced up the hill when, from behind the new-built American fortifications, a torrent of rifle and musket shots exploded. There were constant spits of flaming red as rebel gun after rebel gun was discharged, a continual clattering, pounding, and banging so that great clouds of gun smoke billowed, filling the air with the stench of gunpowder even where we stood. The shooting was only partially returned from British lines as redcoats tumbled like bowling pins, horrifying to see. From people standing near us, I heard groans and gasps.

To our amazement, we saw the line of redcoats retreat, regroup, then move up anew, only to drop back into another retreat. The British were failing.

We didn't see what was happening to the rebels, how many, if any, were killed. Nor did we see them retreat.

It was clear we were witnessing a huge battle, spectacular and frightening at the same time. That's to say, we, along with the other people on the hill, remained transfixed by all unfolding across the channel. From our hilltop elevation, we could see that many others watched from Boston rooftops. There was little talk but much hushed gazing, hands clapped to ears against the booming cannons.

Meanwhile, the British ship *Somerset* had come into place and began to aim its cannon fire right at Charlestown and its wooden houses. At the same time, a new British line moved up the hills, only to fall back again.

Now longboats—with more British soldiers—pushed farther up along the peninsular shore, this time closer to Charlestown. Once landed, the redcoats began to move forward in battle lines, bright bayonets thrust forward. They were trying to get behind the rebel lines. They were succeeding.

It wasn't long before all Charlestown was ablaze, sending up towers of gray, black, and white smoke. Poking through were church spires, twisted fingers of flame. A few tumbled, bringing a collective gasp from onlookers.

As the redcoats persisted in advancing up the hills, we saw the rebels begin to retreat. (I later learned they had run out of ammunition.) They went slowly at first, then faster and faster, firing much less. Meanwhile, the British were trying to reach the Charlestown Neck to cut off the withdrawal. In that, they failed.

The banging sounds of guns and drumbeats began to diminish, until, as daylight started to fade, the battle appeared to be over. We, along with hundreds of others, had been watching all day.

But even before the fighting ceased, we saw that the longboats that had brought the British troops to the fight had begun to return to Hudson's Point and Long Wharf. They were loaded with bleeding, wounded, maimed, and dead soldiers. We heard appalling cries and wails, sometimes screams.

The wounded were carried ashore, then brought into the town in carts or on horses. I saw one soldier transported in a wheelbarrow.

"Where are they taking them?" I asked Jolla.

"They'll have many places. You forget? The Dragon is one of them. Come on. They'll need us."

When Jolla and I got to the Green Dragon, soldiers were carrying out tables, benches, and chairs.

"We work here," Jolla said to a soldier guarding the door.

"You still can. We can use you."

We went inside. Muted lantern light revealed a transformed place. Almost everything that pertained to the tavern had been removed. Folded blankets had been put down on the open floor. Buckets were set out, along with stools and rolls of cloth. On the one remaining table, surgeons' tools had been laid: scissors, pincers, and saws, plus devices that seemed so gruesome I didn't want to know their use. The air smelled of strong vinegar. Waiting surgeons and their assistants wore leather aprons.

We were given rags and leather buckets and told to wash floors. As we scrubbed, wounded soldiers were constantly led or carried in and laid down. Their uniforms were torn, ripped, and ragged. So were their bodies. We saw shattered arms and legs, appalling gunshot wounds, wounds still bleeding, wounds coated with filth, wounds encased in congealed blood, wounds to the body, wounds on faces and heads. It was a slaughterhouse for men.

The injured were moaning, crying, muttering, and praying, all with unending calls for help. For the most part, pleas were ignored, as there were so many hurt and dying and not enough surgeons. Blood pooled on the floor, attracting swarms of flies. People slipped on it. Jolla and I were forever cleaning.

We found cups and gave water to some of the soldiers. More than one man died when I was with him.

With amputations taking place on the second floor, we heard constant screaming and ghastly shrieking. The medical men were spattered with blood. Lead musket balls crushed by clamping teeth to bear pain bounced down the steps, *tap, tap, tap.*

We carried out buckets of vomit, cutoff limbs, and excrement, as well as the bodies of those who died. We laid them out on Union Street. Simultaneously, more wounded were brought in. As we would learn, some 50 percent of the British troops had been cut down in the battle. To be sure, I knew of hell and had heard it described. I never thought I'd see it. That day in the Green Dragon, I did.

There was a rumor that Doctor Warren, the rebel leader, had been killed during the battle. Later, we learned that it was true. Indeed, the list of people who had been killed kept getting longer. So many died that General Gage ordered that church bells not ring their normal peals of death. It was what I had foreseen. Death was rendered silent. It filled me with unending horror and sorrow.

By nighttime, Jolla and I were spent, unable to work or talk, but we managed to get home, avoiding two night watch patrols. Once inside, we collapsed and fell asleep. In the early morning, we returned to what had been the Green Dragon. The suffering was terrible. The soldiers who lived were carried to transport ships to be taken back to England. Those who died in transit were left in the sea. Those who died in Boston were taken to be buried in earth, I didn't know where.

For twelve days we worked there, fed now and again. At night we returned to Hog Alley, exhausted in body and soul. On the thirteenth day, the army shut up the tavern. It had become, they said, too filthy with blood, gore, and stench.

With the tavern closed, our source of food was gone.

Sunday, July 2, 1775
In the aftermath of the Charlestown battle, a deep despair settled over Boston. Streets were clogged with exhausted, limping, and broken British soldiers. They claimed victory — they *had* driven the militiamen from the Charlestown hills. But, as I heard it said by a British officer, "One more victory like it, and we'll lose the war."

Most important of all, Boston was still ringed by the rebels, who clearly intended to stay and, so it was said, were ready to attack again. In other words, the siege continued.

We learned that a great number of British officers had been killed, so many it was obvious that the militiamen must have targeted them. It meant that regular English troops had few commanders to enforce discipline, which added to the disarray in town.

Two days after the Dragon closed, as Jolla and I were out searching for food, we passed a sergeant who, along with some other soldiers, was herding a group of boys and young men down the street. The next moment, without explanation, we were collared and pushed into the group and told to come along. It happened so fast we were unable to protest or do anything about it.

Fearful it was a press gang, we were marched to the southern end of the Commons. Once there, shovels were put into our hands. Orders were shouted out. It soon became clear we had been brought there to dig graves for British soldiers. We did so all day. Once, bread was given out. Some water, too. That night, we were made to sleep there under guard. The next day, the work continued. Only then were we let go. We had stopped counting how many graves we dug.

Tuesday, July 4, 1775

We heard that the new commander of the American army, the man named George Washington, had come among his troops in Cambridge and was now leading them. As we were going to the Hog Alley house for the night, Jolla said, "At the White Horse I learned some things about that Mr. Washington. He comes from Virginia. He's rich. And he enslaves Black people."

In a tone of disgust, Jolla continued: "All this talk of liberty, and they choose a leader who acts otherwise."

"That's bad," I said, knowing too well how weak my response was.

"Remember how I told you I had this notion of a liberty bird bringing me to a free land?"

"Think so."

"Well, it just flew by again without stopping. Didn't even drop a feather."

Monday, July 24, 1775

Now that the army had made Boston safe from attacks from Charlestown—by occupying it—they were worried about possible assaults from the southern end of Boston, Dorchester. There was talk about securing the area, but nothing came of it that I saw.

General Gage did send troops, via transport ships, to Connecticut to find needful food. When the ships returned with almost two thousand sheep and a hundred cattle, such was the joy that town bells rang.

One of the results was a ditty that circulated:

> In days of yore the British troops
> Have taken warlike kings in battle.
> But now, alas, their valor droops
> For Gage takes naught but cattle.

It provided a rare smile.

Monday, July 31, 1775

It was claimed that Boston now had less than seven thousand civilians. When I first came, there had been sixteen thousand. As for British soldiers, when I came to town, there had been four thousand. Now it was said there were more than thirteen thousand. It was like living inside a fortress.

The only way the army could get out was by attacking and defeating the Americans who ringed the town. To do so, they would have to cross the Charles River, a dangerous undertaking. In any case, they didn't have enough boats. To march out in substantial numbers over the narrow Neck to attack would be equally precarious, since the American militiamen outnumbered the British. And more rebel militiamen, it was rumored, were arriving in Cambridge all the time.

With fears of more fighting, I could not rid my mind of what I had seen at the Green Dragon—turned-hospital. People talk about being haunted by ghosts. I was haunted by the memory of living men who had been torn apart.

Tuesday, August 1, 1775

As the days' summer heat grew intense, nights were much the same. Drunkenness and disorder increased among the British soldiers. Brawls were common.

When we went out and about, we avoided main streets.

"You sorry you ever came to Boston?" Jolla asked as we headed home one afternoon.

The question surprised me so much I stopped walking. I tried to think back. Our arrival in Boston seemed so long ago. But it had been only a year and a half.

"I wouldn't say that," I finally said. "Before my father's death, there was a lot I didn't know."

"And now?" asked Jolla.

"Sometimes it feels like I know too much. Hard to understand it all. I admit it seemed easier before."

"Hate to tell you, but it's hard to unknow things."

"Almost as hard as it is to get out of Boston," I said, and we laughed.

Saturday, August 5, 1775

By night and day, we heard random bursts of gunfire, though we never knew the cause. Either the British troops were making forays to push back the American militia, or the militiamen were poking at the British. Most of all, it changed nothing. It merely frightened people.

It surely frightened me.

Thursday, August 10, 1775

In the middle of the night, there was a thunderous cannonading from the militia into Boston from across the Charles River. We went down to the basement and waited for an attack that never came.

Thursday, August 24, 1775

All Black Bostonians, free and enslaved, were summoned by the army to meet in Faneuil Hall. Jolla went. He had to. I went with him. To some hundred or so Black men in attendance, a British captain announced that thirty would be chosen and required to clean Boston's streets. They would receive no pay. They had to do it. I was relieved Jolla was not selected.

One of the Black men—Jolla told me later his name was Caesar Merriam—stood up to make a strong objection. He was immediately arrested and put in the courthouse jail and kept there until the work was done. Black Bostonians brought him food and drink.

That day, as we walked back to the house, a livid and dejected Jolla said, "Outside or inside of Boston, it doesn't matter where I go.

There are always white people who think they can tell Black people what to do."

I hated to hear his pain. Trying to change the mood, I said, "Well, at least with us, you're the one always telling me what to do."

The look Jolla turned on me made me flinch. "Of all the dumb things you've ever said, Noah, that is the dumbest. Don't you get what I just said?"

"I'm sorry, Jolla," I said. "I was just . . ." There was no way to finish that sentence.

Silence reigned. Then Jolla said, "Did it ever occur to you that I have better things to do than tell you what to do?"

He walked on, and only after a moment did I follow. *Think for yourself,* I self-scolded over and over.

For a time after that, the streets were cleaner. But it didn't take long for them to become what they had been: filthy and cluttered. That forced cleanup was not repeated.

Tuesday, September 12, 1775
News spread that Doctor Church—who had been so thick with the rebel leadership, Mr. Adams, Mr. Hancock, and Doctor Warren—had been spying for the British all along.

Jolla and I talked about how mean and dishonest an act that was.

"But you did the same thing," he reminded me.

"What do you mean?"

"You spied for Captain Brown."

Embarrassed, I could give no response. It made me think how

tangled everything was. The rebels claimed they fought for liberty but tyrannized those who disagreed with them, such as my father. The British said they upheld English rights but denied them to others. Both sides supported slavery.

"I wish things were simple," I said.

Jolla snorted. "Simple is for simpletons."

Wednesday, September 20, 1775

As the siege continued, we spent more and more time scavenging for something to eat. We begged at tavern doors. At barracks. At wealthy homes where people still lived, we learned to go to back doors and ask servants for food. Sometimes we received it and were grateful. Once, we came upon a wagon that was bringing food to a barracks. For whatever reason, there were no guards or drivers. I'll not deny we stole some food. We ate well that day, but there were days we found nothing.

Now and again, having naught to do, we wandered about wharves in search of boats. Though we doubted we could escape, the looking gave us something to do. As for our searching, we were either warned off or never found any boats at all.

One night, sitting on the far edge of a deserted wharf, we stared out into the bay at the British ships riding at anchor.

"We keep looking for a boat," said Jolla after a while. "But what if we did find one? Where would you go?"

The question had been asked so often I merely shrugged.

"What do you know about other places in the world?" he asked. "I mean, far away."

"Not much," I admitted. "England. Canada. At the Dragon, I heard someone talk about a place he called the Sandwich Islands."

"Where's that?"

"The other side of the world. Whalers go there."

"Think people who live there ever talk about us?"

"Why should they?"

This time it was Jolla who shrugged. "Then the way I see it," he said, "if we stay here we'll die of starvation, sickness, get killed in an attack, or be pressed into the army. I leave out anything?"

I shook my head.

Jolla said, "If you had your choice to do anything you wanted, what would it be?"

I thought awhile. "To live," I said. "You?"

"The same."

We didn't laugh.

Tuesday, September 26, 1775

News was confirmed that General Gage had been relieved of his command and called back to England. General Howe was put in charge. I talked to some soldiers who were pleased because they thought Gage was weak. They admired Lord Howe. No reasons were given that I heard.

As for Gage, he received much public saluting.

The praise baffled me. He seemed to have failed at everything.

But as we went about town, we noticed the British army had new energy. Uniforms were scrubbed. Streets were cleaned. Those on guard seemed to be more alert, ready for good things to happen.

There was talk of going on attack, and a tension mixed with excitement spread through town.

Thursday, October 5, 1775
One of the last things General Gage did was put a variety of cannons — some twenty or so — around the Neck fortifications. It was clear: they expected the next assault from the Americans to come there.

Wednesday, October 11, 1775
General Gage left Boston for England on the ship *Pallas*. He had come to pacify the Americans and protect Boston. He had achieved neither. No wonder he left at night.

Inspired by Gage's departure on the *Pallas*, Jolla and I spent the day inventing ways we could steal a great vessel for ourselves and sail it to freedom. We argued as to who should be captain. Since we could never decide where we might go, the notion of living upon the ocean — cut free from land — was most appealing.

Later that day, I was stopped on the street by some soldiers who asked me to identify myself. Once I had satisfied them — Uncle William's name still helped — I asked them if they were sure the Americans would attack. They said it wasn't a question of *if*, only of *when*.

Tuesday, October 24, 1775
It was night, and we had gone as far as Foster Lane, not an area we usually went to, but we needed food and wood. Not finding anything,

we made our way home in the dark, me carrying a lantern. The slow tolling of church bells sounded desolate. On the way, we came upon a group of Loyalists patrolling the streets. In their hats, they wore cockades—knots of ribbons—which proclaimed their authority.

They quickly surrounded us and demanded I tell them if I was a rebel or Loyalist.

I could feel Jolla's eyes on me. "Loyalist," I felt obliged to say.

They pointed at Jolla. "This boy your slave?"

"I am a freeman," he said.

"Can you prove it?"

"He's speaking the truth," I said.

"Who are you?"

"Noah Cope. I live on Hog Alley with my uncle, Mr. William Winsop."

Their looks showed doubt, but fortunately, one of the men said, "I know Mr. Winsop. A solid Loyalist."

"Get off the streets," they ordered.

We walked toward home. Jolla exploded with great bitterness: "You ever wonder why I spent so much time at the Dragon? They liked me well enough there because I was waiting on them. But soon as I stepped away, people wanted to tell me what I should do or be.

"I don't have papers to prove that I'm free, and it's not likely anyone is going to take my word for it. You know what I hate? Having to depend on white persons to define what I am."

His face was full of anguish, and I saw something I had never seen from him before: tears.

Not knowing how to respond, I kept thinking of what had happened. While it may be strange to say—after all our time together—it was only then that I saw how greatly different Jolla's world was from mine. In time (if I lived), I could leave Boston. I could go back to my old home, join my family, if I chose to. It would be hard, and it might not be what I wanted, but I could do it. I'd survive, I supposed, freely. Jolla, though a freeman, could assume none of those things.

I felt the gulf between us I had never recognized before. I remembered trying to make light of Jolla's comment about white people telling him what to do some weeks before, and I winced.

Saturday, October 28, 1775
General Howe, the new commander in chief, made his first proclamations, designed to tighten his control. All Tories must officially organize themselves into watch groups to preserve order in the town. They were given fancy names to puff them up: The Loyal American Associators. The Loyal Irish Volunteers. There was even a group called the Royal Fencible Americans.

On the street, I came upon a watch group. I approached and asked about the word "fencible."

"It's from Scotland. Means a soldier used for defense."

Later, Jolla and I talked about how men from different parts of the British Empire were defending the army.

It didn't seem to make a difference.

At night we stood on the banks of the Charles River and tried to count the campfires of the Americans in Cambridge. There were too many. We gave up.

Wednesday, November 1, 1775

The British regulars, unhappy with bad barracks, often broke into deserted homes and lived in them.

"What if they try to take our place?" I mused one night.

"We'll have to fight them off."

"How?"

"Not sure."

I went and found Abner's gun.

Monday, November 6, 1775

A new proclamation came from General Howe and was read out upon the streets: citizens were now allowed to ask to leave Boston. Depending on who and what you were, permission *might* be granted. People said it was because the army expected an attack and once again wanted to ensure civilians were not in their way.

Jolla said, "They'll let you go now."

"I'm not asking."

"Why?"

"Staying with you."

"What about your family?"

I was silent for a long moment. Then I began to voice thoughts that had been forming for months. "That letter I got back in May. It told me Mercy is taking better care of our family than I ever could—ever will. They seem safe in Tullbury." I tried out my ideas slowly. "Going back there would be, for me . . . like going back in time. I can't do that. My mother told me not to be like my father. That I need to think for myself—you said so too. I'm still trying to learn how, and I'll never be able to do it there.

"It's hard here, but at least I've figured out I can't go back." We kept walking on, me stealing glances at Jolla. "Sometimes, Jolla, I think the only thing I have left to be loyal to is you."

"That a joke?"

"No. It's true. You know what else I was thinking? We should start our own tavern."

Jolla's face lit up. "I'd like that."

"You'd be in charge. Sit at a table like Mr. Simpson did, collecting money. I'd do the rest."

He laughed. "All of it?"

It was my time to grin. "Sure."

"Fine with me. I might even give you a salary. What are we going to call it?"

I thought for a while. "What about . . . the Freeman?"

We both laughed.

We spent a long while working out all the details.

Before we went to sleep, Jolla said, "It's fun, but hard, too, working out a future we'll never have."

After the good time we'd had planning, that made me sad.

Monday, November 13, 1775

In the afternoon, Jolla went off but soon came back, greatly excited. "Have you ever heard of Lord Dunmore?"

"Never."

"The royal governor of Virginia. He's offered freedom to any slave or indentured servant who joins the British forces."

"For all the colonies or just Virginia?"

"Don't know. Let's go to the White Horse and see what people are saying."

The tavern was crowded and noisy, with everyone talking breathlessly about Lord Dunmore's offer, debating what it meant for Massachusetts.

One man said he had read Dunmore's proclamation that was printed in the *Post-Boy*. "He proclaimed freedom for all enslaved Black men and indentured servants *if* they joined the British army and fought for the Crown."

"That it, exactly?" someone demanded.

"Close enough."

That was followed by lively debate: Some men wanted to support the British in hopes Lord Dunmore's offer was meant for all enslaved people. Others wanted to support the rebels, believing their talk of freedom would lead to slavery's end. There were arguments every which way. But in the end, the general sense was that Dunmore's offer did not apply to Massachusetts. The talk settled into a mixture of wishful hope and despair.

When Jolla and I walked back to Hog Alley, I asked him, "What do you think?"

"Guess the offer is just for the southern colonies," he said. "Not here. Still, that's better than the Massachusetts congress. Massachusetts people don't want any slaves in their army. They aren't talking about freedom for Blacks at all."

He was not simply disappointed but indignant. I thought him right to be.

Monday, November 20, 1775

It was night, and by the light of a thin moon, we had been out scavenging but had met with ill success. As we went down along Cooper's Alley, not so far from Fort Hill, we came upon a British soldier lying in the street.

Smallpox had spread. When people were discovered with the symptoms, they were forced out of town at the Neck. Between smallpox and dysentery, it was said that twenty to thirty people—soldiers and citizens—died each day. That meant dead bodies had become common in Boston.

When we saw the soldier lying there, our immediate thought was that he was dead of the illness.

We approached him with great care. Only when we drew close did we realize he was asleep and, from his smell, drunk. How or why he came to be in such a spot, we had no idea.

Though in full uniform, he had no gun with him. Perhaps someone had already taken it. What we did see was his pouch, which might hold cartridge rolls. It was closed.

We stood there, staring at him.

"Abner's gun," I said. "I have no cartridges."

Jolla reminded me, "Get caught stealing from a soldier and you'll be shot."

I looked up and down the street. No one else was there. In haste, I knelt, put a hand into the pouch, felt a few paper cartridges, and plucked them out. No sooner did I have them in hand than we ran and kept going until we got into our house.

Once inside, Jolla said, "That was reckless."

"Wasn't. If anyone tries to take the house, we can fight them off."

"Did you ever learn how to load that gun?"

I shook my head.

"Then you aren't reckless. You're stupid."

We both laughed.

Friday, December 1, 1775

I became fifteen years of age.

When I informed Jolla, he said, "I wish you the compliments of the day."

I asked him, "What day were you born?"

"I have no idea."

"Do you ever wonder about your family, mother, father, brothers or sisters?"

"Sometimes I fancy I pass my father on the street. I think, *Maybe that man is my father.*"

"Is it hard living without a family?"

"Just if I live or die, it won't matter to anyone."

"I'd care."

"You told me you buried your father."

"I did. What of it?"

"You can do the same for me."

"And you for me."

We shook hands to honor the agreement.

Tuesday, December 5, 1775

The miseries of Boston continued as winter temperatures froze the town. From time to time food arrived, but it was given first to army officers, then regulars, and then—if any left—to townspeople. If we heard rumors that food was available somewhere, we'd rush to the place, only to find others already there. Lines were long. If we got anything, it was meager.

As for wood for heat, almost all trees in town had been cut down, including the Liberty Tree. Old wooden buildings were torn apart. Pews from some churches—no Church of England struc-tures—were ripped out and burned as fuel.

One cold night, Jolla led me to a little street—Hills Lane —which ended at the bay. No soldiers were there, so we tried fishing. We caught nothing. Jolla said the fish were smarter than we were, since they found a way to escape Boston.

"How long do you think the siege will last?" I mused aloud.

"Until someone gives up."

"Which side?" I asked.

"For us, not sure it matters."

Friday, December 15, 1775

It was night. Having no fuel to lessen the cold, we sat wrapped in blankets, the front door locked against wind and drifting snow. Boston, it seemed, had sunk to the bottom of a cold sea. The only sound I heard was my chattering teeth, which I tried to clamp down to keep silent. Jolla had his eyes closed, but I don't think he slept. The ink on Uncle William's desk was frozen.

During the silence, we heard a sudden crunch of footsteps before the house. Next came low, murmuring voices. Men were at our door. The door rattled.

I rushed to get Abner's gun and the cartridges.

When I rejoined Jolla, he whispered, "You ever figure out how to load that thing?"

I shook my head.

The door rattled again.

Jolla leaped up, went to the hearth, dragged down two iron pots, ran back, and began banging them together.

The rattling at the door stopped.

Jolla banged again.

We heard the steps recede.

There were no more break-in attempts.

"Jolla?"

"What?"

"We can't keep on like this."

"What are we going to do about it?"

"Hope something happens."

He said, "Now you're waiting for my liberty bird too."

Sunday, December 31, 1775

Jolla and I wandered the slush-mucked streets. When we spotted people quitting their houses for good, which we knew by the things they took out and left on the street, we marked the place in our minds. At night, we'd return and find a way to push open doors at the back. Once inside, we took such scraps of food as we found. We had to be careful. The night watch was patrolling. The last thing we needed was to be taken up.

Neither of us said so, but we would starve if things did not change.

Thus, the year ended with no promise of any change. I wondered how long it would be before one of us died.

PART 7

1776

Monday, January 1, 1776

As the day dawned, Jolla and I stood on the edge of the Commons and looked across the Charles River. It was so cold I was sure my bones had turned to ice. My teeth chattered. My feet stamped. To herald the New Year, the American army, still laying siege from the Cambridge side of the river, had hoisted a new flag. In one corner the Union Jack, then came thirteen alternating red and white stripes, which we guessed represented the colonies in rebellion against Great Britain. On the Commons, we saw Great Britain's flag flying. In other words, the Charles River was a border that separated two countries.

Jolla said, "Which country do you belong to?"

"Not sure," I answered. "You?"

"My own."

I bent down, picked up a stone, and skipped it over the water. It bounced five times.

"You've been practicing."

"Nothing else to do," I said.

Saturday, January 13, 1776

The harsh freeze continued, as did the lack of food. A British soldier was publicly hanged for having stolen something to eat. We did not watch the execution.

Then we had some luck. In our scavenging, we came upon a wagon on Pleasant Street. It was delivering bread to an army barracks and had become stuck in muddy snow. We offered to help push it free, and for our efforts, we each received a loaf of bread, which, though stale, carried us through the day. The soldiers on the wagon told us that the British had sent out thirty-six ships from Ireland with food. But because of Atlantic storms, only thirteen got through. The ships, the soldiers said, would provide only a few weeks of nourishment.

That night, in our cold, empty house, we again talked about the possibility of escape.

Jolla said, "Half the time, I think that maybe I can find a way to stay here in Boston. The other half, I think I need to get away from here."

"You keep saying that. But where would you go if you could?"

"Far away as I can get. Could be a time to start something new as a free man. Maybe the French up north would let me live in peace."

"The British are there now. And they support slavery," I said, not that he needed the reminder.

He said, "That mean you're ready to try the Americans?"

I shook my head. "I can't, Jolla . . ." I couldn't go on. So much had happened, and I viewed both sides differently than I once had, but still: "I can't," I repeated. Jolla was looking at me, silently challenging me to tell him more. I took a deep breath: it was time. "I never told you everything that happened in Tullbury, did I?"

"When you saw your sister?"

"No, when this began for me. My family. Almost two years ago."

He waited for me to continue. I was still finding it hard to talk about.

"After my father was killed in Tullbury," I began, "from that tar and feathering, the Sons of Liberty — two of them anyway, Ezekiel Trak and Richard Poor — came after me.

"They beat me. Hard. Remember you asked about the scars on my back? They tried to get me to talk about hidden guns and powder. I didn't know anything about it. Not then. All I . . . I wanted was to be loyal to my father and do as he did. Remain silent. But the beating was so terrible I said things I didn't believe. People knew about it. I was ashamed of myself. I think about it often."

Jolla, his legs drawn up to keep warm, nodded. "Nothing binds tighter than bad thoughts."

"Thing is," I continued, "those men who beat me, I keep worrying that if the rebel army comes into Boston, they or other Tullbury men might come too. Even if it's not them, people like them might be in charge. Someone might recognize me. Grab hold of me, and this time . . . keep me. Or worse. That scares me. Jolla . . . do you think I'm a coward?"

"Why would you even ask?"

"Those men forced me to say things I didn't believe."

"No shame," said Jolla, "in fearing people who want to kill you."

I said, "I hate being scared."

"If nothing scares you," said Jolla, "you're not paying attention."

"I used to think loyalty to the British Empire would protect me. Now I just want to get to where I feel safe." I tapped my chest. "Safe inside."

He said, "How long since you came to Boston?"

"Told you: almost two years."

"You've said you think differently now. Good. Do you think you *look* the same as you did then?"

"I don't have a mirror."

"Noah, you're at least a foot taller since you first walked into the Green Dragon. Your face has changed. You wear different clothes. You used to have that brown jacket."

"Fell apart."

"Even your voice is different," Jolla continued. "If those Tullbury people saw you now, they wouldn't recognize you. You know how caterpillars turn into butterflies? Same thing: get older and you become something different. Want to know what your problem is?"

"Tell me."

"You're free, but you don't know it. You've built a cage out of notions and fears, but you don't see that the gate is open. It is. The least you can do is try to do whatever it is you want."

I didn't know what to say. I felt that gulf between us again as Jolla's words rang loudly in my ears: "You're free, but you don't know it."

Sunday, January 14, 1776

After all that talk about Tullbury, I had the notion that I should go to church. I was trying to see if any shred of that part of my life, which had once been so important, remained. But when I observed that the only people going into the church were British troops, I remembered my father used to say, "The church is England, and England is the church."

I turned away, wanting nothing to do with it.

Instead, under heavy gray skies, I wandered to a place called Windmill Point. Deserted, it faced the bay, where a low tide exposed flats of brown mud. On the old windmill, four canvas blades hung motionless, like the arms of an empty shirt. To the southeast, dull Dorchester Heights overlooked all, including the anchored British warships and Castle William. A few puffed-up gulls walked clumsily across the flats, looking cold and miserable, the way I felt.

I thought of Father. The terrible thing that happened to him seemed distant. But since that time, I had seen many terrible things. I recalled his words: "Our church, country, and family deserve your total loyalty."

All that was gone.

Jolla's words came back to me: "You're free, but you don't know it."

But, I told myself, *I can't live without believing in, without being loyal to, something. To what?*

As I sat there, I so wanted something to believe in. I felt like that motionless windmill, needing a wind so it—and I—could turn.

Thursday, February 15, 1776
In search of food, Jolla and I decided to split up and look separate ways. After some time, I found an empty house on Spring Street in

the north part of town, near the Charles River. It had been a fine brick place, but when I came upon it, the front door had been ripped out. The shutters were missing. As far as I could see, there was no light inside.

I entered and found the rooms bare and barren, all furniture gone, wainscoting ripped away. Gaping holes in the walls told me where other wood had been. The steps to the higher floor were missing as well. If the outside walls had been made of wood, no doubt they, too, would have been removed. Everything burnable had been taken. In its wreckage, the house appeared like an ancient ruin, a discarded shell. A monument to Boston.

As I was wandering about in search of something worth taking, three British soldiers walked in. Their faces were gaunt, their eyes dark. They carried their guns, and their uniforms were dirty. In an instant, I realized they were blocking my only way out.

One of them, I saw, was carrying a broken chair. Another carried a partially filled sack. That told me what they were doing: searching for burnable things and food.

When I saw them, they saw me. Fearful of what they might do, I stood still.

They considered me in silence until one said, "Anything here?"

"Nothing," I said.

"Bloody town," said another of them.

With that, the soldiers turned, but the man nearest me paused. He reached into his sack and pulled out a chunk of hard salted meat. He held it out toward me.

After a moment, I went forward and took it. "Thanks."

As they headed out, I heard "Good luck" called back to me.

I stood there, alone, and I understood that it didn't matter who you were; the whole town—citizens and soldiers—wanted to leave Boston.

At that moment, more than anything, so did I.

Saturday, March 2, 1776

We woke to a morning bombardment from the Americans across the river. When we stepped upon the Commons, we saw they were aiming at the north end of town. We went up Beacon Hill, trudging the muddy road, past John Hancock's mansion. From across the river, the rebels were firing on North Point, which lay below Copp's Hill.

Other citizens had come to the same place, trying to make sense of what was going on.

Someone said, "They're going to make a landing down there."

Another: "If they can silence the batteries on Copp's Hill, they can command the town."

"They can't do that."

"They're going to try."

Sunday, March 3, 1776

The bombardment continued. Some Boston houses were destroyed. It was said four British regulars were killed. But the Americans, as far as we could see, made no move. It was the English who made troop movements, massing around the North End for defense.

Jolla and I were sure the siege was coming to an end, and that what would come next would be worse.

Monday, March 4, 1776

During the night, there was almost a full moon. No cannonading. A scary silence settled over all. All we heard was the tramp of soldiers moving through the streets. Boston held its breath, bracing for the American attack.

Tuesday, March 5, 1776

In the morning when we went out, we saw people rushing toward the eastern wharves. Clearly something important had occurred. Following along, we saw that overnight, like magic, the Americans had placed themselves on Dorchester Heights, the high peninsular south of Boston that overlooked the bay. Behind large fortifications, they had set up multiple cannons.

The Americans now dominated Boston and the bay. It wasn't only the town that was in cannon range, but the Royal Navy fleet was in jeopardy too. So was Castle William in the bay. If all that were destroyed, the entire army would be trapped. Great Britain would be forced to surrender.

There were endless questions. Where had the Americans gotten the cannons? How did they build fortifications on the Heights so fast? How would they use them? No one knew, but the cannons and fortifications were surely there. It was now obvious that the previous days' bombarding in the north had been a deception, fooling the British into looking one way while the rebels occupied the Heights. As we watched, panicky troops rushed everywhere.

Moreover, it soon became clear that the cannons the army had placed at the Neck couldn't be elevated to any degree to dislodge the Americans from the Heights. The British tried. The efforts proved useless.

After months of shifting fortunes, after Lexington and Concord, after the battle on Breed's Hill, after so long with nothing happening, overnight, *everything* had happened. The Americans had gained a decisive advantage. General Howe and his army were in danger of being destroyed.

We hurried out on Long Wharf and watched the army make frantic efforts to put together a force capable of storming Dorchester Heights and dislodging the Americans. They began to assemble, bringing ladders with which to scale the Heights. Then the weather changed and grew worse with every moment. A fierce storm struck with rain, hail, and high waves.

The British attack was called off.

The Americans remained on the Heights, dominating Boston.

Friday, March 8, 1776

Things moved with astonishing speed.

At the White Horse Tavern, we learned that, under a flag of truce sent out from the town, General Howe had made an offer to the Americans: if his army was allowed to leave without being attacked, they would not burn Boston.

News came back: the Americans agreed.

Word swept through town: Great Britain was about to give up Boston. The Americans would take over.

The British had been defeated.

The questions started immediately.

Would the British army and navy take all the troops?

Would they take anyone else?

What would the remaining Loyalists do?

When the British army left, would the Americans march right in?

What would the Americans do then?

And what would Jolla do?

What would I do?

Feeling great urgency, Jolla and I made a quick decision: we'd go separate ways about town, find out as much as possible, and meet later in the day. Figure out what to do.

I don't know where Jolla went. I hurried to the north end of town, then to the Commons, where the troops were scurrying about, pulling down tents, packing things. Next, I went to the British Coffee House. The officers there were in a great froth. They cursed the Americans, cursed General Howe, and cursed their own troops. From what I heard, they would have loved to burn all of Boston down. Instead, General Howe was preparing the immediate evacuation of the army.

"Will they take citizens?" I asked a young officer.

"Just Loyalists, their families, and their slaves."

"What about freemen?"

He shrugged with indifference.

I went out on Long Wharf. There were more than a hundred

merchant, military, and transport ships already tied up, being loaded with goods as fast as possible. All ships had guards posted by them. The British were fleeing.

By late afternoon, Jolla and I were back at our house.

"What I learned at the White Horse," he told me, "is that the army will take only as many Loyalists on their ships as there is room. Not saying how many. No one knows if they'll take freemen. And once their ships leave, the Americans will come in."

"Did you find out where the British are going?"

"Maybe New York Town. Or up north, Halifax. Might be a southern place called Charles Town. What did you learn?"

"Same as you," I said. "I could see it: the army can't get out fast enough."

Jolla was quiet for a long time. Then he said, "Noah, I have to leave. When those militiamen come in, what will they do about Black people? They've offered nothing like the freedom that governor in Virginia did. And I told you, that George Washington, who heads the Americans' army, he's a slaveholder. I have to try and get on one of those ships."

"How?"

"Don't know. Just must. No choice." Then he asked, "Are you going or staying?"

I said, "I don't want to fight with either side. You said I'm free to do what I want. I want to leave. Get somewhere else. Not even sure it matters where. Just something new."

"We'll have to find a way to get on a ship. They're guarded."

"Jolla, it's the only way out."

"We won't know where we're going."

"Maybe that's the best place to go."

Saturday, March 9, 1776

Early the next morning, we set out for Long Wharf in search of a ship that we might try to board. The whole third-of-a-mile length of the wharf was in disarray, crammed with wagons and carts, both military and civilian, stuffed with every imaginable object — from household items like mirrors and trunks to army supplies like barrels of muskets and piles of collapsed tents. With the goods were hundreds of people, women, men, children, laborers, and gentlemen, all frantic to get on ships. Guards were turning them away. No civilians were being allowed to get on — not yet.

Near the end of the wharf, we came upon a smaller ship, a two-masted brig called the *Hunter,* sitting low in the water. She appeared to be a merchant ship, as we saw no armaments on her. She, too, had guards on her to keep anyone from boarding, but fewer than other ships had.

The *Hunter* could not have been more than thirty feet wide and maybe eighty feet long. Which meant she wouldn't carry many.

We stood there, staring at the ship.

"She might be the easiest to get on," I said. "People will be trying for the bigger ships."

"Agreed," said Jolla.

That was as much a plan as we made.

In silence, we returned to the Hog Alley house for one — hopefully — last wait.

Monday, March 11, 1776

During the night, the watch marched through town and proclaimed that by order of General Howe, all citizens must, on pain of death, remain in their houses from eleven in the morning until sunset, lest they hinder the troops in their embarkation.

Jolla and I agreed that we'd try to board the *Hunter* at the last moment. "By then there should be so much confusion, no one will pay attention to us."

In the morning, before the curfew, we searched for food. We found a clay pot of cooked rice, along with half a roasted fish. We hurried home and devoured it.

For the rest of the day, hungry and restless, we stayed in the house.

I recalled how much relief I had felt when my family and I first entered Boston. Now I knew I would feel even more when I left. Then it crossed my mind that I was about to take that ocean voyage I had long dreamed about. I would do what I always wanted to do. It lifted my spirits. I was even excited.

Saturday, March 16, 1776

It was night when we closed up Uncle William's house as he had requested. We locked the door and hid the key where he had told me to. Finally, we folded the shutters in and walked away. I left Abner's gun behind.

In the faint moonlight, we discovered that many streets had been barricaded by the army. Furniture was heaped up, along with things like doors, tables, and trunks, anything to hinder movements. Wagons were overturned. I saw General Gage's fine carriage had been flipped on its side, wheels stripped off.

"To block the Americans coming in," said Jolla.

Many cannons had also been abandoned, made useless by rods of barbed steel that had been put into their touchholes. Multiple houses and businesses—those that had somehow escaped destruction—now stood desolate and looted. It was like an abandoned battlefield. We had to pick our way through the wreckage with care.

We discovered that despite the hour, the town population was in great commotion. Some people were still trying to get out by way of the Neck, ahead of the incoming Americans. I had no idea if they succeeded.

On Long Wharf, there was, as I had anticipated, a panicky crush of civilians, more than a thousand, all proclaiming themselves Loyalist, mingling midst the British troops who were already there, standing in restless formation.

Everyone was nervous. Lit lamps were everywhere. Whether for illumination or heat, it was hard to say.

Civilians had no choice but to remain on the wharf with mounting frustration and impatience. Many had their belongings with them, fine things too. Some had blankets in their arms. Others carried bulky bags of who knew what.

Jolla and I, jumpy and alert, stood in the middle of the crowd, trying not to be noticed.

Army soldiers had been told to assemble at four in the morning. Then they marched to Long Wharf, to the fighting and transport ships. Their arrival created more confusion. We became a crowded mass of frightened, hungry, and cold people all pressed together, desperate to get away. There was constant pushing, shoving, seeking place, many crying, others shouting, complete bedlam. The British army had made no plan for citizens, and there was no order of any kind. Many of the goods people wanted to take were being abandoned.

In all the chaos, none of the guards bothered to ask who we were or why we were there. Talking to no one, we moved slowly toward the end of the wharf, gradually drawing closer to the *Hunter* and our departure.

Sunday, March 17, 1776
Until daylight fully arrived, we and all the agitated Loyalists waited on Long Wharf. I ached to put my feet upon the deck of the *Hunter*, to be gone from Boston once and for all.

The civilian loading finally commenced. We saw some people being turned away. We didn't know why, save that the ships were filling up fast. Jolla and I inched forward. Looking ahead, we could see the line had begun to narrow, forced between soldiers as it neared the *Hunter*.

"Hello, boys."

It was Mr. Simpson, the owner of the Green Dragon. We had not seen him since before the tavern had been turned into a hospital.

"Wanting to go too?" he said to us.

"Yes, sir," I said.

"Got a letter of appreciation from General Howe." Mr. Simpson held up a piece of paper. "It's for me and another. I was going to take Ephraim, but he's disappeared. Still, this'll get me out and one more. Did anyone tell you where we're going?"

Jolla shook his head.

"Halifax," he said. "Up north."

"What is it like?" I asked.

"Don't really know. But I'm going to set up a tavern there. You boys can work for me again."

It was tempting, though I wanted something new. I said nothing and looked to Jolla. He hid all reaction and gave no reply, but I knew him well enough to guess his fury.

We edged forward. It was maddening. In a matter of moments, I'd step on deck and be on my way to a new life. My heart thudded.

We reached the guards. As we came up to them, one of the soldiers stretched out an arm, blocking our way. "Stop."

We had no choice but to halt.

From on board, an officer came forward and spoke into the guard's ear. The guard turned back to us.

"Only room for two more," he announced.

"These two are mine," said Mr. Simpson, as if he owned us. He held out his letter from General Howe. "They work for me."

The soldier refused to look at the paper. He shook his head. "No more than two," he repeated. A second guard joined him to reinforce the decision. Then a third.

We stood there. It was obvious the soldiers were not going to budge. Their eyes shifted from Mr. Simpson to me. It was clear they expected I would be the one to board the *Hunter*.

Jolla and I looked at each other. I don't know what expression I wore, but his face showed no emotion, only a hint of resignation. I could almost hear our conversation from nearly a year ago:

"What happens if I get into a spot that isn't easy to get out of?"

"I'll help you."

"I don't want to have to put that loyalty to the test."

"Come on, boys," pressed Mr. Simpson. "I can use either of you. Make up your minds. I'm going." With that, he moved forward, leaving Jolla and me.

Though Jolla made a point of not looking at me, I recalled his words: "You're free, but you don't know it. You've built a cage out of notions and fears, but you don't see that the gate is open. It is. The least you can do is try to do whatever it is you want."

I had to think fast.

"Jolla," I blurted out, "you go. You'll have a better chance to stay free if you leave."

He did not move. Still without looking at me, he said, "What will you do?"

"Stay here and try to keep out of cages."

He swung about and gazed at me for a long moment. I saw a trace of a smile. Then he held out his hand, which I grasped, until, with an impulsive move, we hugged each other. No words were spoken. Next second, he turned and hurried forward onto the ship's deck.

The gate snapped shut behind him. Just as he was about to descend into the *Hunter*'s hold, he looked back at me. I knew that expression so well. He was challenging me one last time, charging me to keep challenging myself.

It was about noon when the *Hunter* dropped her sails and caught enough wind to move out—one among many—toward the ocean and Halifax.

I was not alone. A large gathering of Bostonians who had survived the siege were there. I recognized several. Whigs. Tories. There was no cheering. No celebrating. They were too tired. Too hungry. But I could read hope on their faces, hope that change would bring better fortunes. I wondered what my face showed.

I remained on Long Wharf until the ships left the bay, all those departing sails looking like a migrating flock of birds. Maybe, I thought, they were, at last, Jolla's liberty birds.

I told myself I had been loyal to Jolla.

That felt right. The best decision I ever made, and surely the first important one I had made truly on my own.

Then, from a distance, I heard the thump of drums and the shrill shriek of fifes. The Americans were coming into Boston. The crowd on the wharf, suddenly energized, hastened away, ready to welcome the Americans.

And me? I pushed my hair out of my eyes and headed back into town too, wondering how I'd make a new life for myself, but knowing that it was only me who would make the decisions.

As I walked away, the question *What should I do?* came into my head. It didn't just come: it insisted I find an answer. I suddenly realized I could do what I had always wanted. It would take time, but I supposed the port would reopen and start working again. Wasn't my name Noah? Like the great seaman? I would become a sailor on a ship — on my own terms — and sail away. I didn't care where I went, save that it was far. Maybe it would be to those whaling islands.

And I knew there was only one thing I absolutely needed to do: stay out of cages. I'd be loyal to that.

Author's Note

Loyalty is a work of fiction based on as much historical fact as I could provide. The essential chronology of events is true. That said, not everything that happened in the years depicted has been included. It was, to say the least, a tumultuous time.

The American Revolution has inspired a vast library of personal accounts, letters, memoirs, and histories. In many cases, these sources agree on the facts, but there are differences and disputes. Perhaps the most famous example is the question of who fired "the shot heard round the world," at the Battle of Lexington. There are many guesses, conjectures, and opinions, but no one truly knows who pulled the trigger, or why. Each side blamed the other for that shot. No one ever took responsibility for it. No one took credit. It has even been suggested it was an accident.

"The shot heard round the world" is a phrase created by Ralph Waldo Emerson in his poem "Concord Hymn," written in 1837. Only in retrospect did it seem as if that moment in 1775 started the actual war, which lasted until 1783.

There is also much debate as to who supported the rebellion. There seems to be a consensus that the population was divided into thirds: one-third in favor, one-third against, one-third neutral and shifting with the tides of war. In other words, the War of Independence was also a civil war—family members against family members (Benjamin Franklin and his son were on opposite sides), neighbors against neighbors, with violence in communities. That the Boston Sons of Liberty circulated a broadside listing Loyalists, noting which ones had not been born in the colonies, is true.

The best (but not only) account I know of all this is *Scars of Independence: America's Violent Birth* by Holger Hoock (New York: Crown, 2017).

Noah Cope and Jolla Freeman are invented characters.

"Jolla"—an African name—I found cited among many names on a ship's list of enslaved people brought to American shores. Enslaved people first arrived in Massachusetts in the 1630s. Slavery was made legal in 1641. "Freeman" was a name free Black men and women often took to inform others of their status.

The War of Independence was fought—on the American side—for high ideals that Americans can recall with pride. "All men are created equal." But ideals are one thing; realities are another. Thomas Jefferson, the man who wrote those words, enslaved Black people.

At the time of the Revolution, Black Americans constituted some 20 percent of the total colonial population. It's vital to understand what happened and did not happen to them at the time. Free African Americans did fight on the patriot side. No doubt some enslaved people did as well. But, as depicted here, enslaved people were not welcome in American armies. It has been suggested the rebels did not enlist Black men in fear that it would upset the pro-slavery southern colonies, whose help and alliance they desired.

At the same time, the royal governor of Virginia, Lord Dunmore, issued a proclamation in November 1775 offering freedom to enslaved and indentured men who joined British forces. Thousands moved to do so. Simultaneously, enslavers reacted by supporting the anti-British revolution.

Vermont, while still seeking independence, outlawed slavery in 1777, the first of the thirteen colonies to do so. Massachusetts abolished slavery in 1783, eight years after the Revolution began, at a time when John Hancock was governor. But slavery was not ended in all states until 1865.

Whereas the town of Tullbury is a product of my imagination, all the other places in this story are real and are depicted to the best that my research provided. Boston street names are given as they were. Boston's Green Dragon Tavern was real. The White Horse Tavern was real. They no longer exist. But other colonial structures still stand in Boston, including the powder house near Charlestown, which is considered the oldest stone structure in Massachusetts. That said, over the years, Boston's topography has changed radically.

The rough treatment Noah received at the hands of American rebels comes from a memoir written by Walter Bates, *Kingston and the Loyalists of the "Spring Fleet."* In 1774, Bates suffered far more brutality in real life and ultimately fled his home in Connecticut for Canada. I used a reprint of the small book, published in 1889, for my retelling of the incident.

Abner Hosmer was the name of a young man killed at the North Bridge during the Concord Battle. He was buried in Acton, Massachusetts, with a memorial that reads: "Here lies the Body of Abner Hosmer . . . who was killed in Concord fight April 19th, 1775 In defense of the just rights & Liberties of his Country, being in the 21st year of his age."

This is the way historical fiction works in my book: Young Abner was real, as was his age at his death on the North Bridge. I know nothing else about him save that. But I married him to a fictional Mercy Cope. Thus, the fiction is placed in a framework of what truly happened and brings realism to the story for both the writer and the reader.

Captain Brown and DeBérniere were also real people, though I never found a description of them beyond names and ranks.

The Sandwich Islands, to which Noah dreams of traveling, is the name the English gave to what are now called the Hawaiian Islands.

The prayer spoken by Noah's father in the opening pages of this novel is from a contemporary British prayer book.

How the rebels secured the cannons that ended the siege of Boston is an extraordinary story. Under the command of twenty-six-year-old Henry Knox (a former bookstore owner), the cannons came from captured forts at Ticonderoga and Crown Point in New York State and were dragged some three hundred miles through snow to reach Boston.

When you look at how and why the American Revolution unfolded, it seems to me that it is still going on, with much, such as "All men are created equal," still to be fully achieved. And when you consider events such as the storming of the U.S. Capitol building on January 6, 2021, it is clear that the definitions of "patriots" and "traitors," and of "loyalty" itself, are also still being debated.